PRAISE FOR THE SA[...]
GARAGE SALE MYSTERIE[...]

I KNOW WHAT YOU BI[...]

"*I Know What You Bid Last Summe[...]* engaging cast of characters and a[...]
—**Susan Santangelo, author of** *Dieting Can Be Murder,*
for *Suspense Magazine*

"Fans of Harris will appreciate both the clever mystery and the tips for buying and selling at garage sales."
—*Kirkus Reviews*

"This is book 5 in the popular series. Sarah is a likable character . . . the mystery is a good one, keeping readers guessing until the end. Readers will also crave lasagna after the first few chapters. Included in the book are two fun items: Garage-sale tips about selling food at the event, and tips for setting up a pretzel bar . . . both delightfully informative."—*Kings River Life*

"Whether garage sales are your thing or not, this is a series you will certainly enjoy. *I Know What You Bid Last Summer* is a fantastic addition to the series that will keep you turning pages until the end. Now comes the long wait until we can visit Sarah again."—**Carstairs Considers**

A GOOD DA[...]

"Harris's fourth is a slam [...] [lo]ve antiques and garage sales. The kn[...] [intere]sting premise and some surpri[...] *Reviews*

"Sarah's [...] curves as the appearanc[...] [m]akes up her world. This fast-m[...] with a bang and keeps the twists and [...] Sarah is a likable protagonist who sometim[...] bad decisions based on good intentions. This [...] the action and drama as she tries to extricate herself from dangerous situations with some amusing results. Toss in a unique cast of secondary characters, an intriguing mystery, and a hot ex-husband, and you'll find there's never a dull moment in Sarah's bargain-hunting world."—*RT Book Reviews*, **4 stars**

THE SARAH WINSTON
GARAGE SALE MYSTERY SERIES BY SHERRY HARRIS

THE GUN ALSO RISES

I KNOW WHAT YOU BID LAST SUMMER

A GOOD DAY TO BUY

ALL MURDERS FINAL!

THE LONGEST YARD SALE

TAGGED FOR DEATH

Published by Kensington Publishing Corporation

THE GUN
ALSO RISES

Sherry Harris

KENSINGTON BOOKS
KENSINGTON PUBLISHING CORP.
www.kensingtonbooks.com

KENSINGTON BOOKS are published by

Kensington Publishing Corp.
119 West 40th Street
New York, NY 10018

All Kensington titles, imprints, and distributed lines are available at special quantity discounts for bulk purchases for sales promotion, premiums, fund-raising, educational, or institutional use.

Special book excerpts or customized printings can also be created to fit specific needs. For details, write or phone the office of the Kensington Sales Manager: Attn.: Sales Department. Kensington Publishing Corp., 119 West 40th Street, New York, NY 10018. Phone: 1-800-221-2647.

Kensington and the K logo Reg. U.S. Pat. & TM Off.

First Printing: February 2019
ISBN-13: 978-1-4967-1696-5
ISBN-10: 1-4967-1696-5

ISBN-13: 978-1-4967-1697-2 (eBook)
ISBN-10: 1-4967-1697-3 (eBook)

10 9 8 7 6 5 4 3 2 1

Printed in the United States of America

To Bob
May all my sunrises be with you

Acknowledgments

Thank you to my agent, John Talbot of the Talbot Fortune Agency, for your continuing support and career advice. Gary Goldstein, my editor at Kensington, had the idea for a garage sale series. Thanks for trusting me to bring it to life.

To my dear Wickeds, Jessica Estevao, Julie Hennrikus, Edith Maxwell, Liz Mugavero, and Barbara Ross, thanks for always having my back—and front and all the bits in between. I cherish your advice and friendship.

Bruce Coffin is a retired detective sergeant from Portland, Maine. He writes the best-selling Detective Byron Mystery series. Bruce answered many questions for me, so any errors are entirely on him. Kidding! They're entirely on me.

Vida Antolin-Jenkins has been a great supporter of my series and has talked through many aspects of the relationships in the story with me—thank you so much.

Aubrey Hamilton shared her expertise on running a book sale and all that entails.

Ashley Harris (no relation, but dear former neighbor) talked to me about issues facing military spouses, and pointed me to where Tracy could get help.

Barb Goffman read an early draft and, thankfully, didn't tell me to burn it. After returning the manuscript to me, she continued to provide support and advice.

Honestly, I'm surprised she didn't block my phone number. Thank you for your professional eye, your friendship, and for making the books so much better.

Mary Titone, friend, fellow military spouse, beta reader, and also my publicist—thank you for all you do. Your reading eye has helped me so much. You set up events, get my name out there, and cook up adventures for us.

Clare Boggs is another friend and beta reader. I feel as if we've grown together, and that your insightful comments have greatly improved my writing. Thank you for taking the time!

To the crime writing community—you are amazing— I wish I could buy you all a drink. I have to give a special shout-out to Sisters in Crime and Mystery Writers of America, along with all the bloggers and reviewers. Thank you.

To my family, who love me even at my worst. Life is an adventure with you in it.

Chapter One

A drop of sweat rolled down my back as I rang the doorbell of the mansion. I wanted to blame it on the hot sun pummeling my shoulders, but it was nerves. As I listened to the deep gong echoing inside the house, I thought, *for whom the bell tolls; it tolls for thee.* I didn't know the rest of the poem, only that Hemingway used it for a title, or why the lines swirled through my head. They sure sounded ominous.

I'd been summoned here via a thick cream envelope delivered by a messenger yesterday at noon. The card inside read:

Mrs. Belle Winthrop Granville, III
Requests the presence of Miss Sarah Winston
at 10:00 a.m., July 25

It was impossible to refuse such an invitation. Okay, so I could have, but curiosity would have killed me if I did. I'd been running a garage sale business for over a year and a half, here in Ellington, Massachusetts. But I'd never worked for someone as wealthy as Belle Winthrop

Granville, III. Miss Belle, as she was called around town, which was a very Southern thing to do for a bunch of Yankees, was a legend in Ellington. I couldn't imagine how she'd even heard about me. Or that she needed me to do a garage sale for her.

But I knew about Miss Belle. In fact, everyone in Ellington knew her story because who didn't love a good love story? She was from an elite Alabama family. She'd met Sebastian Winthrop Granville, III at spring break in Key West in the early sixties. Sebastian was from a wealthy Boston Brahmin family. Both families were dead set against the union, but the two snuck off and married. They were like Romeo and Juliet without the entire star-crossed business.

The story went that Miss Belle had brought her Southern hospitality up north as a young bride, but never won over Sebastian's family. To escape the cold disapproval, Miss Belle and Sebastian moved to Ellington, where Sebastian opened a bank and made his own fortune. This all happened in the sixties, long before I'd landed in Massachusetts three years ago when I was thirty-six.

I stared at the door, willing it to open. I was beginning to feel twitchy, which wasn't a good way to make a first impression. When it finally swung open, a twenty-something woman in a black knee-length dress with a crisp white apron stood there. For a moment, I wondered if I'd been invited to a costume party and that I should have worn something other than my blue and white sundress. "Hi, I'm Sarah Winston. Mrs. Winthrop Granville is expecting me."

"Yes, ma'am, follow me."

I detected a bit of a Boston accent in her voice. We trekked across what seemed like miles of marble flooring, under chandeliers, and past a staircase that would suit Tara from *Gone With the Wind*. She led me to a room with a massive desk near tall windows lined with dark green velvet curtains. For a moment, I wondered if I was on the set of a remake of *Gone With the Wind*.

"I'll go get Mrs. Winthrop Granville," the maid said.

"Thank you." I turned slowly around after she left. The room was two stories high and filled floor to ceiling with shelves of books. There were two library ladders and a small balcony. It was a reader's dream room. Except for a lack of comfy chairs.

"How do you like my library?"

I turned at the sound of the soft voice with a Southern accent, where the word *my* sounded like *mah* and the word *library* was drawled out from three syllables to about five. A petite woman with silver hair twisted into a neat bun stood behind me. "Mrs. Winthrop Granville," I said. I recognized her from photographs in the newspaper. "It's an amazing room."

"If you are going to work with me, please call me Belle," she said. She wore a twinset that looked like Chanel and tan slacks. A scarf draped gracefully around her neck.

I was going to work with her? She really wanted to have a garage sale?

Miss Belle laughed. "You look flabbergasted."

"Trying to keep my emotions from showing isn't my strongest suit. It's why I rarely play poker. Apparently, I don't have just one tell, I have a multitude of them. What did you have in mind?"

"Let's sit," Miss Belle said. "Would you like me to have Kay get you something to drink? Tea or a Coke?" She gestured to the maid, who stood in the doorway of the room.

"No, I'm fine, thank you." The idea of having

someone wait on me had always made me slightly uncomfortable.

Miss Belle sat in a leather chair behind a desk that almost dwarfed her and gestured for me to sit across from her in an equally massive chair. She ran a hand across the smooth mahogany of the desk. "This was my Sebastian's desk. He loved this silly thing. It's ridiculously big, don't you think?"

"It's lovely." What else could I say?

"It was his grandfather's. One of the few things he wanted from his family when we moved to Ellington in the sixties." She sighed. "But I'm guessing you are wondering why I've asked you here."

Boy, was I. I nodded. I realized I'd crossed my legs at my ankles, had my hands folded neatly in my lap, and sat more erect than usual, like I was in the presence of a VIP.

"It's time to do some downsizing."

I didn't realize rich people worried about downsizing too.

"We never had children, so there's no one to leave all of our things to. Although a few pieces will be returned to Sebastian's nieces and nephews." She wrinkled her nose on the last bit.

"I'm not sure I'm the person to do a sale for you." I hated turning away business, but . . . "I think you need Sotheby's, not me."

"Oh, dear. I'm not being clear at all. It's my massive book collection. I want to put together a sale to raise money for the Ellington Free Library."

I craned my head around the room. The books were all bound in leather, some looked old, most looked valuable. I had no expertise with old or rare books. I didn't even know anyone who did. "I don't think I'm qualified to do that."

Miss Belle looked surprised. "Oh, not these books." She waved her hand around. "I have an expert coming in to deal with them."

"What books, then?" I asked.

Miss Belle's cheeks reddened. "I'm addicted to mysteries. Come with me."

Chapter Two

"Nothing wrong with that. I love them myself."

Miss Belle smiled. I followed her down the hall and into an office. This one was a smaller-scale version of the first. Tall windows, a smaller desk with graceful curved legs, and paperback books everywhere, on shelves, on end tables, even some stacked on the floor. A bunch of hardbacks were on the shelves too. I spotted a complete set of Sue Grafton books, all the Louise Penny's Armand Gamache novels, and books by Sara Paretesky. This room had several comfy chairs to sit in with a good book.

"I don't bring everyone in here," she said, "but you don't seem like the judgmental type." She took a quick glance at me, and I gave her my best nonjudgmental smile. "Some people look down on mysteries, you know."

I may be a lot of things, but snooty wasn't one of them. Besides, who wouldn't love mysteries?

"There's everything from Agatha Christie to Trixie Beldon to Donna Andrews in here," she said.

"I think I could handle this," I said.

"This isn't all of it," Miss Belle said. "Follow me, please."

We climbed the curving staircase to the second floor. Halls led off on either side with the plushest, longest Oriental rugs I'd ever seen. Their reds glowed against the dark paneling.

"There's another staircase at the end of this hall" —she gestured to her left—"but we'll go up here."

She opened one of the multiple closed doors and we climbed another set of stairs. The rug on this floor wasn't as plush but looked much loved. In the center of the hall, Miss Belle opened a door to a steep set of stairs to an attic. The big house was very quiet. I could hear Kay vacuuming somewhere on another floor.

The attic was as clean or cleaner than my apartment. Not a cobweb or mouse to be seen. To the left was a room with large windows spaced evenly around the room and plenty of lighting from fixtures in the ceiling. It certainly wasn't like most attics I'd been in, with low-sloped ceilings, a light bulb on a string, and rickety stairs leading up to it.

Miss Belle showed me around the room. We passed what looked to me like a treasure trove of antiques: an old radio, a gramophone, and an ice chest. I would have loved to linger and explore. For a small woman, Miss Belle could move quickly, and I hurried to keep up with her.

We arrived at a small hall with three closed doors. "Kay, my maid and housekeeper, lives up here. It's her choice. There are plenty of rooms on the second and third floor."

She opened the door that was straight ahead of us. The hinges squeaked just a little, and Miss Belle frowned. It made me realize again how very quiet this house was. This room had dress dummies, suitcases, trunks, shelves of books, and boxes with books spilling out of them. I spotted a box of Nancy Drew books and another of Bobbsey Twins.

Miss Belle shook her head. "I should have parted with some of these long ago. It's silly keeping them up here, where only I can read them. And it's a bit of a mess. I'm not sure what's in the trunks and suitcases. Probably more books." Miss Belle looked me over. "Are you up to the task?"

"Can I just poke about for a bit before I answer?" I asked.

"Very sensible. Of course. There's a bathroom just outside to the left. Kay's room is on the right. Stop by the study before you leave."

"Okay." I watched as Miss Belle left. When she was out of sight, I turned back to the scene before me. Books, glorious books.

I found a box full of Agatha Christie's books, including my favorite, *And Then There Were None*, and a trunk filled with Mary Stewart, Phyllis A. Whitney, and Victoria Holt books, which my mom loved. I flipped through a few of them but had to stop myself, more than once, from sitting down to read. None of them were first editions, but this might be the best project I'd ever had.

I spent about fifteen minutes poking around in Miss Belle's attic before I headed back downstairs. I heard voices coming from the library, so I knocked lightly on the open door before going in. Miss Belle stood next to an older man in a black suit who wasn't much taller than her and at least an inch shorter than my five-six.

"Sarah, let me introduce you to Roger Mervine. He's an old friend and a rare book dealer from Boston."

Roger strode over to me and took my hand. For a

minute, I thought he was going to kiss it with his waxed, mustachioed mouth. But he shook it instead. Vigorously. "Belle tells me you'll be handling the lesser books."

Lesser books? Yeesh.

"And of course I'll be here to answer any of your questions should you find something rare or valuable."

I managed to maintain a pleasant expression. "That hasn't been decided yet." If I had to work with this guy around, I wasn't sure I wanted to. Although I'd come down here with every intention of saying yes.

"Oh, Roger, don't be such a snob," Miss Belle said. "He's harmless, really. Roger has a fabulous bookstore on Beacon Hill in Boston."

Beacon Hill was a neighborhood full of beautiful brick row houses, exclusive shops, and restaurants north of Boston Common, America's first public park, and the Public Garden, the first public botanical garden in America. It was a world for John Kerry and the Kennedys and Seth Anderson's family, but this was no time to think about Seth. Good grief, now I was starting to sound like Scarlett O'Hara. He had caused me a lot of heartache and I'd done the same to him. I shook it off. "I've been in your shop. Mervine's Rare and Unusual Books?"

He did a slight bow instead of saying yes. His thick white hair swept forward, momentarily covering his face. It was hard to peg his age, but I'd guess somewhere north of sixty-five. Geez, it was like he was playing the role of lord of the manor. Roger probably had a smoking jacket and crystal decanters full of port at home. He'd probably never tasted a fluffernutter, my favorite sandwich, in his life. Although if he was connected to Belle, he might really be a lord of a manor somewhere, or at least the American equivalent of one.

When he raised his head, his light brown eyes had a bit of a twinkle in them.

"So delighted you've been in. Did you purchase anything?" he asked.

I almost said no to be ornery. "Several things. My father was thrilled with a history of coastal California I gave him for Christmas one year. Also a book with early California maps. They were beautiful." I'd grown up in Pacific Grove, California, which was sandwiched between the more famous Monterey and Carmel. My parents still lived there.

"Wonderful. It's the best part of having the store, knowing that the books end up in the hands of someone who loves them. I must be off. Sarah, I hope we'll meet again, and Belle, *enchanté* as usual." He swept out of the room as if he was exiting stage left.

"Sorry about that," Belle said. "I was hoping to have you on board before you met Roger. He's always overly assertive when you first meet him, but then he's just a big old teddy bear."

"I don't scare that easily," I said. That might not be true, but if I said it out loud often enough, maybe it would be.

"Good. That's what I heard, and that you're clever."

Oh, dear. People had been getting the craziest ideas about me since I'd helped solve a few murders. "Don't believe everything you've heard."

"I did a lot of checking before reaching out to you. After all, you will be in my home all day for some length of time going through my treasured things. I had to find someone trustworthy."

"How did you hear about me?"

"Other than the newspapers? I asked around. I know your friends the DiNapolis, among others."

Angelo and Rosalie DiNapoli owned DiNapoli's Roast Beef and Pizza, my favorite place to eat in Ellington.

They had become my extended family since I'd moved to the area.

Belle clasped her hands together. "Back to my books. What do you think?"

"I'd like to do it. If I find things I can't easily price, I can look them up."

"Or you can ask Roger."

"Yes, of course." Over my dead body. I explained to Belle that I'd have to work on an hourly fee basis. I hated charging someone when they were doing something for charity, but I'd recently done an event for the school board for free. I was still trying to recoup the money I'd lost by turning away other paying jobs during that project. I also had another charity function in the works.

"No problem," Belle said. "When can you start?"

I pulled out my phone and checked out my calendar. "I could come by for a couple of hours in the morning, if that works for you."

"Of course it does. Thank you so much. This is going to be wonderful."

At noon, I sat across a table from Stella, my landlady and friend, at DiNapoli's. We were sharing my favorite bianco pizza, a white pizza with four cheeses, Angelo's secret garlic sauce, and basil, and sipping a nice cabernet sauvignon. I kind of missed the days when DiNapoli's didn't have a liquor license and would sneak me wine in a plastic kiddie cup with a lid and a straw.

"How is practice going?" I asked Stella. She taught voice classes at Berklee College of Music, private lessons at home, and had a minor role in a fall production of *The Phantom of the Opera*.

"Good. The cast is fantastic. The director has a clear vision. So far, it's been amazing."

"I hope it stays that way," I said.

"They asked me to be the understudy for the lead role, Christine." Stella's dark green eyes were wide with excitement. And her olive skin was a bit flushed.

"That's wonderful news. Now we just have to figure out how to get rid of the lead actress. I could wish her good luck instead of saying *break a leg*." It was a theater superstition not to tell an actor good luck.

"No. I'm content with my role. It's been so long since I've been in anything professionally. I'm fine with this." Stella had toured Europe with an opera ten years ago, when she was in her twenties. "What about you?"

I picked up a second slice of pizza. The piece was about the size of my head. Angelo didn't believe in small slices. He thought it threw off the toppings-to-crust ratio. The cheese dripped over the edges as I slid it onto my plate.

"I have a new job I'm excited about."

"For who?" Stella asked.

"Belle Winthrop Granville. She has an enormous collection of mystery books she wants to sell and then donate the money to the Ellington Library."

"Miss Belle? Wow. How did you manage that?"

"She found me," I said. "Her house is amazing. Right out of a magazine. And her attic. It's a treasure trove. I wish I had time to explore it all."

"Let me know if you need any help. I'd love to see her house."

"That would be fun. I may just need an assistant for a day or two."

A police officer walked over to the table. Usually that meant trouble for me, but this time it was just

Nathan Bossum, who I called by the nickname I'd accidentally given him, Awesome.

"Want some pizza?" I asked.

"If you have extra," Awesome said.

Stella scooted over a chair and Awesome sat next to her, flinging an arm across the back of her chair. They'd been dating since they'd met last February. After giving her shoulder a squeeze, he snatched a piece of pizza, folded it, and took a bite.

"So, how about those Red Sox?" I asked with a grin. Awesome used to be a NYPD detective and was a die-hard Yankees fan. They weren't doing well this year and the Red Sox were well on their way to making the playoffs, if they didn't have a fall collapse.

Stella laughed. "They're amazing this year."

Awesome just chewed and didn't take the bait.

I scooted my chair back. "I'll leave you two to the pizza."

"You don't have to leave on my account," Awesome said. "I have to get back to work soon."

"I have a meeting to get to at two." A meeting with Seth Anderson, onetime love interest, that had me on edge. Now there would be no avoiding thinking about him. "I'll catch you later." I waved goodbye to Rosalie and Angelo as I left.

Chapter Three

I sat across a large desk from Seth Anderson, the district attorney for Middlesex County, and one of the assistant DAs. The office had a serious feel to it and was a bit austere. There was no vanity wall with photos of Seth with famous people. Ones with the Kerrys, Kennedys, and Krafts. People his family knew and associated with. Instead, his diplomas hung off to one side, along with some other certificates I couldn't read from here.

Seth, along with the assistant DA, had prepped me for the upcoming trial of the person who'd stalked me last February. They'd told me what to wear, what to say, and when to let my emotions show. They'd warned me the defense attorney would try to twist things. The pressure was terrifying. The stakes weren't just high, they could impact my life. If something went south, my stalker could be back out on the streets again.

The assistant DA gathered her things to leave after we finished going over my testimony. I stood when she did.

"Can you stay for a minute, Sarah?" Seth asked.

I nodded and sat back down as the assistant DA left and closed the door behind her.

"It's going to be okay, Sarah," Seth said.

What would be okay, him, me, the trial? The last time I saw him was a month ago at a party at DiNapoli's, where I'd apparently misinterpreted a look he gave me. I thought it was one of interest, but hadn't ever had a chance to talk to him that night.

Seth leaned back in his chair and loosened his tie. Geez, he was handsome. He looked every bit the Mass-achusetts's Most Eligible Bachelor he'd been named by a magazine two years running, all broad shoulders, dark hair, and delicious smelling. We'd dated after I split up with my ex-husband, CJ, the first time. As much as I didn't want to react to him, my body always seemed to have other thoughts. Seth grinned at me. It seemed like he knew what I was thinking. *Snap out of it.* Quit staring at him like a teenage girl drooling over some hot movie star she'd stumbled across.

Thankfully, I hadn't spilled pizza or soda down my front when I'd had lunch with Stella. And I was still all dressed up from seeing Miss Belle.

"You'll be a great witness."

"I hope so." Thinking about seeing my stalker again scared me beyond reason.

Seth leaned forward. "I'm leaving in the morning to go to the Berkshires."

"Because of the change of venue?" I finally managed to ask. The defense had persuaded the judge to hold the trial on the western side of the state—three hours away—because the case had gotten a lot of local press coverage.

"Yes. We have several motions pending with the judge. I was hoping . . ." Seth paused and cleared his throat.

Why was Seth nervous? I was nervous, but I'd been

telling myself going through my testimony, reliving all
that had happened, was what had rattled me.

"That when the trial is over I could, maybe, take you
out to dinner."

Oh, boy. That wasn't what I'd been expecting. Not
at all. He looked as anxious as a parent sending their
kid off for their first day of school. I felt the same way.

"But if it's too soon, I understand," he said. "I realize you've been through a lot since we first met."

Heat rushed up my face at the memory of the night
I met Seth. At a bar. In Lowell. After CJ and I had first
divorced. We'd had a one-night stand that was totally
out of character for me. We'd dated on and off until
CJ and I had tried to make our marriage work again in
May. Seth had even told me he loved me last winter.
Now that CJ had moved to Florida and our marriage
was clearly over, maybe now was the right time for
Seth and me. But I hesitated.

Seth's phone rang. "You don't have to answer me
now. Just think about it." He reached for the phone.
"Please."

At four o'clock, I stopped at the Visitors Center at
Fitch Air Force Base to get a pass for the afternoon so
I could meet my friend James. He had to sponsor me
on. Even though I'd been a military spouse for almost
twenty years, after CJ and I divorced a year and a half
ago, I was no longer considered a dependent. Because
of that, I didn't have an ID to get on base. It felt a bit
like being locked out of one's own home.

James was sitting at a table in the food court outside
the Base Exchange, or BX as Air Force people called
it. I waved to him before ordering an iced coffee and
joining James at the table. It was quiet in here this

afternoon. A few people were going in and out of the BX, which was like an all-purpose department store with everything from baby clothes to sheets to furniture to grills. But I wasn't allowed to shop there anymore. Even buying my own iced coffee was probably stretching the rules.

I'd known James for almost three years. First, when he had worked for CJ when CJ had been in charge of the base security police, and then as a friend during our ensuing divorce. James had gone through a lot in the past year and a half too. He'd returned from a deployment a different, angrier, sadder person. James was still fighting through the PTSD, but had found helping others and therapy helped him.

"Hi," I said as I settled in across from him. A deep line creased his forehead. His shoulders seemed tense. "Are you okay? Or worried about the sale for Eric this weekend?"

Eric Hunt was deep in the throes of PTSD. He'd bonded with a street dog in Afghanistan and they had been injured by a suicide bomber. Eric had been hit with shrapnel and medevaced out, his dog left behind. Eric's life had spiraled downward. Drinking, drugs, anger issues; it was a classic PTSD scenario, although when it happened to you there was nothing classic about it. James had met Eric at a bar one night, taken him home, sobered him up, and gotten him to join a group of veterans who shared similar stories. It had helped, but Eric mourned the loss of his dog.

He would love to bring the dog home, but it was prohibitively expensive for a man with a wife and four kids surviving on a sergeant's wages. That's where I came in. I was in charge of arranging a fund-raiser on Ellington's town common this Saturday to bring the dog here. I'd been in a bit of a downward spiral myself;

second-guessing had become a terrible middle-of-the-night sleep spoiler. Doing something for someone else had helped lift part of my spirits as well.

"I'm fine. I've got a few more things on my to-do list for the sale, but that's not why I called." He took a sip of his coffee. "I asked Eric to join us too. He should be here any minute."

"There he is now," I said. I waved to Eric as he looked around for us. Eric was lean, with high cheekbones. As he got closer, I could tell something was on his mind.

"How's King doing?" I asked Eric when he sat down.

"Okay. I'm hoping we can get him out of there before my buddy's deployment ends," Eric said.

His friend who'd been caring for King since Eric came home was leaving Afghanistan in a month. The thought of King being back out on the street made my stomach churn. "It's going to be okay," I said. "We'll get the money. Any recent pictures?"

Eric grinned and whipped out his phone. "Here he is." King was a big dog, some kind of mixed breed.

"He looks good," I said. "Very handsome."

"Did I ever show you the photos of the first day I found him?" Eric asked.

"No," I said.

Eric flipped through some more photos. He shook his head. "Look." He handed me his phone.

The dog was so emaciated, I could see every rib poking through some loose, hanging skin. Patches of fur were missing, and there were some lesions on his shoulders. I blinked back tears. "That's heartbreaking."

"The day I found him, I promised him if he'd hang in there, if he'd be strong, he would live like a king for the rest of his life."

"Thus the name King?" I asked.

Eric swiped at his eyes. "Yes. I don't want to break my promise."

"Sarah's doing everything she can to make sure you don't," James said.

"Will you be there on Saturday, Eric?" I asked.

He stared down at the picture of King. "I'll try."

We all took a sip of our coffee, but I could tell something else was bothering Eric and James.

"Spit it out, you two. Not the coffee, but what you're worried about." I smiled, trying to ease the obvious tension radiating from James. I hoped something hadn't triggered another bout of PTSD. I remembered a Vietnam vet who was a friend of my parents. We'd been having a cookout when a helicopter flew overhead. He had screamed at everyone to run for cover.

"I'm worried about Tracy," Eric said.

"Your wife?" I knew her because we both volunteered at the base thrift shop. But I didn't know her well.

Eric nodded. The alarm on his phone went off. Eric stood. "I've got to go. James can explain." Eric grinned. "My oldest has a soccer game and it's good to be home to go to them."

We said our goodbyes, and after Eric left, I turned to James. "What's going on?"

"I'm not sure. I've been over there a lot. Eric and I've been playing tennis and going for runs."

"That's good."

"For both of us. Tracy wasn't too keen about it at first because it meant Eric was away from the family after a yearlong deployment. But after she saw that it helped to relax Eric, she called me, asking me to schedule our games as often as necessary."

"So what's the problem?"

"I'm not sure. She always seems on edge when I'm there."

"Do you think he's abusing her?" I asked. "Because

if he is, you have to report it, no matter how much you don't want to."

James shook his head. "I haven't seen any signs. No bruises, no cowering. But I know that Eric's gone through some bouts of anger and depression. I think it's affecting her. How can it not? I'm just not sure to what degree."

"Ah," I said. Here's the thing about being a military wife: there's an unspoken rule about keeping a stiff upper lip when things are tough. Not big things like injuries or death; people rushed in to help in those circumstances. Sometimes it was too much help. I remembered a woman whose young daughter lost her battle with cancer. I'd seen her across the room at the Officers Club but hadn't spoken to her since her daughter had died. As I headed her way, an expression passed over her face that seemed to say, *oh, no, someone else that wants to express their sympathy.*

Anyway, it was often the day-to-day problems that wore spouses down: sick kids, bad grades, a disciplinary problem, getting into trouble on base. Anyone could have similar problems, but adding on having a spouse in a war zone who was gone for months at a time made it worse. It could really weigh on a person. Most spouses bore it silently, even when you asked how they were doing. As a commander's wife, I'd been responsible for the well-being of the spouses under CJ's command. Sometimes people were so good at hiding what was really going on, they fell through the cracks. Spousal depression was a real and rarely talked about issue.

"What can I do?" I asked. I drank some of my iced coffee.

"Would you just go talk to her?" James asked.

"Sure. I'll give her a call."

James's brow crinkled in a way that made me think more was coming.

"I don't want her to know I was worried. If she finds out and it gets back to Eric that I asked you to do this, it might make things worse for both of them. Can you arrange to bump in to her?"

"Of course."

"She's at the thrift shop right now," James said.

"I'll swing by there on my way home."

"Thank you."

Chapter Four

When I got to the thrift shop, I threw a blue bib apron over my head, which identified me as a worker. Even though I was no longer a dependent, I could still volunteer here as long as someone sponsored me on base. They usually needed all the help they could get. Base thrift shops were run by spouses' clubs. Membership in spouses' clubs was dwindling. No one was quite sure why, but more women worked than in the past. Kids were in more activities. And there was still a perception of officers' wives being snotty.

Way before my time, spouses were separated by rank. There were clubs for officers' wives and clubs for enlisted wives. It was all about teas, luncheons, wearing hats and gloves, helping to promote a husband's career, and raising money for scholarships. Things morphed over time, but sadly, there were still some who lorded their spouses' position over others.

"Sarah," the new manager said when she spotted me, "thanks for coming. We need to get out the back-to-school supplies."

I followed her through the maze of rooms, where things were sorted before they were put out on display.

Once upon a time, this thrift shop had been a Chinese restaurant. When the restaurant was forced to close due to health violations, nothing had been cleaned. So, when we got to take over the space, it meant hours of scrubbing grease off surfaces. Some days it seemed like there was still a scent of sweet and sour chicken wafting around.

Tracy was working the register, which wasn't conducive to chatting. Her dark red hair was pulled back in a ponytail, exposing an almost painfully thin neck. It was surprising it could hold up her head.

I helped set up a back-to-school display. It enabled me to keep an eye on Tracy while I worked. I hauled out backpacks, notebooks, and art supplies. As far as I could tell, she seemed okay. I didn't know her all that well, but she was smiling and interacting with customers. Now I felt really awkward. I'd promised James but didn't want to be intrusive. How did I get myself in to these situations?

I worked until two, when the shop closed, and managed to walk out the door with Tracy.

"Thanks for setting up the sale to bring Eric's dog home," Tracy said.

"I'm happy to do it."

"Yeah, just what we need is a dog in our small place with all the kids and their things." She shook her head.

Ah, an opening. Base housing was assigned according to rank. The higher the rank, the bigger the house. Some consideration for number of dependents worked into the formula, but if a base had limited housing it was take what they offered or leave it. You'd be offered two units; if you didn't like either of them, your name went to the bottom of the waiting list. In the summer, when most people moved, the waiting list could be fairly long.

"Where do you live?" I asked.

"In one of the older three-bedroom town houses."

"That's near where I used to live." I didn't add that it had been in a single-family house with plenty of room for just the two of us.

"At least the kids love it. They can run around outside without a lot of supervision."

"I miss base. Instant family. People around to help out."

Tracy nodded but didn't add anything.

"How are you doing?" I decided being direct would be best. After all, she was aware that I knew Eric was having problems. It was the whole reason for the fund-raiser.

"Great."

She said it reflexively and without any enthusiasm.

"I know how tough it can be to have them gone and then back. And I didn't even have any kids to take care of." I wished I had. We'd wanted kids, and some days I think it would have made the time go by a lot faster when CJ was deployed.

"How'd your husband do when he got back? Your ex. Sorry."

"It varied from deployment to deployment." I stopped in the parking lot. "CJ never had PTSD, but he came back in various moods. Sometimes he was all gung-ho happy to be back, and sometimes he felt guilty for leaving when others were still stuck in a war zone."

"Eric's been deployed four times. He volunteered once because of the extra pay."

I nodded.

"Eric barely knows our youngest because he's been gone so much." Tracy shook her head. "And he's not getting a very good impression of his daddy right now. It's heartbreaking." Her voice caught on the word *heartbreaking*.

My heart ached for her. "Who's taking care of you?" I asked.

She barked a bitter laugh.

"So, no one," I said.

Tracy shrugged. "I have a couple of neighbors who take the kids sometimes. But some days I just want to run away."

"There are resources that can help you."

"Yeah, that's what Eric's commander's wife said too." She shrugged again. "But those resources aren't going to cook the meals or clean the house." Tracy's eyes filled with tears. "Or—" She clamped her lips together.

"Or what, Tracy?"

She attempted a smile. "It's not that bad. I've got to go pick up the kids from school." She hurried to her car.

My heart felt heavy. I had to figure out how to help her.

At seven a.m. on Tuesday, I rang Belle's doorbell. Running my garage sale business meant a lot of early mornings. I'd already worked on my virtual garage sale site, showered, and run through Dunkin's for an iced coffee. I wished there was an entrance I could use without dragging Kay away from whatever she was doing. After a few moments, Kay opened the door. She gave my outfit—khaki shorts and a Red Sox T-shirt—the once over. Even though Belle's attic was immaculate, I didn't want to wear a dress to work in. Cataloging and moving books around might not be as easy as I'd originally thought. But now I felt a bit underdressed.

"Hi, I'm Sarah Winston. We didn't really meet yesterday." I stuck out my hand.

"Kay Kimble," she said after she reluctantly shook my hand.

She managed a smile and gestured for me to follow her. We went to Sebastian's library. Belle sat behind her desk, and Roger was nowhere in sight. Somehow, that made me happy.

"Good morning," Belle said. She stood, and I saw she was dressed in a simple rose-colored sheath dress. "Thanks for coming today."

"Thank you. I'm excited to get started." I glanced behind me. Kay had left. "Is there an entrance I can come in where I won't have to bother Kay?"

Belle frowned. "Well, you could come in the kitchen entrance. It's usually unlocked during the day. But it's Kay's job to answer the door. Was she unpleasant?"

"Not at all. I just might be in and out a lot the next couple of weeks until the sale, and I don't want to be a bother."

"You do whichever suits you," Belle said.

"Great. Thanks. I'll head on up."

I decided to tackle the Nancy Drew books first. Although I looked longingly at a jumble of old suitcases. Who knew what treasures they held? I'd read up on the Drew books last night, and the different editions. They debuted in the thirties and different iterations followed through the late 2000s. Nancy's personality seemed to reflect the times. In the thirties, she was jaunty and daring, in the fifties she became more the perfect girl, in the nineties, the books focused on her somewhat dysfunctional relationship with Ned. The thirties Nancy sounded the most interesting to me, and I was secretly hoping to find one up here to take home to read.

I worked through them, but they all looked to be

regular editions from the fifties and sixties that were sold by the thousands over the years. There weren't any first editions or rare old ones among this pile anyway. I didn't have any luck finding a single copy of a thirties Nancy Drew. Now that my interest was piqued, I wondered if I could find one at a garage sale or online. Or maybe Miss Belle had some down in her study. That's where I'd keep my best books if I had a study. I organized the books by edition, number in the series, and price. There was something so satisfying about working with books for a change. I loved the smell and feel of books old and new.

I took a break to stretch and moved about a bit. I was much more used to being active than sitting. Thank heavens it was air-conditioned up here. Not only for my well-being but for that of the books, and Kay too because she lived up here. I wandered around the big room for a bit. Books were tucked under the eaves and some sat on rickety shelves. There were also the trunks and suitcases I itched to open. I peeked in a couple of the trunks. One was empty, which was terribly disappointing, and one was full of vintage clothing. I'd love to take time to look at it, but that wasn't what Miss Belle was paying me for. Maybe she'd let me take a look when I was off the clock.

Instead, I tackled the Bobbsey Twins books. My mom had a bunch of them from when she was growing up and had read them to me when I was little. I always loved the younger set of twins, Freddie and Flossie. Flossie had blue eyes and blond hair like I did, although hers was curly and mine was straight. And she was mischievous, always getting into some kind of trouble. It was the polar opposite of how I'd been when I was young. I normally wasn't a rule breaker. But now, trouble seemed to find me. It's not like I sought it, but I did have a hard time saying no when someone asked me to help them with a problem. Maybe I'd gotten in touch with my inner Flossie.

I spent another thirty minutes sorting through the Bobbsey Twin books. Occasionally, I had to check the price of an edition online. Belle had a few that were quite old. I set them aside to ask Roger about them. From what I'd learned, they didn't seem extremely valuable, but better to err on the side of caution. I glanced at my phone. It was already nine.

I glanced again at the stack of precariously piled old suitcases and smiled. Maybe the thirties Drew books I was interested in would be stuck in one of them. There were seven in this particular pile but more scattered around the room. Which one to open first? It was almost like Christmas morning. The brass latches and locks twinkled at me. The scent of their leather filled my nose.

Lots of people stacked old suitcases like these to use as an accent table in their homes. It was a look I loved. I used an old trunk as a coffee table in my apartment. It had so much character, plus it provided extra storage that was so important in a one-bedroom place like mine. When I'd decorated Seth's house for him, I'd used a Louis Vuitton trunk I'd found in his basement as a coffee table.

I lifted the top one off. It was heavy. A leather behemoth with straps that buckled it closed. It made the whole pile sway. I didn't want them to fall over. It would make an enormous racket in a house that was always so quiet, and I didn't want anything to break. How embarrassing would that be? I hastily set down the big one and managed to stop the swaying pile by leaning them against my body. I unstacked the rest of them to keep them from falling over. Some were covered in beautiful, aged leather, others in hardcovered vinyl; one had what looked like a fake alligator print stamped on it. I took a better look. It was real alligator. Wow. The smallest was a battered overnight case with travel stickers from Paris, Spain, and other European cities.

The behemoth was full of Agatha Christie paperbacks. I set it aside after I tapped a note in my phone of its contents. The overnight case intrigued me. The travel stickers made it look like it had been on lots of adventures. If only it could talk. I snapped open the brass metal locks and lifted the lid.

It was filled with manila file folders. I took one out and flipped it open. It held typewritten sheets of eight-and-a-half by eleven pages, complete with carbon paper and copies. The print on the copies was slightly blurred. The paper had yellowed a bit but still looked sturdy. It looked like a short story. My hands begin to shake as I flipped through the pages. I stared down and blinked a couple of times before reading a few paragraphs. The protagonist's name was familiar, Nick Adams. There was a title, and after the title it said, "By Ernest Hemingway."

Chapter Five

I lifted more and more folders out of the suitcase. Each one contained a story that said it was written by Ernest Hemingway. I was so shaken, I had to find a chair to sit on. After staring down for several minutes, my mind worked furiously to recall what I knew about Ernest Hemingway. I had a degree in literature I'd piecemealed together as CJ and I'd moved around the country. I'd taken a class on Hemingway. I confess he wasn't my favorite. I'd always been more of a Twain and Steinbeck fan. Maybe it was my California roots. I looked through the typed pages again.

Then it came to me. The story had fascinated me when I'd first heard it. In the twenties, Hemingway had traveled to Switzerland. His wife, Hadley, stayed behind because she had a cold. She set out to join him a few weeks later, packing his works in progress, which were the Nick Adams stories set in Michigan. Everything he'd worked on for months. She boarded a train, stowed her luggage, and went off to buy water. When she returned, the bag was gone. Never to be seen again. Until now, if I was right.

I put everything back and snapped the latch closed.

I carried it reverently down the stairs. Miss Belle wasn't in the library. No one was. I found her in her small study.

"Are you okay, Sarah? You're quite flushed. I need to have Kay bring you up a fan."

I set the overnight case in front of her on her desk.

"What's this? I don't recall seeing it before."

"You aren't going to believe this." I shook my head, still not believing it myself. "Maybe it's some kind of hoax, but I don't think it is."

I watched as Miss Belle opened the case and looked through the folders, frowning.

"Hemingway stories?" she asked.

I explained what I thought they were. She turned so white, I thought she was going to faint.

"Do you want some water?" I asked. When she nodded, I dashed to the kitchen, found a glass—thank heavens for open shelving—and poured the water before hustling back.

"Don't bring the glass too close. We don't dare spill on these." She sipped some water before setting it on a shelf five feet from the desk.

"What would you like me to do?" I asked.

"Give me a few minutes alone. Please." Her voice shook as she took a seat at her desk and lifted one of the folders.

As I left, I heard her say, "How can this be?"

I left the various doors that led to the attic open so I could hear Miss Belle if she called out to me. I restacked the suitcases and immersed myself back into the Bobbsey Twin books. I noticed some of them had the name "Winnie" written in them. I wondered who she was. Miss Belle had a first-edition copy of

The Bobbsey Twins at the Seashore, but it wasn't worth very much even in good condition. Not nearly what a first-edition copy of *The Secret of the Old Clock*, the first Nancy Drew, would bring.

At eleven, the alarm on my phone went off, telling me it was time to go. I gathered my things and headed down the stairs. A cry came from below as I was halfway to the second floor. Followed by a thump and a door slamming.

That didn't sound good. "Miss Belle?" I yelled. I ran down the last flight of stairs, leaping off the bottom two, and ran into Miss Belle's study.

She lay on the floor by the desk. The overnight case was gone. Miss Belle struggled to sit up.

"What happened?" I asked. I kneeled beside her. A large bump was swelling rapidly on her temple.

"Kay. She grabbed the overnight case and hit me with it."

"Don't get up. I'm calling for help." I dialed 911 and gave a quick explanation of what I thought happened.

Miss Belle grabbed my arm. "You have to go after her. Get the overnight case back. We can't lose it."

I hesitated. "I don't think I should leave you."

"Please, you have to."

I handed her my phone. "Stay on the line with the dispatcher. I'll go see if I can spot her."

It doesn't seem like she went out the front door because the slam I heard would have been louder. I dashed out the back and ran down the path around the detached garage. The long lawn sloped down toward the woods. It was hot, the humidity hanging hazy in the air. I didn't like all the freaking woods, but I saw movement through the trees. "Stop," I yelled. A blur of black and white pushed through bushes.

I glanced over my shoulder. I didn't hear any sirens. No one else was around. I shrugged. Kay was a petite little thing that should give me an advantage. I took off running. At the edge of the woods, I paused and listened. I heard movement. It sounded like it was coming from straight ahead. I plunged in too. Branches and brambles grabbed at me, scratching, pulling. It almost felt like they were trying to hold me back. I kept pushing forward, stopping occasionally to listen.

"Kay, just stop. Give the case back and we'll forget this ever happened," I yelled. I wouldn't, but maybe she would buy my story. "It's not too late to make this go away." Nothing. No response, but more movement ahead and to my left. Sweat poured off me. Mosquitoes and gnats surrounded me, buzzing away. I pushed on until I came to what looked like a small trail. Not one the city had put in but something the deer used. Left or right? All seemed quiet. I chose left after hearing something. Some kind of crack, like a branch breaking or a deer running. It made the most sense to head toward noise instead of away from it.

I trotted along for a couple more minutes, hot, sweaty, panting. I saw a blur of black on the trail ahead and picked up my pace. It was Kay. Sprawled facedown on the path.

Chapter Six

I gave one final boost and ran to her. "Kay?" I asked. No response. A big limb lay beside her. Had it fallen and knocked her out? I didn't see the overnight case, but Kay had to be my first priority. A large crack sounded as I leaned down to check on her. Bark sprayed on me. I looked up, hoping another limb wasn't falling. It took me a bewildered moment to realize the noise hadn't been a branch falling but a gunshot. A tree about two feet from me had been hit.

I leaped up, dodged into the woods, and ran back the way I had come. The woods were thick and hopefully provided more cover than the path. But it slowed me down. That, and I'd already run more this morning than I normally did in a month. My side ached. I gasped for air from a combination of fear and exertion. I plowed ahead, trying to clear limbs and brambles away with my arms.

I thought I heard movement behind me. But maybe it was just the blood pounding in my ears. The noise I created as I ran. I was too scared to look back. If something bad was going to happen, I didn't want to see it coming. I finally came to the edge of the woods behind Miss Belle's house. I eyed the long expanse of lawn between me and the house. The house represented safety. By now, the EMTs must be there. Maybe even the police. I had, after all, reported the overnight case as stolen.

I slipped behind a tree and peered around me. I didn't see anything, but with the density of the woods it wasn't surprising. I didn't hear anything either. Not a twig snapping. Not a bird chirping. An unusual silence, as if the woods were holding their breath, waiting for someone to make the next move. To show themselves.

A police officer came around the corner of Miss Belle's garage; I was too far away to tell who. He shaded his eyes and scanned the tree line. To my right, I heard crashing in the woods. It sounded as if it was moving away from me. That was my cue. I burst out of the woods, running to the police officer as if my life depended on it. And maybe it did.

As I ran, I made a waving motion with my hand. *Go back to the garage. Take cover.* Instead, the officer ran toward me, looking, scanning. It was Awesome. When I got to him, he started to shove me behind him. But I grabbed his arm and dragged him along with me until he got the idea. He ran, pulling me along with his faster stride, until we rounded the corner of the garage. I bent over sucking in hot air.

"What happened?" Awesome asked.

"Get someone out to the woods," I gasped out. "Kay. Miss Belle's maid is out on the trail. She's hurt."

Awesome talked into his shoulder mic.

"There's someone out there with a gun. They shot at me. Tell them to be careful."

Awesome frowned as he updated whoever was at the other end of his mic. "Someone shot at you?"

"Me, Kay, the tree near us. I don't know. I heard a crack and then was sprayed with bark. I took off."

"The EMTs are still here. Let's have them look at your cheek."

I swiped at my cheek and then looked at blood on my hand. My arms and legs were covered with scratches. "Miss Belle?"

"She's going to be okay. Her personal physician just arrived a few minutes ago. Come on, before the EMTs take off."

The EMTs swabbed my scratches and bandaged the small gash on my cheek. If I kept this up, I was going to know every EMT within a ten-mile radius, with the experiences I'd been through over the past year. Awesome stayed with me but wandered away every time his radio crackled.

"Any word on Kay?" I asked after the EMTs finished up and left.

Awesome looked down and away. A sure sign he didn't have any good news. I sat quietly, trying to figure out how I felt. Exhausted, scared . . . lucky to be alive.

I sat on a chair next to Miss Belle, who was resting on a chaise longue in the sitting room off her bedroom. Her personal physician had just left. She held an ice pack to her head with one hand and gripped my hand with the other as I caught her up what had happened in the woods. Scott Pellner, an officer with the Ellington Police Department, stood near us. I'd met Pellner over a year ago and had seen more of him than I'd ever thought possible. I'm sure he felt the same way about me. He'd just confirmed that Kay was dead.

"Officer Pellner, would you please give Sarah and me a moment alone?" Miss Belle asked, her Southern drawl more pronounced than I'd ever heard it. But there was a strength in her voice that belied the question. It was a command.

Pellner looked back and forth between us for a moment before giving a short nod and leaving the room. He shut the door.

"This is going to sound tacky at a time like this, but was the overnight case with Kay?"

"No. It was gone. Maybe she hid it somewhere in the woods. Or maybe she gave it to someone who double-crossed her." That sounded so dramatic.

"Must we tell them what was in the overnight case?" Miss Belle asked, but this time it was definitely a question. "I can't imagine how the manuscripts came to be in my attic."

"You didn't know they were there?" I wanted to double-check her reaction.

"I've spent the last few hours thinking about it. And what came over Kay?"

"Had she worked for you for very long?"

"Only a couple of weeks. But Kay came from a highly recommended agency." Miss Belle slipped her hand from mine. "You didn't answer my earlier question. Do we have to tell the police right away about what was in the overnight case? I'd like some time to sort this out on my own."

I shook my head. "It's not an option."

"Please hear me out."

Miss Belle paused until I nodded.

I'd kept a lot of secrets over the years. Some I should have and others I shouldn't. Secrets cost a person one way or the other. But the least I could do was listen.

"I need some time. Just a day. To figure out where the papers came from. They're priceless." She set the ice pack aside.

"A woman is dead. I don't think we can lie to the police. They're going to ask what was in it."

"They've already asked me."

"What did you say?" I asked.

"I'm an old, injured woman. I had a brief relapse, so I was unable to answer their question."

At any other time, I might have been amused, and I *was* impressed. Miss Belle was the epitome of a Steel Magnolia.

"Kay is dead. Probably murdered. I just can't lie about this." I'd justified a few sins of omission in the past. But this didn't fall into that category. We both knew well and good what the contents of the overnight case were.

Miss Belle studied my face as if she was looking for a crack in my conviction. She finally sighed. "You're right."

"They might be able to keep it quiet. But they won't be able to promise even that."

"Will you go get Officer Pellner, then?"

I stood. "Where's Roger today?" I hadn't seen him, but the library and attic were far enough apart that we could easily avoid each other.

"Why, I don't know. With all that's gone on, I hadn't even given him a thought."

"Was he supposed to come?"

Miss Belle nodded.

"Could Kay have let him in without you knowing?"

"It's possible. I Skyped with my brother this morning about some family matters and asked not to be disturbed."

I walked over to the door as I pondered that bit of information and gestured for Pellner to come back in.

Chapter Seven

I went back and sat next to Miss Belle again. Pellner looked a little out of place standing a few feet away from us in such a feminine room. The wallpaper had big pink cabbage roses on it. The chaise was tufted pink silk with silk fringe dangling. There was a white French provincial dressing table with a large mirror and a cabbage rose upholstered stool tucked neatly underneath. A pink needlepoint area rug with more cabbage roses topped the mahogany floors. It was a stunning room. Not meant for police officers. It didn't seem like anything bad should ever happen in a room like this.

"Won't you have a seat, Officer Pellner," Miss Belle said.

"I'm fine, thank you." Pellner pulled out a notebook and flipped it open. "When Sarah called 911 she reported something had been stolen. What was it?"

"An overnight case she found up in the attic." Miss Belle spoke before I could open my mouth.

"What was in the case?" he asked.

This time Miss Belle didn't speak up right away. We exchanged a look.

"What?" Pellner asked.

Miss Belle nodded at me.

"Manuscripts that were written by Ernest Hemingway and stolen in 1922." I smoothed my hands over my shorts. "They must be worth millions."

Pellner stared at me. "Hemingway."

I nodded. "The author."

"I know who he is. How'd they end up here?"

I looked at Miss Belle.

She lifted her chin. "I have no idea."

"You didn't know they were in your attic?" Pellner asked.

"Not until the moment Sarah brought them down and showed them to me. My family has been piling stuff in that attic for years."

"Sarah?"

"I believe Miss Belle. She was shocked when she saw them." Then I realized maybe he was asking me if I'd known they were there. "How could I know they were up there? Miss Belle just hired me yesterday."

Pellner nodded. "What were you thinking, chasing after Kay?"

What had I been thinking? I think I'd just responded to the tone of Miss Belle's voice. I took off for the same reason Pellner left us alone in the room earlier. "I was thinking we couldn't lose those manuscripts. Although it looks as if we already did." It made me so sad. A few hours ago, I'd handled something written by Ernest Hemingway, something maybe only a couple of other people had ever read. If only I had read more of them before I brought them down. Words hardly anyone else had seen slipped right through my hands. I looked down at them accusingly.

"Officer Pellner." Miss Belle's drawl deepened just a bit. "If there is any way we can keep the contents of the

overnight case a secret for now, I'd be very grateful."
She smiled at him. "I realize there's been a murder, but
I can't think this would reflect well on the town of
Ellington. Or, I have to admit selfishly, my family."

"Was anyone else here this morning?" Pellner asked.

The nonanswer. Even a woman like Miss Belle couldn't
get that promise out of Pellner. Miss Belle looked at
him thoughtfully for a moment.

"There's a possibility Roger Mervine was here. He is
organizing the more valuable books in my library."

"But you don't know for sure."

"No. I was tied up in a meeting with my brother."

"So your brother was here?"

"No, we met via Skype."

Pellner's eyes widen a bit at that.

"Just because I'm old doesn't mean I don't keep up
with technology."

"My apologies if I offended you," Pellner said. "Can
you tell me what the overnight case looked like?"

Miss Belle nodded at me, and I gave Pellner a brief
description.

After that, he fired off a whole litany of questions.
Have there been any threats? Anyone hanging around
who shouldn't be? Was Kay in some kind of trouble?
Miss Belle answered *no* or *not that I know of* to each
question.

"So Kay entered the room while you were looking
over the manuscripts."

"Yes," Miss Belle said, but she didn't add anything.

"Did she say anything?" Pellner asked.

Miss Belle closed her eyes for a minute. "She hesi-
tated in the doorway and said 'Excuse me.' I told her
I needed some privacy. Kay came in anyway. I stood.
She picked up the case and hit me on the temple

with it. Next thing I remember was Sarah asking me if I was okay."

"You didn't hear Kay talking to anyone or any other voices?" I asked. Pellner gave me a look like I should quit asking questions.

"Not that I can recall."

Pellner slapped his notebook shut. "Let me know if anything comes to you," he said. "Either of you." He stood to go. "The state police will show up later today or tomorrow and want to question both of you again. So please be available."

I looked at his back as he walked out. As if we had any choice.

Miss Belle slumped against the back of the chaise and closed her eyes.

"Would you like me to get you some more ice?" I asked.

"Yes. If you would, please."

I trotted down the main staircase. An occasional creak of the house was the only sound as I made my way to the kitchen. It was almost noon, but I wasn't even hungry. I took a moment to lock the back door and wondered how many other entrances the house had. I refilled the bag with more ice and took it back upstairs. The quiet was giving me the willies. Miss Belle snored gently on the chaise longue. I set down the bag beside her and tiptoed out of the room. I didn't feel comfortable leaving her alone while she was sleeping so I sent a text to my other client, telling her something had come up and that I'd get back in touch soon. Fortunately, she was agreeable to that.

I decided I might as well work on cataloging more

books, so I headed back up to the attic. I passed Kay's
room on the way by. The police surely had been here.
There wasn't any police tape around the door, so I
tried the knob. The door opened easily. I'm not sure
what I'd been expecting; maybe something like a
scene from *Downton Abbey*: a narrow bed with an iron
headboard and a washstand. But this room looked like
something out of a luxurious bed-and-breakfast. There
was a bed with a pale blue silk canopy and matching
comforter, a sitting area with a window seat and piles
of books, and a fancy, old-fashioned-looking brass
telescope stood in front of a large window. What the
heck did she use that for? Maybe she was a birder.

I snooped, opening drawers, looking under the
bed, and going through the pockets of clothes hanging in the closet. I wasn't even sure what I was looking
for. A diary, or flash drive, or signed confession. But I
didn't find anything remotely suspicious. Maybe the
police had already found whatever it was I thought I
was looking for.

I went over to the telescope, peering through it.
Everything was a blur. It took me a few minutes to
adjust a bunch of dials to bring my view into focus. It
was pointed toward the woods. I could see police tape
and thought how ironic it was that the telescope was
pointed at the very spot where I'd found Kay's body.
Why? Had she been planning to meet someone there
or was it just a coincidence? The answer to that had
died with Kay.

From up here in the attic I could see the woods
were narrower than I'd realized when I was in the
thick of them. On the other side lay a fairly busy road.
There was a police car parked on the shoulder of the

road and some sort of utility van. I wondered if that was crime scene people from the state police.

I returned my focus to the woods. I scanned back and forth with the telescope, hoping to spot the over-night case sitting out in plain sight. But the density that had protected me earlier today now blocked my view of anything helpful. Or did it?

Chapter Eight

On the last pass, I glimpsed something in a small clearing that didn't look as if it belonged in the woods. I twisted the knobs and made everything blurrier as I madly tried to swing the telescope back to the black blob I'd thought I'd seen in my last sweep. Modern electronics had spoiled me with their ability to auto-focus. I finally got things somewhat focused and moved the telescope slowly inch over inch of woods. It seemed painfully tedious when my heart was racing because I thought the black blob might actually have been the overnight case. Cast aside, lying in the mud.

But there, there was something out there, though it was too blurry for me to know for sure what it was. Screw it. I didn't have the patience to use all the knobs on the telescope. I charged down the stairs and patted the back pocket of my shorts to make sure I had my phone. Once again, I ran out of the house and across the broad lawn. I stopped for a moment. Looking down from three stories was a lot easier than being on eye level. I glanced back at the third-floor window and tried to picture an imaginary line from the end of the telescope that glinted in the window to a spot in the woods where I thought I'd seen the case. The telescope had been angled to the right, away from where I'd found Kay's body. I walked along the edge of the woods, tracking the angle of the telescope. It was tedious—take a few steps, look toward the house, a few more steps, double-check the house—but I did it until I came to a small path.

Kay must have known it was here and entered the woods at this spot, unlike the place I'd plunged through earlier. I took one last look at the telescope and felt fairly confident if I entered here, then headed right again, I'd find the overnight case. But as I eased into the shadowy woods, I worried that maybe I'd gotten it all wrong. Why would Kay leave the overnight case in one direction and then end up in the opposite? Maybe because someone besides me had been chasing her? Someone she didn't trust entirely.

I took out my phone and called Pellner. Yes, I had him on speed dial. It just seemed easier these days. He might still be in the vicinity, or know that someone else was. For all I knew, they were still over by where Kay's body had been, searching for clues.

"I might have spotted the overnight case in the woods," I told Pellner when he answered.

"How?" he asked.

"There was a telescope in Kay's room. I used it."

I heard Pellner sigh.

"I'm not going to ask what you were doing in there because I know. You were snooping."

"Maybe it isn't clear to you how important those papers are."

I heard another sigh.

"I get it. I'll come back to the house so you can show me."

"I'm not exactly at the house."

"Where are you?"

"In the woods. Heading for the spot where I think the case is."

"What? Someone shot at you."

"I know, but I saw a police car parked alongside the road when I was looking through the telescope."

"Get out of there. Back to the house."

I reached a bend in the narrow path. "I'm almost to where I think the case is." I held the phone away from my ear as Pellner swore. After a moment, I listened again. "Pellner?"

"Sarah. Don't do that. When you didn't answer, I thought something awful had happened. I'm on my way over there and have called for backup." Through the phone, I could hear his siren come on. "And don't hang up either."

"I won't. I called you, didn't I?" The path curved again. I couldn't see the house any longer, so I slowed to search for the case. I slapped at a mosquito that landed on my neck.

"What was that?" Pellner asked.

"Just a mosquito." I didn't tell him to calm down because little made me madder than someone saying that to me.

Ahead of me, there was a lot of rustling in the woods, which I reported to Pellner. "It's probably a tiny bird or squirrel. It's kind of dry out here. One time a tiny bird flew out of a bunch of leaves and made such a ruckus, I thought I was going to be attacked by a bear."

"Or maybe it's whoever took a shot at you earlier."

Now I could hear a siren through the phone and air. "I guess that's possible. Although with all the police around, you wouldn't think they'd come back right away."

"Given the value of what's in the case and the fact

that it looks as if they already killed someone for it, it seems like a distinct possibility to me. You didn't wait around."

"But I'm not a bad guy who's afraid of the police. I *called* the police."

"Maybe you don't get how bad guys work."

I rounded a corner just as someone burst out of the woods about fifty feet ahead of me. Overnight case in hand. I gasped and almost dropped the phone. The person ran straight ahead and hadn't even noticed me. I started running too.

"What? What?" I heard Pellner yelling from the phone.

"Someone has the case. They burst out of the woods like a lighted bottle rocket."

"What are you doing?"

"Chasing him." I knew my voice sounded incredulous.

"Stop. Run the other direction."

I ran around a bend. I could see the man ahead of me on a wider path, one that ended at a road with a few cars whizzing by. I pushed myself forward. A black sedan was parked on the shoulder. The man leaped in the driver's side. The car screeched off. Gravel spurted up as I got to the road, which forced me to turn my back.

"Damn it. He got away," I said. I took a good look around. "I think I'm on Nutley Road." My voice panted between words. "Black sedan, Massachusetts plates, heading toward Bedford."

"License plate number?" Pellner yelled. I heard a siren.

I shook my head, then remembered Pellner couldn't see me. "I didn't get it. Maybe a six at the end."

"What did he look like?"

"I'm not sure. He was far away. Pants. Maybe jeans.

And a Tshirt. I didn't get a glimpse of his face. Pick me up."

A few moments later, Pellner approached. I stood on the shoulder, flagging him down. He roared past me.

"Hey, what about me?"

"I'm in pursuit." Then he hung up.

I kicked at a rock and stubbed my toe. I bent over to rub it as I heard a car slow. I glanced over and noticed an SUV. Its right-turn signal came on and it pulled over on the shoulder behind me.

"Need a ride?" Ryne O'Rourke, my next-door neighbor and friend, poked his ridiculously good-looking head out of the window of his red SUV.

I dashed over to the car, yanked the passenger-side door open, and hopped in. "Go, go, go." I pointed in the direction the car and Pellner had taken.

Ryne gunned it without asking questions. And soon we were flying down the road past Nutley Lake in Bedford. There was no sign of Pellner or the black sedan. Hopefully, Pellner had it in his sights. I turned one of the air-conditioning vents on me. I was a sweaty mess for the second time this morning.

"Want to tell me what we're looking for?"

"A black four-door sedan, Massachusetts plates, possibly ending with a six."

"And why exactly are we pursuing it?"

Just as I opened my mouth to answer him, I spotted the car. Heading toward us. I jabbed my finger at it before I could get the words to come. "There it is. He must have pulled in a driveway or something because Pellner didn't see him."

The car whizzed by us, but I couldn't make out who was driving or if anyone else was in the car. I turned in my seat, but a jumble of chairs in the back seat blocked my view, so I didn't see the car. "Turn, turn. Go back."

Ryne signaled, pulled into a drive, and reversed directions. "Hurry," I said.

"Why? Hot date escaping? You looked like you tangled with someone recently."

"Rough morning." Ugh, I'd forgotten the scratches from earlier. Ryne could drive me nuts at times. He'd moved here a few months ago to help his uncle with his antique store in Concord, which probably explained the chairs in the back of the SUV. Ryne was extremely popular with the ladies, with his dark hair, green eyes, and occasional Irish accent. I heard lots of laughter and jazz music coming through the thin walls between our apartments. But at least he sped up.

"You seemed to have had quite a few rough mornings since we've been neighbors."

"Yeah, but not the good kind."

Ryne laughed.

I called Pellner. "The car just passed us going the other way. I'm with my neighbor, Ryne O'Rourke. We're heading west on Nutley."

Pellner blew out a snort of exasperated air. "I'm calling it in. You two knuckleheads stop trying to pursue them."

I hung up. If there was any chance we could find that car, I wasn't about to stop.

"You have the police chasing down dates for you?"

"As if."

A few minutes later, Ryne pulled over as Pellner flew by us, lights flashing and siren screaming. Pellner's car disappeared over a hill as Ryne got back on the road.

"Can you go any faster?" I asked. My foot smashed down on the floorboard like there was some imaginary accelerator I could use to make Ryne speed up.

"I've found that it usually isn't a good idea to go chasing after the police. At least not where I've lived."

A couple of miles later, we saw a black sedan pulled over on the shoulder. Pellner and two other cops approached the car and yanked open the doors. Another officer flagged us down and made us detour onto a side road. As we turned, I could see that the car was empty.

"Another one bites the dust," Ryne said.

"He has to be around here somewhere." I leaned back in my seat, exhausted.

"He must be really desperate to get away from you if he's gone to those lengths." Ryne's tone was light, but there was no mistaking the curiosity in his voice.

"Aren't they all." It made me think of Seth.

"Where to, me fair lass?" Ryne's Irish accent seemed to come and go in waves. "Home?"

What if Miss Belle had woken up? It's not like she was some frail, old woman, but today's events had been frightening. And if she woke and I disappeared too it might freak her out. I know it would me.

"My car's at Belle Winthrop Granville's house. I'm working for her."

"And your work includes chasing after black sedans and police cars? It must be an interesting job."

I shook my head and gave him the address. He hadn't been in town long enough to be impressed or to know anything about her. "She's probably wondering where I've disappeared to and why my car is still parked at her house."

"Anyone that knows you realizes they're going to constantly be surprised by you."

"I'm not sure you meant that as a good thing," I said. Ryne grinned. "Take a left here."

Ryne followed my instructions, heading down a side street that would probably lead us back to Nutley. I sent a quick text telling Miss Belle I'd be back in a little while, that I'd gone for a walk. She might decipher the subtext that I didn't want to put in a text.

As I looked up from my phone, I saw movement to my right out of the corner of my eye. A man was sprinting through a backyard with the overnight case. I couldn't have had better luck if I'd had a tracking device on the case. It made sense that he couldn't have gotten too far after abandoning the car and having to hoof it.

"Stop," I yelled to Ryne. "There he is."

Chapter Nine

"I've heard of chasing a man before, but you've taken it to a whole new level," Ryne said as he braked.

I flung my door open, ready to jump out before the car stopped. Ryne grasped my arm and held tight.

"Where do you think you're going?" he asked. "If the police are chasing that man, it's not safe for you to."

I slumped against the seat. "You're right." I blamed the heat and adrenaline and craziness of the morning for skewing my judgment. I called Pellner for a third time.

Ryne looked over at me when I disconnected. "Next time, you might want to let me fully stop the car before you try to bail out. You took years off my life with that move."

A police car skidded around the corner. Pellner slowed next to us. Windows were rolled down.

"He ran that way," I said, pointing.

Pellner looked at Ryne. "Do me a favor and take her home." Then he tore off.

* * *

"What's with all the chairs in the back?" I asked as we headed toward Miss Belle's house.

"Garbage day. I found a particularly amazing pile of goods along the road and grabbed a bunch of chairs. My uncle will be pleased with my finds, even though some of them need a bit of love. That and upholstery fabric."

For me, one of the delights of living in New England was the way people put their old things out on the curb for other people to pick up. "Oh, that sounds like fun."

"Want me to take you by the place I found the chairs? It's not too far from here."

"I wish, but I really need to get back to Miss Belle." Oh, for a morning of driving around to look for treasures.

"What's going on with you and this Miss Belle?" Ryne asked. "I may have joked that you were chasing after a man, but we both know that's not the truth."

I told him a little bit about what had happened this morning. Ryne deserved some kind of explanation after driving me all over the place. He'd peppered me with questions the whole way over to Miss Belle's. I was too depressed to answer most of them. The biggest literary find in years had slipped through my fingers three times in a few short hours. I'd failed to protect it. Hemingway must be rolling in his grave.

I trudged into Miss Belle's kitchen after Ryne dropped me off. Miss Belle sat at a round walnut kitchen table next to a bay window. A glass of iced tea sat in front of her. She held another ice bag to her head.

"You need to keep your doors locked," I said.

"You're right. Would you like some sweet tea?" she asked. "It's my grandmother's recipe."

"I'd love some. But don't get up. Just point me in the right direction."

"It's in the glass pitcher on the shelf in the refrigerator. Glasses are to the left of the sink."

I settled across from Miss Belle after helping myself. I took a long drink of the tea and sighed. "It's delicious." It was the good kind. Miss Belle must have used a simple sugar to make it instead of just dumping sugar into brewed tea. It made me think of CJ's mom, who prided herself on her sweet tea. They lived in Fort Walton Beach, Florida, aka LA, aka Lower Alabama.

"I take it you didn't just go for a walk," Miss Belle said.

I looked down at my smudged clothing and pushed back a strand of sweat-dried hair. "No." I filled her in on what had happened since I'd left her napping. Her eyes grew wider as I told the tale, and she put the ice bag down on the table.

"Sarah, you put yourself in danger."

"I know. On the surface, it seems foolish." I reached across the table. "But it's Hemingway and now it's lost. Maybe forever." I blinked my eyes to keep the tears that were welling at bay.

Miss Belle didn't try to offer any words of comfort, and I respected that. What was there to say?

"Why does Kay have a telescope in her room?" I asked. I was trying to go through all the questions swirling through my head. I needed answers to anything that seemed unusual.

"My former caretaker was a birder. He put it up there and used it frequently. No one ever thought to take it out."

"So that was his room before Kay's?" I asked.

"No. He and his wife had a suite of rooms on the third floor. My caretaker thought the line of sight was better up in the attic." She paused and studied me. "We have to put our heads together," she said. "Between the two of us, surely we can think of some way to find the manuscripts."

"Did Roger ever show up?" I asked.

"Not that I know of."

"Do you think if we went in to the library you'd be able to tell?"

"It's worth a try." Miss Belle took a long look at me as we walked down the hall. "What are you thinking? You sound suspicious of Roger."

"Maybe he overheard us talking when I brought you the case with the manuscripts."

"Was he the man you were chasing?"

"No." Roger was on the pudgy side, with soft hands and a pasty complexion. "The man I chased was lean, taller. Roger, I could have caught." That put a bit of sparkle in Miss Belle's eyes.

We looked around the library. Some books were pulled off shelves. There was a box on the desk filled with books. All of them had been priced, and many were worth more than I paid for rent in a year.

"As far as I know, this looks just as it did last night."

We trekked back to the kitchen as a car pulled up. Pellner knocked on the kitchen door.

"Ice tea, Officer?" Miss Belle asked when he came in.

"Yes, please."

I got him a glass and watched his Adam's apple bob up and down as he drank.

"Sarah, you put yourself at risk," he said.

"I know, but it was—"

"Hemingway, I get that," Pellner said. "Anyone would have done the same."

I was astounded. I'd expected a lecture. Maybe he wanted me to help. I felt a bit tingly all over. "Any luck finding the man or the overnight case?"

Pellner shook his head. "We canvassed the neighborhood. A man who lives near where you last saw the thief reported his old Jeep had been stolen. Someone probably hotwired it. It was found later in Carlisle. The trail is dead." He looked at Miss Belle. "I'm sorry. Thank you for the tea." Pellner stood.

"Thank you for all you've done," Miss Belle replied.

Pellner looked at me. His dimple was in its deep, unhappy position, which I was all too familiar with. "Stay out of this. If either of you think of anything helpful, contact me." He walked to the door, but turned back to us. "Don't let her get you involved in any crazy schemes, Miss Belle." With that he left.

"What a mess," I told Miss Belle. "If you want to look for someone else to run your sale, I'll understand." The weight of today's events settled over me like a steel shroud.

"Piffle. I was thinking maybe we should go visit Roger at his store because he isn't answering his phone."

I smiled. "Excellent. Let me go home and clean up and then I'll come back for you."

Miss Belle insisted that I needn't drop her off in front of the store. We'd both changed clothes, me into a green sundress and her into beige linen pants and a gold twinset. The Red Sox were playing tonight, so traffic into the city at four had been a nightmare of inching forward, lots of honking, and hand gestures I was embarrassed to have Miss Belle see. Until she made one herself when someone tried to cut us off.

"I've lived up here a long time," Miss Belle said when she noticed my sideways glance at her. "You become used to the local customs."

I laughed. "I guess you do."

After driving around the block several times, I found a space about a block from Roger's store. It was a brick building with a large plate-glass window. His door was painted a deep red. We swept into the store, which was "a clean, well-lighted place," to borrow the title from a Hemingway short story. Somehow, I always expected rare bookstores to be dim and musty.

A woman with silver hair in a loose bun on top of her head looked up as we entered. She set some knitting aside.

"Miss Belle, how delightful to see you." The woman looked past Belle at me, and then beyond me. "Is Roger with you?"

"No. We were hoping he was here," Miss Belle said.

"He left early this morning and said he'd be at your house all day."

Miss Belle and I glanced at each other.

"Has he called you since?" I asked, keeping my voice light and friendly while my mind went through frantic scenarios about his disappearance.

"No. Is something wrong?" she asked.

Miss Belle smiled. "Just a mix-up in communications. Sometimes I can be a doddering old woman." She grabbed my arm and clung to it, as if to prove her point. We left the store. I didn't think Roger's assistant bought our story for one minute. No one would mistake Miss Belle for some doddering old woman. The assistant was probably speed-dialing Roger right this minute.

Chapter Ten

As soon as we were several steps away from the store, Miss Belle quit the weak-old-woman act.

"What are you thinking?" I asked her. I knew what *I* was thinking. Roger had been in the house, heard Miss Belle and me talking, and somehow had convinced Kay to make off with the overnight case.

"I'm thinking I need some tea. There's a place just beyond where you parked."

Minutes later, we sat at a small bistro table by a large-paned glass window. Miss Belle had Earl Grey tea and I had a double shot of espresso. Not my usual order, but today seemed to call for an extra boost of energy. I picked at the blueberry scone sitting in front of me while Miss Belle added milk and sugar to her tea. She daintily stirred the tea before taking a sip and visibly relaxing.

"It seems to me if Roger had been in the house this morning, someone would have seen him. Certainly, he would have come to my aid when he heard me cry out."

Unless he was in on it, I thought again.

"Did you see his car this morning when you arrived?" Miss Belle asked.

I shook my head. "No. There weren't any other cars around." That gave me another thought. "Did Kay have a car?"

"She did," Miss Belle said. "A black sedan. She keeps it parked in the garage next to mine."

"A black sedan? That's what I saw this morning on the road. The car I told you we followed."

"Oh, dear. I never thought to check the garage."

"Neither did I. Excuse me." I pulled out my phone to call Pellner. Maybe he'd know about Kay's car. It could be the one that was abandoned on the side of the road. All I got was his voice mail. He wouldn't necessarily have answered my question, but I left him the information anyway. I nibbled on my scone for a moment. "When did you decide to do a sale for the Ellington Library?"

"A couple of months ago. Roger had been over visiting and mentioned doing something like that. That it was a shame to have all those books sitting around when they could be appreciated by so many."

"Really? He was such a snob about them the first time we met."

Miss Belle laughed. I didn't want to add that he said many cretins would appreciate them.

"Maybe he was hoping you'd sell them through his store." I shook my head. "Then again the way he feels about them, probably not. Unless there was something valuable or rare." I did my best impression of Roger's voice.

Miss Belle smiled. "He might have been. But I'd rather help the library."

"He loses a lot of income by not being able to sell them."

"I'm paying him an exorbitant fee. I'm worried

about him. It's unlike him not to be where he said he was going to be."

I couldn't help but feel as if no fee would match getting a commission off the sale of the books. Maybe he resented that, but how would he even know about the Hemingway manuscripts to be in on stealing them? The whole thing seemed like a spur-of-the-moment crime. I found the manuscripts and Kay, realizing their value, took off with them. But that didn't explain the man in the woods with the car. Maybe Kay had ThugsRUs on speed dial.

"What's our next move?" Miss Belle asked. Her appetite seemed intact as she forked a bite of scone into her mouth.

I opened my mouth while I tried to process her question. It's not as if we were Cagney and Lacey out on a case. If anything, I felt as if I needed to get Miss Belle home and safely tucked in bed.

"I see you're surprised at my question. I'll invite you to my next poker party. My card-shark pals will make a fortune off you with that face."

It was hard to picture Miss Belle with a pack of card-shark friends smoking cigars and placing bets. "As I said the day we met, no one has ever accused me of having a poker face."

"And you aren't going to answer me? Just give me a hypothetical. What would be your next move?"

"Going home?"

"That doesn't sound like the woman I've read about in the papers."

"Yes. Well, the woman you've read about in the papers might be a fictional version of the real me. A big old scaredy-cat that's stumbled into a few bad situations and managed to come out on the other side."

"I see. What would that woman do?"

"You're very stubborn."

"So I've been told."

I took a bite of the scone to hold her off. It was moist and delicious. The blueberries were still plump and juicy. "I'd go to Roger's house and see if he was there."

"Excellent idea. We can walk over when we're finished."

There was no dissuading Miss Belle once she had her mind set on something. I'd refuse to go. Miss Belle would tell me fine, she'd walk to Roger's house and Uber home. Uber! Home! Of course I couldn't let her do that, and as we walked over I berated myself for even mentioning going to Roger's in the first place.

"Oh, stop," Miss Belle said when we'd walked a block.

I did.

"I didn't mean stop walking. I meant stop torturing yourself. You keep making hand gestures that I assume go along with some internal debate you're having with yourself."

I didn't even realize I'd been making gestures, but the debate had been going on the whole time.

"I would have suggested going to Roger's house even if you hadn't," Miss Belle said.

"We could call the Boston PD and have them do a welfare check." I should have thought of that when we were having tea.

"It will take them hours to send someone and we're almost there."

Miss Belle had a point. I started moving again. "Okay, then. Let's do this."

"He's just two up in the lovely brick with the wide steps."

All the brick houses looked lovely to me. On any

other occasion, I'd be enjoying this walk. The weather had cooled a bit since noon. I followed Miss Belle up the steps and she rang an impressively large brass doorbell in the shape of a book. We waited a moment. I studied the lion's head door knocker. The kind in the Mr. Magoo version of *A Christmas Carol*. I expected it to turn into a face and say something any moment. Instead, nothing happened.

"Knock, please," Miss Belle said.

I did. Nothing.

"A bit harder, perhaps?"

This time I put some power behind it, and the door opened. Miss Belle was through it before I could say anything. It took me a minute to realize it hadn't been pulled open from the other side, but swung open with the force of my knock. It must not have been latched securely, which worried me. By that time, Miss Belle was through a foyer and disappearing down a hall, calling for Roger.

"Miss Belle, come back." I hesitated, fearing what awaited us in there. She didn't return. I stepped in, leaving the door wide open and hustled after her. By the time I caught up with her in the kitchen, she was drumming her fingers on an old-fashioned linoleum countertop and frowning. What a contrast to the entrance hall and marble stairs. It made me wonder if Roger didn't have the money to update the kitchen or if he just didn't care.

"Where the devil could he be?" she asked.

"We shouldn't be in here. What if something's wrong, or someone else is in here?" We both stopped moving around and listened. All I heard was a bit of traffic noise from the street. She pivoted and headed back to the front of the house. I grabbed her arm as she started up the marble staircase in the foyer.

"Wait. I don't think that's a good idea."

"Then stay here by the door and I'll yell if I run afoul of anything."

I sighed. "You stay. I'll go."

"Okay."

As I trotted up the first couple of stairs, eager to get this over with, I realized Miss Belle had manipulated me in to doing this very thing. I looked back down at her, but her face was all innocence as she nodded encouragingly at me. The house was so quiet. The steps were marble, so they didn't creak. The baluster was cool under my sweaty hand. Sweaty from nerves, because it was unusually cool in here.

"Roger? Mr. Mervine?" I called out every few steps, hoping for an answer but hearing nothing. I got to the top and looked down the hall. Of course, all of the freaking doors were closed. There were five to choose from. I knocked, waited, called out, and opened the first door on the left. An empty guest room. I headed across the hall to the right, repeated my knocking routine, and opened the next door. A lovely study filled with shelves and old books. I went back into the hall and opened more doors. A linen closet full of neatly folded towels and sheets on the right. A sparkling white bathroom across from it.

That left the door at the end of the hall, which must be the master bedroom. I stopped in front of the door and gave myself a shake. I could do this. Better me than Miss Belle, although I was starting to feel like a bit of a lapdog doing her bidding. I knocked, called out, and waited. Nothing. I reached for the doorknob. Maybe it would be locked and I could scamper back down the stairs and out the door. But it turned in my hand.

Chapter Eleven

I decided to use the ripping-off-a-bandage approach and flung the door open. A bed with a light gray tufted headboard was the focal point. A gray comforter with an assortment of pillows including European shams and a neck roll were propped up. The only thing out of place was a large suitcase with clothes thrown haphazardly into it. Some only partially in. Closet doors were open and hangers were in disarray, as were the rows of shoes on a shoe rack.

Thankfully, there were no dead bodies. A half-filled suitcase I could deal with. Everything about Roger was neat and particular. This hastily filled suitcase was telling of something. I hustled back down the steps and explained the situation to Miss Belle.

"I don't like it," she said. "The door not locked or closed. The suitcase. He would have mentioned leaving town to his helper at the store or me. We were both counting on him."

Something was up, but my plan was to get Miss Belle home and figure out what to do. We weren't supposed to be in his house in the first place.

"What do we do now?" Miss Belle asked.

"Lock the door and go home." I heard the hint of a question in my voice and wanted to slap myself.

Miss Belle pounced faster than a kitten on a ball of yarn. I needed to quit thinking of her as a kitten and more of a lion, strong, determined, and fierce. Then she wouldn't keep getting the upper hand on me.

"I know where Roger's favorite restaurant in the North End is. We both need to eat, and we can look for him at the same time."

The North End was the Italian section of Boston near the harbor, well known for its numerous Italian restaurants. My mouth almost watered at the thought. I was still hungry; the scone and tea had been my breakfast and lunch. "Okay." I did it partly to humor Miss Belle. If we were at a restaurant, we'd be away from that partially packed suitcase. It made me uneasy. I couldn't decide if I should mention it to Pellner or not. If I did, I'd have to fess up that we hadn't exactly been invited in to roam around a private citizen's house. Although maybe the extenuating circumstances were solid ground for doing so.

After I locked Roger's door, we retrieved my car from where it sat by Roger's store and headed to the North End. The parking gods were with us and I found a spot two down from the restaurant. I managed to squeeze the Suburban into the tight space. The restaurant was just up the block from Il Formaggio, a cheese shop owned by Mike "the Big Cheese" Titone. Mike was connected to the mob, had done me the occasional favor, and wasn't what he seemed. I'd asked him for help in the past, but had come to realize that staying far away from him was my best policy. Being so close to his business raised my anxiety level another notch. As if I needed that.

I glanced over my shoulder a couple of times as we walked down the street. The unease of finding Roger's door unlatched hadn't left me. The buildings were brick, four or five stories, and connected to each other like LEGOs. Windows were open, people sat in front of the now-closed stores on aluminum lawn chairs, the conversations following us in Italian. On any other night I'd stop to listen.

We entered the dimly lit restaurant. It was small, like many restaurants in the North End, where space of any kind was at a premium. A kitchen on one side and about ten tables on the other. Roger didn't appear to be sitting at any of them. The host recognized Miss Belle, kissed her cheeks, and led us to a table. He handed us heavy menus with a flourish. As he left, a young man hurried over and filled our water glasses. A waitress with lush dark hair and a lush figure came to see if we wanted wine.

"None for me," I said.

"Are you sure?" Miss Belle asked.

"It's been a long day and I have to drive us home."

"I don't need any either. Will you just tell Chef Sal to pick an appetizer and entrees for us?" she asked the waitress. After the waitress retrieved the menus, Miss Belle turned to me. "I hope you don't mind. But his specials are superb and aren't always listed on the menu or the specials board."

"It's fine. Roger isn't here," I said, pointing out the obvious. "Is there a back room or upstairs to this place?"

"Not that I'm aware of."

"Are you going to ask for him?"

"All in good time. Sal is the owner and chef. We'll eat, compliment the food, overtip, and then ask for information."

I smiled. "Excellent thinking. Who knows, maybe he'll show up while we're here."

"Yes, with a logical explanation for the half-packed bag and unlocked door."

Miss Belle was as worried as I was.

The food started to arrive. First bread with olive oil, balsamic vinegar and herbs, followed by a bread-crumb-and-parmesan-stuffed artichoke.

"Pace yourself," said Miss Belle. "When Chef Sal gets going, it can be quite the feast."

A caprese salad of beautifully red tomatoes, fresh basil, and a mozzarella as creamy as butter arrived next. Then came osso buco with polenta. When I thought I couldn't eat another bite, the tiramisu showed up. I glanced outside. Long shadows were cast on the street by the setting sun, so I checked my phone. We'd been there for almost two hours. I could have had a glass of wine early on if I'd known we'd be so long.

"Will Chef Sal be upset if I ask for the tiramisu to go?"

Miss Belle leaned forward. "He'll be insulted. He thinks there's only one way to serve and eat tiramisu and that's in the moment." She took a big bite, then looked over her shoulder to the kitchen. She put her fingers to her lips and kissed them. The woman had a hearty appetite for someone so fit. "Sip some coffee to stall. And pray he doesn't send out any of his famous gelato after this."

I sipped my coffee. "I wish Roger had shown up."

"Me too. Although it seems unlikely now."

"We'll drive by his house on the way home to see if there are any lights on."

"Do you mind if we make one other stop?"

"Where?"

Miss Belle sighed. "My mother-in-law's house. She doesn't live too far from Roger."

Her mother-in-law was still alive? I did a quick calculation in my head. She had to be in her midnineties.

Miss Belle leaned in. "She's ninety-five and going strong, except for some memory problems. I think she'll outlive me. And if she heard what happened today at my house, she'll be angry."

"Is she one of those people who comes off as angry when she's really worried about you?" CJ had been like that. Sometimes breaking bad news over the phone had worked better than telling him in person.

"No. She'll be angry if the family name is besmirched by some kind of scandal."

"It's hardly a scandal. A woman stole something and was killed."

"It's a scandal to her. Her memory problems are making her reactions worse. One minute she's fine and the next some strange, unrelated thing will come out of her mouth. It's gotten worse since my father-in-law died last year. She keeps threatening to send me away. As if she could."

I took a big bite of my tiramisu to try to cover any expression of horror that could creep across my face. My family and I had had our differences, but we always supported one another. Even when I married CJ at nineteen, my mom hadn't been thrilled, but she hadn't tried to cut me out of the family. "Okay. We can go. Let me check my phone to see what's on the news so we'll have an idea of what she might have heard." I scrolled through a couple of news sites for Ellington. "All it says is there was a suspicious death in Ellington. No names or circumstances mentioned."

"Yet," Miss Belle said.

"You're right; it will come out. Are you going to tell her about the contents of the suitcase?"

"Not tonight. She'll probably think I stole them somehow."

The police might think that too. I took another bite

of my tiramisu. "This is delicious," I said. "Not soggy, not too much coffee flavor."

Miss Belle nodded, and we ate our desserts in silence. Thankfully, it wasn't a gigantic piece.

As we finished our last bite, Chef Sal came over. He kissed Miss Belle on both cheeks and held her hands.

"How was it?" he asked.

"The best meal I've ever had," she said. "Italian or otherwise."

I thought that was a bit over the top, but I knew from my experiences with Angelo DiNapoli that chefs' egos could be large and fragile. They both looked at me expectantly.

"This is my new favorite restaurant. I'd need a thesaurus to find enough words to describe this meal." Apparently, that did the trick, because soon I was being introduced, kissed on the cheeks, and invited back. A table would always be open for me. I wondered how many people had heard that line.

"Have you seen our dear Roger tonight?" Miss Belle asked. "I was so hoping to catch up with him."

"Don't speak his name in front of me," Chef Sal said.

"Whyever not?" asked Miss Belle.

"The staff told me he had a reservation. For six, and he didn't show up."

"For six people or for six o'clock?" I asked.

"Six o'clock for two. I heard he sounded very pleased with himself when he called. I thought he was bringing someone special."

"Any idea whom?" Miss Belle asked. "Wouldn't it be charming if he'd finally fallen in love after all these years?"

The chef hmpfed. "I suppose it would. But he didn't say who." There was a clatter from the kitchen. "Excuse me, ladies."

"I don't like it," Miss Belle said to me. "Roger is very responsible. If he says he's going to be somewhere, he is." Two lines formed between Miss Belle's brow.

We left soon after with well wishes from the host and our waitress.

Chapter Twelve

Thirty minutes later, we sat across from a stiff-looking woman, Miss Belle's mother-in-law. Her back was ramrod stiff, her hair coiffed to a silver helmet, a large diamond sparkled on one hand, an emerald on the other. No one would ever guess her age from her appearance. I sat on the edge of the chair I'd been pointed to with my back straighter than normal. Miss Belle had a fake smile plastered on her face as she introduced me to Mrs. Winthrop Granville II.

She only gave me a quick glance before what seemed like a dismissal. "I assume you're here about something important given the late hour."

It was just past nine thirty and probably not the best time to call. But it was the way she spoke, barely opening her mouth as if her jaw had been wired shut, that gave away her status as a Boston Brahmin. One of the elite families of the city. The room was expensively furnished but cold. Its only saving grace a scattering of books here and there, mostly expensive, leather-bound classics. They looked worn, which softened my attitude toward Mrs. Winthrop Granville.

"Mother, there's been an incident at my home in Ellington."

Never had the word *mother* sounded so strained.

"It's not surprising. I've been asking you to live with me since Sebastian died. Missing silver?"

Miss Belle shook her head.

"Not Edward's painting?" She turned to me. "Edward was my dear husband. We had the painting of him commissioned so our son wouldn't forget his roots out there in the west."

The west? West of the 95 maybe, by a couple of miles, but it was hardly Wyoming. But I knew people who thought any place west of the 95 might as well be Siberia.

"It hangs over the fireplace in Sebastian's study," Mrs. Winthrop Granville said.

I thought about the study. I remembered seeing a lovely landscape hanging there. But I had the good sense not to look at Miss Belle. I nodded politely.

"The painting is fine," Miss Belle said. "The maid stole something very valuable."

Mrs. Winthrop Granville sat even straighter if possible. "What? Not the sterling tea set we gave you for your wedding. It's been in the family forever."

"No, Mother. But that's not the worst of it. The maid has died under suspicious circumstances, and what she took is gone."

"I insist you tell me what she took."

If Mrs. Winthrop Granville had a cane I'm sure she'd be pounding it on the ground.

"Some short stories, Mother. By Hemingway."

"I've always loved Cracker Jacks." The angry Mrs. Winthrop Granville had been replaced by a past version of herself. Her voice changed, became lighter, younger. "They have a prize in them. Who doesn't love a prize?"

"I love prizes and Cracker Jacks too," I said. Now I saw what Miss Belle had been talking about at the restaurant, about her mother-in-law losing focus.

Miss Belle leaned toward me. "I'll go get Ruth. Stay with her?"

I nodded. Ruth Stewart had been the woman who'd let us in. Miss Belle had introduced her as the housekeeper/companion. She hadn't worn a maid's uniform, just a simple black dress and sensible-looking shoes.

"You can call me Winnie," she told me. "It's what all my friends call me."

I couldn't imagine addressing this imposing woman as Winnie. But it made me realize she must be the original owner of the Bobbsey Twin books in Miss Belle's attic. The ones with "Winnie" written in them.

"You like to read?" I asked, trying to think of something we had in common, some topic that wouldn't be upsetting, while Miss Belle was off finding Ruth. I figured she wasn't a big fan of garage sales.

"I do," she said. "Did you ever go to a fair? People steal things there. I wasn't allowed to go." She smiled. "But my beau would sneak Cracker Jacks to me."

"I've gone to a fair. You have to be careful, though." I hoped I was saying the right things because I didn't want to upset her. Miss Belle and Ruth returned a few moments later.

Ruth walked calmly over to Mrs. Winthrop Granville. "Winnie, I just noticed the time. Let's head upstairs."

Mrs. Winthrop Granville nodded and stood. She clung to Ruth's arm as they headed toward the staircase.

Mrs. Winthrop Granville paused. "Thank you for coming by, Belle."

"We'll let ourselves out," Miss Belle told them.

* * *

THE GUN ALSO RISES

The outside air was heavy with humidity. I felt its weight on my soul. It had been a long and tumultuous day. "I'll drive by Roger's house one more time on the way home," I said as I pulled onto the street. I looked up at the beautiful brownstone as we left and thought of Winnie. Even money couldn't stop the ravages of time.

Two blocks later, I slowed in front of Roger's house. There wasn't much traffic, so I pulled to the side and stopped. The house was dark.

"I'll just check the door and ring the bell. Maybe he's home now and just in the back," Miss Belle said.

"I'll do it," I said. If anything was amiss, I was probably better equipped to handle it. I trotted up the steps and tried the door. It was still locked. Then I rang the bell. After waiting a minute or so, I went back to the car. "Maybe he's sound asleep."

"Could we just swing by his store too?" Miss Belle asked.

"Sure." I had this odd combination of exhaustion and antsiness going through my body. I had to take a left and circle around a one-way before we came to the block his store was on. Halfway down the street, I noticed there was unusual activity: lots of lights and police cars.

"Oh, no," Miss Belle said as I slowed to a stop. She climbed out of the car as a police officer impatiently flagged me to go around. I found a parking space half a block ahead and jogged back toward the store. I'd done more running today than I had all year. I had to cross the street and back again to get to where I could see Miss Belle. She was talking to a Boston police officer.

"Is Roger okay?" I asked when I reached them.

"Sarah Winston," Miss Belle said to the police officer. "The woman I was telling you about." She turned to me. "There's no sign of Roger. It was an attempted break-in."

I was relieved Roger wasn't in there dead. "Was anyone hurt?" I looked at Miss Belle, trying to access what, if any, information she'd given them about Roger, who seemingly had gone missing. I think she shook her head, but it could have been the lights from the nearby police car that continued to bounce around.

"No," the officer said. "The store was closed. Alarms went off. When we got here, the door was open. There's an employee on the way to take a look around. From what we could tell, nothing was disturbed."

"Okay, then. We'll be on our way." I gripped Miss Belle's arm before she could say anything further. If we mentioned our concerns about Roger, we'd be here all night. But if we didn't, we might be accused of obstructing something. Although as far as I knew, leaving a door ajar and a half-packed suitcase didn't constitute a crime. On the other hand, Roger hadn't been at the places he'd said he would. I shook my head. Being tired was getting the best of me.

I took one step before the officer stopped me.

"Why were you driving by here?" the police officer asked.

Rats. He must have noticed my head shake. "We'd been visiting Miss Belle's mother-in-law, Mrs. Winthrop Granville the Second, and we're heading back to Ellington." I hoped name-dropping would stop any more questions.

The officer cocked his head to one side. "Where does she live?"

I gave him the address.

"That seems to be in the opposite direction of the store."

"I always manage to get lost in Boston. Not a local."

I shrugged apologetically. But from the look on his face, he wasn't buying the load I was trying to sell him.

He turned to Belle. "But you must be familiar."

"I explained how to get out of here, but made the mistake of closing my eyes."

"If only I'd listened to her." I smiled.

"Let me just take down your contact information," he said.

I repressed a sigh and gave it to him. "Is it all right if we take off now?"

The officer took Miss Belle's information too before he nodded.

It was eleven thirty when we pulled up to Miss Belle's house. The house was dark as the inside of a bat cave. "I'll come in with you," I said. I realized she was used to having someone else in the house with her. Kay had lived upstairs.

"Thank you. Would you mind just spending the night?" Miss Belle's voice faltered. "It's been an exhausting day. And now being back here, knowing Kay is dead . . ."

"Of course." It really didn't matter where I slept. No one would know the difference anyway. We went through the front. Miss Belle looked so pale, I walked her to her room. "You can stay in the room to the left at the end of the hall. It's all made up."

"I'll just make sure everything's locked up before I go to bed."

"There's a nice bottle of cabernet sauvignon on the kitchen counter if you'd like a drink." She opened the door to her room. "Thank you, dear. For everything today."

I nodded. She closed the door to her room and I headed downstairs, flipping on lights as I went. After,

I made sure all the doors and windows were closed. I circled back to the kitchen and poured a glass of wine. I drank a bit sitting down at the kitchen table that looked over the lawn and down into the woods. The pitch-black woods made me shiver, so I carried the glass upstairs. I'd left a few lights on downstairs to keep the boogeyman away.

I hurried past Miss Belle's door on the thick Oriental carpeting. The lighting in the hall was dim. I almost made it to my room when a figure stepped out of the room opposite mine.

Chapter Thirteen

I turned to run.

"Wait."

It was Roger.

I stopped but didn't get any closer. I was sure I could outrun him if need be. "What are you doing here? Where have you been?" I stuck my hand in my pocket and searched for my phone, ready to call for help if I needed to.

He made a gulping noise. Roger stayed right by the door, his shoulder against the frame as if he was glued there. Only he wasn't, but I didn't realize that until he was pushed to the center of the hall by a figure wearing a ghost mask like you see in the stores at Halloween. I got a glimpse of broad shoulders and a round torso before he stepped behind Roger. That's when I saw he held a gun to Roger's head. Now I wished I'd turned and run when I had the chance. Wished I'd never responded to Miss Belle's invitation to spend the night. Wished I was home in my own bed. With my hand still in my pocket, I used my thumb to try to open my phone. Maybe I could blindly speed-dial Pellner.

"Take your hand out of your pocket," the man holding Roger said.

His voice was muffled by the mask, but I understood what he said. So I did as he asked, well, commanded. In my other hand, I still clung to the glass of wine. I was almost surprised I hadn't snapped the delicate stem in half. "What do you want?" My voice was surprisingly calm.

"The book."

"What book? There are tons of books in this house."

"That's what I told him," Roger said. But he shut up when the man grounded the gun into his temple.

"Tell her which book," the masked ghost man said, "because she claims not to know anything about it."

The man shook Roger. Roger whimpered. "He's looking for one by Hemingway."

I heard a ratcheting sound behind me and glanced over my shoulder. Miss Belle stood down the hall in a long white nightgown and bare feet holding a shotgun that was almost as big as her. The man started to swing the gun toward me. I tossed the wine at him, then the glass. Roger swung an elbow into the man's ribs.

"Duck," Miss Belle yelled.

I dived, grabbed Roger by the sweater, and took him down with me. I covered my head as I heard a shot. Bits of splintered wood and plaster rained down. My ears rang from the blast of the shot. I waited in shock for a couple of seconds before I looked up. The man was gone. But how? Then I remembered the back stairs were at this end of the hall. Miss Belle had pointed them out yesterday. Had that only been yesterday?

I leaped up and whirled around to Miss Belle. She was flat on her back on the floor, so I ran toward her.

My footsteps deadened by the thick carpet. Which made me worry the masked man's would be too. I pulled out my phone. I hadn't managed to dial Pellner or anyone earlier. My fingers fumbled before I pressed the correct numbers to call 911. I gave a dispatcher the address and told him to send an ambulance.

Miss Belle sat up, then. "I don't need an ambulance. But this"—she held up the shotgun—"has a hell of a kick."

Roger moaned.

"Stay there, Miss Belle. But be ready in case that man shows back up."

She stood while I ran back to Roger. Miss Belle flipped on another light and I saw a stain spreading out from under Roger.

"Roger. I think he's hit." I yelled it into the phone.

Roger moaned again and then rolled over. I didn't see any wounds. But even with more light on, it was still dim down at this end of the hall.

I knelt beside him. "Roger, are you with me?"

He snorted out a breath of air. "I'm fine. Don't start yammering on like they do in the movies that everything's going to be okay and to keep my eyes open."

"Stay still. I think you're bleeding." I noticed his sweater had some dark spots on it up near his shoulder.

Roger sat up. "It's only the wine from the glass you threw," he said. "This sweater is cashmere, you know."

Who wore cashmere in the summer? Who worried about his sweater moments after someone had held a gun to his head? "What book was he talking about? Do you know?"

"And why are you here in the first place?" Miss Belle stood behind me, still holding the shotgun. We heard sirens, car doors slamming, and pounding on the door.

"I'll get it," I volunteered. "Just stay here. Together."

I ran down the hall, then the stairs, and flung open the door. Awesome stood there, all big and tall and heroic-looking in his uniform. It made me want to fling myself into his arms and sob. Instead, I gave him a quick description of the man in the hallway: tall, broad-shouldered, dressed in jeans, a black shirt, and a ghost-faced mask. Awesome sent a couple of officers to look around the grounds before entering the house. He stood with another officer.

An ambulance pulled up. "I don't think we're going to need them. But maybe they should check on Miss Belle and Roger before we send them off."

We all trotted up the stairs. Miss Belle and Roger were both sitting in the hall, backs against the wall, legs out in front of them.

Awesome turned to me. "We'll clear the house. There's a chance the intruder stayed in here instead of leaving."

"I can help. It's a big place," I said.

"No. You stay here." He looked at the EMTs. "Check her out too." Then he looked at the other officer. "Let's go."

Thirty minutes later, the EMTs left for the second time today. No one really needed attending, but blood pressures were checked and hearts listened to. Awesome came back into the hall this time alone. "No one's in the house."

We settled in the kitchen, where I made coffee and heated water for tea. Even with Awesome with us, I felt exposed sitting at the kitchen table looking out at the dark woods. Light from flashlights bobbed around as the police searched for the gunman.

"So, what happened here?" Awesome asked.

I explained what I'd seen. Miss Belle added her version. Neither of us mentioned the book. Roger stared down into his tea. I couldn't decide if it was from guilt or terror. After all, there was that hastily packed suitcase.

"Any idea what he wanted?" Awesome asked.

The three of us exchanged glances, but no one spoke up. Awesome sat patiently waiting. He didn't look angry, just interested.

I went first again. "He asked 'where's the book'?" I said. "I didn't know what he was talking about, although Roger said it was something by Hemingway."

"Roger, just spill what you know," Miss Belle said. "I'd like to get some sleep at some point tonight."

Roger threw up his hands. "Kay called me this morning while I was driving to Miss Belle's house."

"She had your cell phone number?" That seemed odd to me.

"It's on my business card. Lots of people have it." Roger frowned at me.

Boy, was he defensive. "What time and what did she want?" I asked.

"It was around nine thirty and she said she wanted to meet me." Roger took a long drink of his coffee.

"Did you think that was odd?" I asked.

"What did she want?" Belle asked.

"She wanted my opinion about the price of something." He looked at me with lowered eyebrows. "It wasn't odd at all. People consult with me all of the time."

That wasn't long after I'd taken the suitcase down to Miss Belle. She must have overheard us, or maybe she knew the papers were there. "Where did she want to meet?" I asked.

"At a Starbucks in Lexington. I went, but she never showed."

"Kay took off from here around eleven." I remembered because the alarm on my phone had gone off about the same time. I glanced at Awesome, worried he might not like me asking so many questions, but he didn't seem to mind. Maybe he wanted Roger to forget there was a cop in the room so he'd talk more freely.

"You never went to your store today," Miss Belle said. "Where were you?"

"While I was waiting for Kay this, this hooligan showed up and threatened me."

"How would he know you'd be there?" I asked. "It had to be through Kay." I rested my elbows on the table, wishing the coffee was a glass of something stronger.

"Tell us about the threat," Awesome said.

"He sat down across from me." Roger shuddered.

That didn't sound too scary. "What did he look like?" I asked.

"Dark beard, dark eyes, thick eyebrows. He wore a T-shirt and jeans. The only thing out of place was an old Yankees baseball cap worn low on his forehead."

Yankee caps always stood out in Red Sox Nation, otherwise known as New England. "Never trust a Yankees fan," I said with a glance at Awesome, "You're the exception, Awesome." I turned back to Roger. "Other than that, what was threatening?"

"Wait until you hear the rest," Roger snapped. "He put his hand over mine, which was weird. I tried to move mine, but he pressed down to trap it there. Then he leaned in. Started asking about a book. I told him he'd have to be more specific because I owned a bookstore. Then he started talking about a rare limited edition of *The Sun Also Rises*."

"A first edition?" Miss Belle asked.

Roger shook his head. "Hemingway did a slim leather volume for his friends. Only five. They were leather-bound and the title was stamped in gold. All of them were numbered and signed."

"What makes them so special?" I asked. So special

that some guy was willing to threaten someone for a copy in public.

Roger just looked at me for a moment. "Beyond the obvious? He handwrote notes in the margins giving further insights into the scenes. Every edition was different, depending on his mood at the time. Most are presumed to be lost. Hemingway wasn't that famous when the book first came out."

"Do you have a copy at your store?" I asked.

"I wish," Roger said. "At the same time he's saying all of this, he started forcing my index finger back with his thumb." Roger grabbed a handkerchief out of his pocket and patted his upper lip. His index finger had a splint on it. "He told me he'd snap it like a twig and then start on the others if I didn't give the book to him. I guess I fainted, because the next thing I remember, there was a Starbucks' employee with water and a woman who was a nurse standing over me."

"Where'd the man go?" I asked.

"The nurse said he yelled for help and said he was going to get my medication from my car." Roger paused. "I don't take anything."

"Did you call the police?" I asked.

"No. Just wanted to get out of there. I told the people in the store I just had low blood sugar and fainted."

"Oh, Roger, that's a terrible experience." Miss Belle patted his arm.

"It gets worse," he said.

That wasn't surprising, considering he'd ended up with a gun to his head a few minutes ago.

"When I got to my car, there was a note on the front passenger seat. Stuck there with a knife."

Chapter Fourteen

"Someone broke into your car?" Miss Belle asked.

"I don't know how they got in," Roger said.

"What kind of knife?" I glanced over at Awesome again. He gave me a little nod.

"A carving knife with a fancy, carved handle. What kind of person carries something like that around with him?"

An evil one, but I wasn't going to say it out loud. "What did the note say?"

"That he wanted the book and I'd better find it fast." He looked at Miss Belle. "Do you have such a book?" He looked at her again hopefully.

She pursed her lips. After a couple of moments, she shook her head. "Not that I know of. Sebastian collected lots of books. And he did love Hemingway. I didn't always pay attention. It seems he would mention such an important book."

"Unless he obtained it illegally," Roger said.

Miss Belle straightened up. "Excuse me?"

Her response made me wonder if she was being truthful. I'd never seen her so upset. Of course, I hadn't spent a lot of time with her. But until now, she'd taken all the day's events in stride. Perhaps too much?

"Let's all calm down," Awesome said. "We need to figure out what's going on here."

"I'm sorry, Belle. I didn't mean to insinuate you or Sebastian would do such a thing. It's been a dreadful day."

Miss Belle nodded.

Roger continued. "But sometimes people buy things inadvertently."

"How would the man even know the book is supposedly here?" I asked.

Everyone thought about that for a moment.

"I don't know," Miss Belle said.

"Is there any chance it's in the house somewhere?" I watched Roger closely. What I wanted to ask was whether he'd seen it and taken it. But I rethought before I did. Roger seemed like the kind of man who would turn something over at the first sign of trouble. What if I'd interrupted him going to get the rare book when I walked down the hall to go to bed? But Roger didn't react to my comment.

"Maybe we should do a search," I said. There were thousands of books in this house between Sebastian's study, Miss Belle's office, and the attic. I wasn't sure the four of us could do it. Then I looked at Miss Belle. Her face was pale and deep shadows had formed under her eyes. "Or we can look in the morning."

Everyone looked relieved at that. We all took a moment to collect our thoughts and drink some coffee. I yawned, setting everyone off.

"Sarah and I went by your house this evening," Miss Belle said.

"You went to my house?" Roger asked. He rose halfway out of his chair, before sinking back down.

Why was he so upset?

"The door was open. I thought something had happened to you." Miss Belle gave him a fierce look. "There was a partially packed suitcase on the bed. It looked like you were fleeing."

"I wasn't fleeing," Roger said. "I decided to go away for a few days."

A couple of moments ticked by while we all stared at Roger. Why was he planning to flee? Why hadn't he?

"We still don't know all of what happened between the time you left the Starbucks and arrived here." Miss Belle might be tired, but her mind was clicking right along.

Awesome perked up at that.

"Right after I left Starbucks, I went to my doctor and had him fix my finger." He held up his hand with the splint on it. "Then I headed straight home to leave until this all blew over."

"But you were interrupted," I said.

"Someone rang the doorbell. I looked out my guest room window. The man from Starbucks was there. I high tailed it out the back." He slapped his hands to his mouth. "That man must have broken in. It's the only explanation for why my front door was unlocked." He shuddered. "Having that cretin in my house is most unnerving."

"It is," I agreed. "Where did you go after you left your house?"

"I hid out at the store while I tried to figure out if it was safe to go back to get my car. Or if I could use my credit cards with no one finding out where I was. I'm not cut out for a life on the run."

"Your employee told us you hadn't been to the store all day," I said.

"She lied. For me. I have a security system set up at the store. I watched the monitor and tried to figure out what to do. Then that ruffian showed up at the store. I ran out the back door." Roger shook his head. "I've never done so much running in my life."

He said *running* with such disdain, I almost laughed. But I knew how he felt because that was how my day had been too.

"Where did you go then? We went to Chef Sal's in hopes of finding you there," Miss Belle said.

Roger got a longing look on his face. "Oh for some of his osso buco. At least I was smart enough not to go there."

"Are you hungry?" Miss Belle asked. "I can throw together something."

"If you wouldn't mind."

"Let me help," I said. In a matter of minutes, we'd put together cheese and crackers, chicken salad, and an assortment of breads. Miss Belle also put out a plate of cookies. Considering the spread, you'd think it was mealtime instead of midnight.

Roger and Awesome dug in. I was still full from our dinner. For once, even the cookies didn't tempt me.

After Roger had eaten, he was ready to talk again. "To answer your question. I went to my happy place. The Boston Public Library."

The Boston Public Library is amazing, and it's massive. For someone like Roger, who loved books, it seemed like a natural. That thought made me frown. It seemed like exactly where a book lover would go.

Roger noticed my frown. "It was stupid. Apparently, it's the go-to place for rare book dealers to hide out. Because that hooligan showed up there."

This tale was so wild, I was beginning to wonder if it might be true. I looked at Awesome. His eyes had narrowed, but he still kept quiet.

"Fortunately, I was sitting in a place where I could see much of the library. And I know it well enough that I once again slipped away." He shook his head yet again. "If I was reading this in a book, I'd have thrown it across the room by now."

I'd had my own wild adventure today, so I didn't feel it was my place to be critical. "What did you do next?" I asked.

"I hopped on the T and just rode around, changing lines, staying underground and out of sight."

The T was what they called the subway system in Boston. Short for trolley; the system was that old.

"So how did you end up here? At gunpoint?" Awesome sounded annoyed. And he looked tired. The lights that had been bobbing around the grounds had long since disappeared. We hadn't heard anything, so I guess the thug had escaped once again. I looked out, wondering if he was out there watching us.

"I came here for two reasons," Roger said. "First, I thought Belle would put me up for the night. Second, I thought perhaps Belle would have the limited edition of *The Sun Also Rises* that man seems to want so badly. Trust me, I'd love to give it to him and return to my normal boring life."

"Of course you're welcome to stay," Miss Belle said. "I wish I knew where the book was."

"What happened?" Awesome's voice snapped out. It sounded as if he'd had it with Roger.

"I took a taxi out here. Let myself in with the key Miss Belle gave me when I took on her project. I went upstairs and entered the room I'd used in the past." He paused.

Awesome made a whirling motion with his hand to keep Roger on track.

"It obviously didn't go according to plan. I got my toothbrush and was heading down the hall to the bathroom when the hooligan nabbed me. He dragged me back to my room and told me to show him the book.

He didn't need to add the *or else.*" Roger yawned. "I thought if I led him to the attic, maybe I'd have an opportunity to escape without anyone getting injured." He spread out his hands. "That's my story."

I wondered again if it was just a story. Made up by a lunatic who was trying to cover his tracks for stealing from Miss Belle. Roger could be working with the man who'd a gun to his head. And that was just an act when they were discovered.

"How'd the man keep finding you all day?"

"I don't have any idea." Lines creased Roger's forehead.

"Have you worn the same clothes all day?" Awesome asked Roger.

"Yes. Why?"

"Empty your pockets," Awesome said.

Roger took off his sweater and patted the pocket of his button-up shirt. Then he pulled out the pockets of his seersucker pants. Something went flying. Awesome bent over and picked up a small, round disk.

"Tracking device," Awesome said. "He probably planted it on you at the Starbucks."

Roger, Miss Belle, and I exchanged uneasy looks. What the heck had we ended up in the middle of?

"I'll call some other departments to see if we can get any security footage of the assailant," Awesome said.

Roger looked at Awesome with eager puppy eyes.

"But security footage is often blurry," he said, "so don't get your hopes up."

"Can't your people edit it to make it clear?" Roger asked.

"Not like they can on TV," Awesome said. "Would you be willing to work with a sketch artist?"

"Anything to find that hooligan," Roger answered. He rubbed his finger.

"What now?" I asked Awesome. "We can't leave Miss Belle here on her own." I looked at her and then out at the woods again. The night was dark. We were sitting in the lighted kitchen. I gave a small shiver.

He frowned and thought it over. "Excuse me a minute. I have a plan."

He left the kitchen, and I could hear him talking. The rest of us were too worn out to speak. We avoided eye contact too. A few minutes later, Awesome walked back in.

"An unmarked car is going to come here and take the three of you to the station. I'll drive Sarah's car back to her place. Hopefully, if the intruder is out there watching, he won't be close enough to see who's driving what car. I'll also put someone here at the house to keep things safe tonight until a search can be conducted for the book tomorrow."

We all nodded.

"The officer will pull into the garage underneath the station. Someone will meet you there. I'll have them put you in one of the SUVs and take you to my place for the night. Miss Belle can have my room, Roger the couch, and Sarah the recliner."

"Where are you going to sleep?" Miss Belle asked.

"I'll head over to Sarah's, turn on some lights, then off, as a decoy. If it's okay with you, Sarah, I'll spend the night there."

"Of course," I said, "if you think that will help."

Awesome nodded. "Maybe we can draw him out and get this shut down tonight."

I started to open my mouth, worried about Stella, her cat Tux, and Ryne.

"I'll have backup, Sarah," Awesome said.

"Why don't I just drive your squad car back to the station?" I asked. "That would save one of your officers some trouble. I could use the lights and siren." How fun would that be? "Roger and Miss Belle could sit in the back like they're in trouble."

Awesome didn't answer, just gave me a withering look.

"Is that a no?" I asked. Joking wasn't lessening my stress the way I'd hoped.

"It's a no way. Too much liability, and right now it might not be safe for you out there, driving around on your own."

"Isn't us staying at your apartment a risk?" I asked.

"Perhaps, but it's so late now, it's only for a few hours. We couldn't find a hotel close by."

Summer was a popular time of year in this area for tourists. While Awesome didn't say it, I got the feeling he wanted us together.

No one else said a word. I guess we really were too tired to argue.

"Wait. Why can't I go home?" I asked. "The man is after Roger, and maybe Miss Belle now."

"He saw you. He may know who you are. I just want to keep you safe until we have more information."

I didn't like it, but I agreed with him. We heard a car pull up.

"Okay, let's head out," Awesome said. "Anyone have any questions?"

There was a knock on the door. Awesome talked into his mic. "That's the officer who'll watch the house tonight. Let's move out."

The transition at the station went smoothly, and soon, the three of us were crammed in the back of an SUV with dark tinted windows. No one could tell we were there. After a bit of circling, we pulled up in front of Awesome's apartment. It was in a big complex to the north of town. He had a first-floor-corner unit.

The officer who drove us went in first. After making sure the place was safe, we trotted in after him.

Awesome's apartment was sparsely furnished with few decorative objects. The couch was overstuffed, the coffee table sturdy, with water rings etched in its surface from glasses, and the recliner matched the dark brown of the couch. Obviously, he hadn't had a woman living with him in some time because there wasn't a feminine object in sight. I knew Awesome spent more nights than not at Stella's apartment.

"Why don't you take the bed and I'll sleep on the recliner?" Miss Belle said to me.

"Absolutely not." I wanted to be near the door in case something bad happened. Not that I had any kind of weapon beyond my purse to fight anyone with.

"I'll take the bed," Roger said.

Yeesh. I know we were all exhausted, but no one had suggested checking manners at the door. "No, you won't. Now go, Miss Belle. Get some sleep." I found a linen closet and grabbed a couple of blankets. I tossed one to Roger and settled in the chair with the other. I closed my eyes, but turning my brain off wasn't as easy. What if Belle and Roger were somehow in cahoots and I'd gotten in the middle of them? And everything I'd seen so far had just been for show? But somehow, I couldn't convince myself that was true. If it was me, I was in the lion's den. Did Awesome suspect anything? Maybe this was some weird form of *The Hunger Games*, where the last person alive won, and Awesome wanted to see who came out of the place in the morning.

Chapter Fifteen

Snoring woke me at seven a.m. At first, I was confused, thought I was home and that CJ was there too. It didn't take long for reality to set back in. It made me think of my marriage to CJ. We had married young. I'd thrown myself into the Air Force life and had done all the things I perceived a good Air Force wife should do to advance her husband's career. I joined the Spouses Club, volunteered on the board, schmoozed the generals' wives, went to dining outs, made sure one or the other of us stayed sober to drive home.

I'd loved it most of the time. I still missed the camaraderie, the instant friendships, the we're-in-this-together attitude. But I'd found a home here in Ellington, a place I belonged. My forever home. I hoped anyway. Part of me felt me sad this morning as I reflected on my failed marriage, Kay's death, the scary man at Miss Belle's house last night. I turned on my side and pulled my blanket over my head. But it didn't begin to drown out Roger's increasingly loud snores. I'd slept better than expected given the circumstances.

Another snore blasted out of Roger, so I gave up and stumbled into the kitchen, hoping for coffee.

Whew, Awesome had one of those single-user cup machines and plenty of little Dunkin's cups. After some fumbling, I figured out how to use the thing. Minutes later, I sat at a tiny round table on a small patio. A six-foot privacy fence kept me from being seen. I was guessing that was a good thing after the day I'd had yesterday, and me without a tooth- or hairbrush. The sun warmed my head, the humidity curled my hair. I was so bleary-eyed, it took me a while to realize it was Wednesday.

Awesome had tomato plants in pots, alongside basil and what looked like garlic sprouts. All the makings of a good bruschetta. I heard the slider open behind me and turned to see Miss Belle step out. She looked a bit more disheveled than normal too. She set down her cup of coffee.

"Good morning," I said as she sat across from me.

"Today's bound to be a better day. Don't you think?"

"It's hard to imagine it being much worse."

We sat contemplating the plants for a few minutes, sipping our coffee.

"Do you think we'll find that book at your house?" I asked.

"Yesterday morning I would have told you no way. But after your other discovery and all that went on after, I'm not so sure."

"Do you trust Roger?"

Miss Belle was silent for a good long time. She finally nodded. "I can't imagine him making up such a wild story. He's never been fanciful or even excitable unless it was about some old book he found."

That didn't necessarily reassure me. The lost manuscripts and book would be priceless. If that didn't make a book lover nuts, nothing would. But if he was in cahoots with the guy who'd held a gun on him last night, he was quite the actor. He'd looked truly terrified. It would be hard to fake that.

"I hate to ask this . . ." I started.

"But you wonder if Sebastian could have stolen the manuscripts and the book, or purchased them on the black market."

I nodded. "Yes."

"He did love Hemingway. Growing up, his family had a second home on Key West, and Sebastian met him once." Miss Belle stared into her coffee cup. "Sebastian was such a straight arrow, though. It's one of the reasons . . . one of the many reasons I loved him so much."

My phone binged. A text from Awesome, asking if we were up. I let him know Miss Belle and I were. He said he'd swing by and pick us up in an hour. Told me there were extra toothbrushes under the sink in the bathroom and to feel free to shower. He also said the state police would be at Miss Belle's house to interview us.

I relayed the information to Miss Belle, who declined his offer of a shower. But I took full advantage of it. When I was done, Roger was up too.

By eight thirty, we were assembled in Miss Belle's living room. I was surprised to find Stella and Ryne were there, along with three police officers, two state troopers, and Awesome.

I sidled over to Awesome. "What kind of shifts are you working?" I asked. "Shouldn't you be off duty?"

Awesome looked down at me. "Not when there's been a murder."

"I thought the state police were handling it." I pointed across the room to them.

"They need our help. Same old story. Short-staffed, too many cases. And this search for the book and manuscript is in response to the attack last night. I convinced them the two might be connected, so I have the extra officers here until they decide they're needed elsewhere."

"So what are Stella and Ryne doing here?" I asked.

"This is a big house and I needed people I trusted to help look," Awesome said. "Fortunately, Miss Belle was agreeable to a search without a warrant."

"She's amazing," I said.

Awesome nodded. "We'll break into teams to search for the missing book," Awesome said. "No one is to talk about this outside of this house. Sarah, Miss Belle, and Roger, the state police will need to talk to each of you. Roger has a photo of what the book should look like."

Roger took his phone around to show each of us the slim volume in its deep green leather and embossed gold writing. Awesome, Roger, and one of the cops took Sebastian's study, the most daunting task. Miss Belle and another officer took her study. Stella and Ryne went with me and the third officer up to the attic, which was no small task either. I noticed Awesome had sent along an officer with each team. Apparently, he didn't trust the lot of us, and I couldn't say I blamed him because I had my doubts too.

The attic looked the same as the last time I was up here. I'm not sure what I was expecting. I guess a small part of me was worried the guy from last night could have sneaked up here and torn the place apart.

Ryne pointed toward a stack of books. "Are those Hardy Boys books?"

"Yes," I said, smiling at the boyish enthusiasm in his voice.

"I'll head over there, then," he said.

"Where do you want me?" Stella asked.

I looked at the officer, but he shrugged. I knew Stella was a big fan of the PBS series *Vera*, based on books by Ann Cleeves. "How about over in the right corner? There's a bunch of Ann Cleeves books over there."

"I love her books. I haven't read her in so long." She looked at the police officer. "*Raven Black* is my favorite. I wonder if there's a copy of it."

That would also put her over near Ryne, so they could chitchat while they searched. At least I hoped they'd search. Ryne was already flipping through one of the Hardy Boys books.

"Look, Stella, it's *What Happened At Midnight.*" A big smile spread across his face.

The officer ambled off to a section near Stella. I looked around for a minute, trying to figure out where I'd stash something so valuable. Something I might want access to, so I could come visit it on occasion. I started with the other suitcases in the stack I'd abandoned as soon as I'd found the manuscripts yesterday morning. I found lots of books and organized them by author as I went along—Ruth Rendell, P. D. James, and more Ann Cleeves—but I didn't find *the* book.

I stood and stretched a little after nine. "I'm going to go look in Kay's room." No one said I couldn't. In fact, Awesome had said *the attic*, not one specific area of it. I was curious about Kay and wondered what actions she'd taken that had led to her death.

The police officer assigned to us got a panicked look on his face. He couldn't watch me and the others all at the same time. It confirmed my suspicion that Awesome thought there could be a thief among us. I wondered who he thought it was. I was guessing he didn't think it was me or anyone else up here. He wouldn't have asked Stella or Ryne if he didn't think they were trustworthy.

"I'll leave the door open," I said to the cop. "You can pat me down after." As I walked out of the room, I heard him speaking into his shoulder mic.

Kay's room was a decent size and really lovely. The big windows let in lots of light. The telescope gave it additional romantic appeal. It didn't look like the room of a criminal. I started with the bookshelves below the window seat. Sometimes hiding something in plain sight was the best strategy. She had volumes of poetry and some classics like Austen, the Brontë sisters, Shakespeare. I wondered if these were her books or came with the room. There weren't any volumes of *A Life of Crime for Dummies* or *How to Steal from Your Employer*.

It was so hard to believe she was dead. Did she have loved ones who were mourning her loss? I'd have to ask Miss Belle more about her when I got the chance. She'd mentioned something about calling the agency to replace her. I'd never heard of such a place here in Ellington. I sat down in front of the shelf, started taking books off the shelf, opening them, and stacking them to the side. I wanted to make sure there wasn't anything hidden behind them.

"Ahem." Awesome stood behind me in the doorway.

Rats. Caught all on mine own. "How's it going downstairs?"

"Very slow. But we're supposed to be on the buddy system and you're in here alone."

"Yeah, if your buddy is a cop."

"You figured that out, did you?"

"We're tired, not stupid. I'm sure everyone figured it out." I took out a thick book and flipped it open to make sure it wasn't a container of some sort. A pink flower petal fell out, but, sadly, no book. I handed the petal to Awesome. "Besides, I'm fairly certain you know it wasn't me. Because if it was, no one would have known I'd found the short stories, right? I would have kept them for myself or taken off with them."

"Yes. You're off the list of suspects."

"But Miss Belle and Roger aren't?"

"No."

Maybe the thought that Miss Belle could have been involved had been whirling around in my head. But I'd kept pushing it aside. What if she'd faked being injured, or had Kay or Roger do it deliberately? She could have sent me out there to get whacked before I had a chance to tell anyone else about my find. Whacked? I was starting to sound like an episode of *The Sopranos*. Maybe I'd spent too much time with, or at least thinking about, Mike "the Big Cheese" Titone.

However, Miss Belle could be faking things. Maybe my return had ruined her plans. It was a terrible thought. I'd spent the night alone with Miss Belle and Roger.

Awesome came over and sat down on the floor beside me. "I know you didn't take the manuscripts. But I have to keep up appearances."

I moved and felt a board give under my leg. "Awesome, there's a loose board here." I scooted over a little and pushed on it. The end closest to Awesome popped up. He pulled it loose and leaned over the space.

"Is there anything in there?" I asked. My heart pounded.

"See for yourself."

I looked in, but nothing was there. It was just a loose board.

We cleared the shelves and didn't find anything out of the ordinary.

"Any luck getting a photo of whoever attacked Roger?"

Awesome shook his head. "I'm setting up a meeting with a sketch artist in Boston later today. Hopefully, that will yield something."

"How about a cause of death for Kay?"

"You know I can't—"

"Come on, Awesome. Someone took a shot at me out there."

He nodded. "Unofficially, the limb fell and hit her, causing an internal injury that caused her to die."

"So it was a freak accident?"

"No. There were bullet holes in the tree where the limb splintered off. We think that caused the limb to fall. I'm not saying anything more."

Had someone tried to kill me the same way yesterday? Death by shot-off branch. Why not just shoot me? I thought about that for a few seconds. "Let's keep searching." I wanted answers, and I was sure Awesome did too. I was surprised to get even that little nugget of information from him.

We took different sides of the room, then together stripped the bed, lifted off first the mattress and then the box springs. Nothing. The closet didn't yield any clues either. To say I was disappointed was the understatement of the century.

I looked at Awesome. "I assume the police went through here after Kay's body was found. Maybe the book disappeared then."

Awesome didn't look happy. "You're accusing someone on the force of stealing?"

Put that way, it didn't sound so good. "Maybe."

"How would anyone know how valuable that book is or to even look for it? At that point we were focused on the manuscripts."

"I'm assuming people on the force read."

Awesome tilted his head. "Of course they do. But with all the books in this house, why that one?"

"It was just a thought."

"Anything taken out of here would have been on an inventory list. How do we even know the book is really here?"

"You're right, we don't," I said. "I'm sorry. I'm exhausted and scared." I hated admitting to being afraid. It made it all too real.

"When I talked to Belle, she said she wasn't even sure they had such a book. She doesn't remember it."

Belle had told me the same thing. When the search was over today, I'd talk to her about that again. And pointing out that she probably didn't know every book that was in the house wouldn't help, because it seemed as if anyone would remember owning a priceless edition of *The Sun Also Rises*.

As we headed out of the room, I glanced back toward the books I'd stacked on the window seat. I grabbed Awesome's arm. "Look." I pointed at the wooden shelves. From this vantage point, I could see a faint line in the shape of a square on the back of the shelf under the window seat. "What's that?"

Chapter Sixteen

Awesome squinted. "It looks like someone cut a space out of the back of the shelf at some point and then painted over it. I guess we were so focused on the books, we didn't notice."

"The lighting is different from this angle too," I said.

We hustled back over, got down on hands and knees, and Awesome pushed on one side of the square. Nothing happened. He pushed harder. A piece of wood about six by six inches popped out. Behind it, I could see the wall just a few inches away. But I couldn't see how deep the hole was. We knocked heads trying to peer in.

"Do you mind?" Awesome asked.

I did, but he was here in an official capacity and I could be sent home at any minute. I backed away a smidge. "Here," I said. I flipped on the flashlight on my phone and held it toward the hole. Nothing was visible from this vantage point.

Awesome put his hand in the hole and fished around. He pulled his hand back out and it was draped with a couple of cobwebs. Better him than me. "There's nothing in there."

I released a long breath. "I guess that would have been too easy."

Awesome nodded. "I'll head back downstairs. The acting chief isn't going to spend too much more man power on this search."

I watched his back as he left the room. Was there some emphasis on *acting* in Awesome's voice? I knew the few officers I'd talked to were unhappy that my ex-husband CJ had left his job as a chief of police in Ellington and had taken a position in Fort Walton Beach, Florida. But it wasn't my fault. No one had been more surprised than me.

It was just after ten when I went back to the other room in the attic and Awesome went back downstairs. My companions had made a lot of progress. Stella came over to me.

"Is everything okay? I heard Awesome's voice." She kept her voice low.

"It's fine." I hoped that was true. "I sort of suggested that maybe someone from the police department had taken the book."

"I'll bet that went over well."

I shrugged. "It could have been worse."

"Did you find anything?"

"A hidey-hole."

"Really? Anything interesting?"

"If you like cobwebs. Awesome didn't find anything else."

"Did you try? Nathan might not have been able to maneuver into the narrow corners. He's got really big hands."

We grinned at each other.

"I didn't. Let's get Ryne to keep our officer busy for a few minutes. We'll sneak over and take another look."

"Hey, Ryne," I called. "Didn't you always love Trixie Belden books when you were a kid? Look at this one."

Ryne looked confused for a moment. Then he glanced over at the police officer. "I did love them." He sauntered over to us. "I really loved them." He lowered his voice. "You two look like you're up to something." Ryne tilted his head toward the officer. "He's going to catch on if you look so guilty." He took the book I was holding. "*Trixie Belden and the Mystery in Arizona* was one of my very favorites. So very American."

"Can you create some kind of distraction so Stella and I can do something really quickly?" I asked softly.

Ryne smirked. I think he remembered the diversion I'd created at an estate sale in May for my friend Carol. It was the day Ryne and I met. "Okay."

Ryne drifted back over to where he'd been working near the police officer. He shuffled books around, acted like he'd finished that box, and moved onto another one, closer to a corner. A minute later, he let out a little scream and grabbed the policeman's arm.

"What was that?" Ryne asked. He pointed dramatically to a box-filled corner.

Stella and I didn't stick around to find out. Ryne looked up as we left and shook his head. I heard his voice as we slipped into Kay's room.

"I think it was a rat," he said in an excellent imitation of a scared elementary school boy. "Look over there."

Awesome and I had left the piece of wood off the hidey-hole, so Stella had her small, delicate hand searching the space seconds later.

"I feel something," she said. She scooted as close

as she could and was up to her elbow in the hole. "It's paper."

"Can you get it?" I asked.

Her face turned pink as she strained. Then she slowly pulled her arm out. Between her two fingers was a four-by-four-piece of ivory paper with some flowery handwriting on it.

"What is it?" I asked. Stella handed it to me. I stared down at it.

"Ladies?"

We turned, and the officer stood behind us, hands on his hips, glowering down at us. We scrambled up. He held out his hand for the paper, but I wasn't about to give it up before reading it first.

"'Loaned to Sebastian Winthrop, one copy of *The Sun Also Rises*, ltd edition.'" Underneath there were two signatures, Sebastian's and one by Harold Mervine. I handed the note to the officer. "Do you think Harold is related to Roger Mervine?" I asked after he read the note.

The officer shrugged. "Just go back in there"—he pointed to the room we'd been working in—"and look for the book we're supposed to be searching for."

Stella and I traipsed back into the other attic room like two naughty children. We'd been scolded by the officer watching us and then by Awesome. He hadn't appreciated it when I mentioned he should be thanking us for finding something instead of being miffed. Ryne rushed over to us.

"Did you find anything?" Ryne asked.

"Proof that the book was in the house at some point," I said. I didn't mention the name on the receipt, and neither did Stella. All of us renewed our efforts to search for the book. I found it hard to concentrate because I was so curious about what was going on downstairs. Awesome must be questioning Roger and Miss Belle. Would that I were a fly on the wall right then. But the officer now watched us as closely as a mother watches over a newborn.

By noon, I was exhausted, and I'd just finished talking to the state police. I didn't know if I could keep going. Stella and Ryne had left at eleven. Both had their own businesses or jobs to attend to. Even the officer who'd been assigned to me had disappeared. I could hear the occasional mummer of voices float up to the attic but couldn't distinguish the words. I wanted to be in the thick of things. Instead, I felt as if I'd been banished to the hinterland.

Awesome came up. "Ready for lunch?" He looked tired too. I stood and nodded.

"Any luck?" he said as we walked downstairs.

"I found a lot of interesting books that will sell well for the library. Miss Belle has every book written by Katherine Hall Page. Even her cookbook. She's a local author who lives in Concord. Then, I found a whole bunch of Joanne Fluke books. There's a Hallmark movie series based on her books."

Awesome didn't look impressed.

"And obviously, I didn't find the book we're all searching for or I'd have come to find you."

"I would hope so." Awesome noticed my frown. "Sorry. I've seen things of a lot less value make people act stupidly."

"Thanks a lot."

"I'm not saying you'd do something stupid." He

rubbed his hand over his face. "No luck downstairs either."

"What about the receipt I found? What did Roger and Miss Belle say?"

"I haven't mentioned it yet. I'm keeping an eye on them to see if something else is going on here."

"That sounds smart." I stopped at the top step that led to the main floor and faced Awesome. "If you don't trust them, why did you let me stay with them last night?"

"Not my best move. It didn't really dawn on me until this morning that they could be trouble."

I felt a chill run up my spine.

"You wouldn't believe some of the characters I had to deal with when I was on the force in New York City. Sadly, people will do almost anything and find some way to justify it to themselves."

We headed down the last flight of stairs but paused in the foyer.

"I slept closest to the door. If someone came in, I'd protect Miss Belle. If Roger or Miss Belle seemed like a threat, I was out of there first."

Awesome grinned. "Good thinking. Come on, Let's go eat."

Chapter Seventeen

We walked into the kitchen. Food was spread across the long kitchen island. Lobster salad, potato salad, lettuce, rolls, beautiful, deep red tomatoes, a bowl of chips, and a plate of cookies.

"I made sweet tea if you'd like some," Miss Belle said.

I filled my plate and poured myself a glass of sweet tea. I took a sip. I hoped the combination of sugar and caffeine would reenergize me. After everyone filled their plates, we sat at the table. We were down to Miss Belle, Roger, me, Awesome, and one other officer. Miss Belle looked tired and stressed. Roger looked shell-shocked. His white hair stuck up like a rooster's comb. He ate methodically—filled a fork, food in mouth, chewed, and swallowed—but he didn't look as if he knew what he was doing. His eyes focused on some spot over my head, as if he imagined a distant future, or maybe, after yesterday, no future at all.

I wondered what, if any, relationship he had to Harold Mervine. He finally looked at me, blinked a couple of times, and returned to the present.

"Are you okay?" I asked.

"I've been on the run and had a gun held to my

head. Then shuffled around like a common criminal."
He shot an angry glance at Awesome. "Of course I'm
not okay."

So, if Roger was a criminal, he didn't lump himself in with the common, run-of-the-mill thieves, kid-
nappers, and murderers. Good to know. Awesome and
the other cop seemed to ignore him as they passed
food around and ate. But I could tell Awesome was listening intently.

"Roger, you're not the only one who has been
traumatized in the last twenty-four hours," Miss Belle
reprimanded gently. She would have made an excellent teacher, with her soft-spoken voice that dared
anyone to argue with her. I noticed she was just sipping her tea and pushing her food around on her
plate. I, on the other hand, was shoveling it in as if I'd
been on a forty-eight-hour fast.

"I'm sorry. I'm so out of my element, I'm not even
close to a periodic table." Roger said it with a tired smile.

"We all are," Miss Belle said. "Sarah hasn't been
home since yesterday morning and was chased through
the woods by a murderer." The word came *muh-der-er*
with the accent on the soft first syllable. With all that
had gone on since, I'd almost forgotten that. I shivered
internally at the memory. It also reminded me that I
wore day-old clothes, and I wondered if I smelled. If
so, everyone, including Stella, had been too polite to
say anything.

"I lead a simple life," Roger said. "I buy books and
sell them. My adventures come through reading or
making a great find. I just want that life back."

I'd like my life back too, although I'm not even sure
what that looked like anymore. Upheaval had become
my new normal since I'd first left CJ when he was
tossed off base over a year and a half ago. I'd been
forced to move off Fitch but had chosen to stay in

Ellington. I looked at Miss Belle and Roger. They didn't even know about the receipt yet, a piece of paper that linked their two families, if Harold was indeed related in some way to Roger. Or did they know, and the superficial affection for each other was a thin layer of ice that covered a roiling, deep ocean of emotion. No one said much after that. I yawned and set off a string of them around the table. After we finished, Miss Belle stood.

"I cannot keep my eyes open another minute. I'm sure Roger and Sarah could use a rest too."

Awesome looked us over. I'm not sure what he saw, but he gave a brief nod. "Okay. We break for an hour. But will you three stay here in the house, please?" He pointed to Roger, Miss Belle, and me.

Roger huffed. "I have a business to run."

I wondered if he just wanted to run. Away. Far, far away. Awesome must wonder the same thing if he wanted us to stay here.

"Can you just run your business by phone for the time being?" Awesome asked.

"I haven't committed any crimes." He whined like a child who wanted something he couldn't have.

"No, but you were the victim of one. Someone was in your home and business. Think of this as protective custody. We haven't found who killed Miss Belle's maid or who attacked you. But if you don't like it, you're more than welcome to leave."

Roger deflated a bit at that. Searching for a book was vastly different from searching for a killer.

"Roger, you can stay in the room across from Sarah," Miss Belle said. They both stood. "And you can use the room you were supposed to stay in last night, Sarah."

I nodded and waited with Awesome while they left. The other cop stood and walked out too.

"Are you going to stand outside his door and listen? Trace his calls? Or do you have some kind of device you can listen in from down here?"

"You must need sleep. I'm not a CIA agent. I'm a cop." But he stood when I did and followed me upstairs. I went into my room but left the door open a crack. Awesome went into the room next to Roger's. Aha! He was suspicious too.

I crept across the hall once Awesome was out of sight and pressed my ear to the door. I couldn't hear anything. No movement, no voices, no snoring. But the doors were solid mahogany, so that might be why. And frankly, I was too tired to wait around to listen. I dragged myself back to my room and collapsed on the bed.

I jerked awake, startled to see Miss Belle beside me, poking my arm. "What? What is it?"

"I'm sorry if I scared you. I just wanted to talk for a minute without anyone else around."

I rested on my elbows for a minute before I swung my legs over the bed. If I were a little kid, I'd be rubbing my eyes with the backs of my hands. I picked up my phone and glanced at it. Two o'clock. I'd only slept for an hour. Another eight would have been nice.

"Okay. I'm awake. What is it you need?"

"Officer Bossum said we were in protective custody."

I nodded, even though I didn't think he meant it in the strictest sense of real protective custody.

"Do you think he means that, or does he think we're guilty and in cahoots?"

I didn't like being looped into the guilty party, but perhaps I could somehow work it to my advantage and find something out. I really wanted to find out if Harold Mervine was related to Roger too. I tried to look surprised.

I shrugged. "I don't know what Awesome is thinking." I paused and bit my lip, trying to act as if I hadn't already thought all of this through. "You could be right. Maybe he thinks I knew all along. We faked your injury, Kay was supposed to hand off the manuscripts to Roger, but something went wrong. That this is all some wild cover story since Kay ended up dead."

I watched Miss Belle. Closely. As I went through all this. She pursed her lips and tugged on her bottom one as she listened. I didn't know her well enough to figure out what she was thinking.

"Or he thinks it's Roger and me. That you were our pawn."

Miss Belle was astute.

"Why would you even need me? It would make more sense to keep me out of it."

"But if you found something we didn't know existed, getting it away from you quickly does make sense."

I shook my head. "I don't think it works. Why send me off after Kay?" Unless I was the one who was supposed to die out there. Or Kay and I both were. In fact, scary as it was, that made a great deal of sense. Then Roger could quietly have sold the manuscripts on the black market. Someone in his world probably knew the good and bad of selling immensely valuable books. He and Miss Belle could split the profits and no one would be the wiser. There were so many variables and possibilities at this point, I couldn't figure anything out. It made my head ache.

"I saw your face when I gave you the manuscripts. You were shocked."

"Maybe shocked you found them."

I tried to figure out why Miss Belle kept on like this. Maybe to convince me she was innocent, or maybe to convince me I was wrong in thinking she could be. With either scenario, I became more convinced that Miss Belle couldn't have been in on the plot to steal the manuscripts and murder Kay. "If you knew I was coming to go through your things, you wouldn't have left them where I would find them."

Miss Belle smiled. "Touché. Now I just hope you can convince Officer Bossum of that."

I smiled back. Miss Belle was a pro. "Before we go back to work, I have a few questions about Roger."

Miss Belle nodded. "I can understand that."

"How long have you known him?"

"What seems like forever. Sebastian went to prep school with his older brother, Harold."

Neutral face, neutral face, don't give anything away. I wanted to shout *aha*, but the information about the receipt wasn't public knowledge yet. "Does Harold still live around here?" I asked.

For once, my face must not have given anything away because Miss Belle didn't look suspicious.

She shook her head. "He died about the same time Sebastian did. At the time, he and Roger were business partners in the bookstore."

"Do they have other siblings?"

"A sister. But I don't think they were close."

"So not business partners?" A sister might have found a similar receipt somewhere. Maybe she knew about the limited edition of *The Sun Also Rises* and sent someone to get it back.

"No. She didn't like old books. They were too dusty for her. She was always a bit sickly."

A light knock on the door interrupted us. I went over and opened it. Awesome stood there.

"Ready to get back to work?" he asked.

Chapter Eighteen

I worked steadily, with only one of the cops as my companion. I couldn't decide if he was there for show or if Awesome really didn't trust me. But many hands made light work, although none of this could actually be called light work. I threw open a humpbacked trunk that still had the original leather handles. The trunk appeared to be full of old scrapbooks. I dutifully lifted them out and stacked them beside me.

I opened each one to make sure it wasn't somehow concealing the book. On any other occasion, I'd have loved to go through them. I got glimpses of vintage postcards, train tickets, photos of women in elegant dresses who looked as if they'd stepped out of an episode of *Downton Abbey*. Pressed corsages and party invitations yellowed but neatly placed on the pages begged to be studied. But there was no time for that today.

At four we took another break.

"I'm leaving," Roger said. "Unless you plan to arrest me." He glared at Awesome with his eyebrows raised and his arms folded.

"You're free to go. I can advise you to stay, but I can't make you."

Roger relaxed.

"I'd like you to meet with a sketch artist if you can," Awesome said.

"Yes. Of course. I said I would." Roger sneered out the words.

Awesome handed Roger a card and told him to call a woman to set up an appointment.

Roger took Miss Belle's hands in his. "I'm sorry to desert you. But my business . . . I hope you understand."

She gently pulled her hands away and patted his arm. "Of course I do. Be careful. I'll let you know if we find anything."

"I'll stay at a hotel tonight and come back in the morning to help search if you haven't found anything." Roger nodded to me as he left.

I wondered if things were as serious as Awesome said, or if he just wanted to keep an eye on Roger. I searched his face, but he had a classic, inscrutable cop face on that gave away nothing. With that face, he was the kind of man who should be playing poker.

Miss Belle turned to me after closing the door behind Roger. "I'm guessing you'd like to go home to?"

I did. Desperately. I wanted to be back in my own home, in my own bed. It would make life seem more normal. But I didn't want to leave Miss Belle alone. And my place wasn't exactly roomy enough for company.

"I can't keep an officer here overnight," Awesome said. "We'll increase patrols. But that's all I can do."

That seemed to seal my fate. I tried not to let my shoulders slump.

Awesome glanced down at his watch. "I need to

head out." He took out a business card and scribbled something on it. "Here's my personal cell. Don't hesitate to call if you need anything."

Miss Belle took it from him. "Thank you." She turned to me after he left. "I'll call the agency that sent me Kay to see if they can get someone over here." She stood straight. "It's not as if I need a babysitter."

"I don't want you here with a stranger, Miss Belle. Especially because we have no idea if Kay acted alone, which seems unlikely, or if someone—maybe even someone from the agency—was helping her. I can stay."

"No. I won't allow it," she replied.

We could probably go back and forth like this for hours. "I have an idea," I said. "I know a woman who has a cleaning business. Maybe if she isn't too busy, she could help out for a few days."

Miss Belle raised her eyebrows at me.

"Her name is Frieda Chida."

"A rhyming name," Miss Belle said with a smile.

"Yes." I'd like to say it suited her, but she was a bit of a curmudgeon. Frieda was strong and not easily intimidated. "I'll have to be honest about the circumstances when I call her, though."

"Of course. We can't have someone here thinking it's business as usual. That sounds like an excellent solution," Miss Belle said.

I made a quick call to Frieda. She said she could come around seven. Miss Belle and I continued to work until six thirty. By then, we were almost too tired to move.

"What do you know about Kay?" I asked Miss Belle.

She was draped across a tufted couch in her study, and I sat behind her desk in her comfy office chair.

We both had glasses of pinot noir in front of us. Even lifting it to my lips seemed like an effort.

Miss Belle frowned at her wine. "As I told you before, I hired her through an agency. She seemed very pleasant. She agreed to live here, which not all help wants to do anymore, and worked hard while she was here. Although she never seemed very happy."

"Which agency?" I asked.

"It's one my mother-in-law recommended to me. Let me think a minute; the name will come to me."

I took a sip of my wine.

"It's the Blackmore Agency for the discerning client in need of staffing." She laughed. "My former house-keeper called. She said the woman who answered the phone was snootier than my mother-in-law, and that's saying something."

"You told me the day Kay was murdered she had only worked here a couple of weeks."

Miss Belle wrinkled her brow. "That's right. The woman before her worked for me for many years. Losing her was terrible. She was a friend. Almost family. Her husband cared for the grounds until he passed a few years ago. She upped and left with two weeks' notice."

"Did she say why?"

"She'd planned to move to Key West, Florida, to be with her sister at some point. But left earlier than I expected. There was nothing I could do to change her mind. Believe me, I tried."

Key West? Hemingway's former home. "What was her name?"

"Rena Accola. Why are you asking about her?"

I wasn't sure I should tell Miss Belle about all the thoughts swirling in my head. But Miss Belle was no one's fool. "The value of the lost manuscripts and book are almost immeasurable." I took a sip of wine for courage. "What if Kay somehow knew they were here?"

"What does that have to do with Rena?"

"Maybe someone paid her off to leave. So Kay would be in a position to find the manuscripts."

Miss Belle took a big gulp of her wine and peered at me over the rim. "That seems pretty far-fetched. If I didn't know the manuscripts were here, how would anyone else?"

I shook my head. "It does sound a bit crazy. How long a gap was there between the time Rena quit and the time Kay started?"

Miss Belle scrunched up her forehead. "About a month. I had temporary help in the meantime."

"Are you still in touch with Rena?"

"We exchange an occasional email. I'll text her email address to you. If you think it will help."

I nodded

Miss Belle whipped out her phone and quickly sent me a text. For someone her age, she handled the phone as well as any teen.

My phone buzzed seconds later with the text. "Do you know anything else about Kay? Did she live nearby, or have any family around?"

"I assumed she lived close, but I don't know that for sure. Kay wasn't chatty. Really, all I had was her first and last name."

"Do you have any paperwork with her social security number or home address?"

"I wish I did, but the agency took care of all that."

"Hmmm. I don't suppose they'll be willing to give any of that up."

"I'm sure they won't."

"What exactly were Kay's duties?"

"Greeting guests, cleaning, some light cooking, that sort of thing."

"Did she act as a secretary?"

"No. I answered the phone and replied to any mail, virtual or of the snail mail variety."

"What about friends of yours who've been here in the past month or so? Maybe even before. Anything unusual?" I asked.

"I had my bridge club over about three weeks ago. But that certainly wasn't unusual. I've known those women forever." Miss Belle frowned as she thought. "People stop by. But other than Kay, nothing out of the ordinary."

"Did Kay have anyone over?" I asked.

"Not that I know of. But it's a big house, and I'm not always home. I suppose she could have had someone over."

There was no way of knowing who. I'd run out of questions. "Maybe there's something more in the news." For a few minutes, we concentrated on our phones. "Nothing," I said. "Her name hasn't been released yet because they're still trying to notify her family."

The doorbell rang. "That must be Frieda," I said.

Chapter Nineteen

Frieda arrived at seven. Miss Belle seemed a little startled when she saw Frieda but covered it well. Frieda was of good German stock. Sturdy legs, thick ankles, and it looked like she could hold eight beer mugs in each hand without breaking a sweat. Quite a contrast to the slim, styled Kay. Frieda still had pink streaks in her hair, but she looked a bit less defeated than the last time I'd seen her. I held back a smile, trying to picture her in an outfit like Kay had worn.

After the introductions, we settled around the kitchen island with more sweet tea for me, decaffeinated coffee for Miss Belle, and full strength for Frieda. She looked around the kitchen, as if she was judging the cleanliness. A frown made me think she didn't approve. Although I had no idea what could trouble her, the place looked spotless to me.

We explained the situation to Frieda. She didn't even flinch or look concerned during the whole story.

"I'll call my son-in-law to come over too if you don't mind. He works security over on base and ain't afraid of nothin'." She studied Miss Belle. "Between the two of us, you'll be safer than a tortoise in its shell."

That made me feel as if I could finally go home. When I'd left almost sixty hours ago, I hadn't dreamed I'd be gone this long. I stood. "I'll be back in the morning. And Frieda, if you need anything, don't hesitate to call. Even if it's in the middle of the night."

We walked to the door together.

"Thanks for thinking of me," Frieda said. "I know I can be a bit cantankerous."

I smiled at that. "Thanks for coming." I glanced back down the hall.

"Go on," Frieda said. "I'll take care of her."

I decided to take a circuitous route home, just to make sure no one had followed me. That route included a stop at Bedford Farms Ice Cream. I figured after all I'd been through, I deserved a treat. Instead of my usual kiddie-sized cup, I ordered a small. It contained two softball-size scoops of Almond Joy, my favorite. Most places you'd get more of a golf ball–size scoop, but I was fine with this.

I carried it to a bench and watched as people swarmed up to the outdoor window where you ordered and swarmed out with ice cream, frappés—what the rest of the world called shakes—and even ice cream pies and cakes. People called to one another, chatted in groups, kids ran around their parents, and teens flirted. But I didn't spot a soul I knew, which made me sad. Maybe that's why I had really come here, to find someone to talk to, to feel normal, to shake off what happened.

After I finished my ice cream, I continued my rambling drive back toward my house. Well, it wasn't really my house; it was Stella's. But I loved my little apartment and was glad to climb the steps up to my second-floor unit. I'd painted the wide-planked floor white, thrown down an Oriental rug I'd found at a garage sale, the trunk I used as a coffee table sat on top of it. The couch, another garage sale find, a couple of end tables, and my grandmother's rocking chair were the only other furnishings in the living room. It could use one more comfy chair, but I hadn't found the perfect one yet.

After a quick shower and throwing on clean clothes, I looked out the window over at the town common. The Congregational Church sat tall and straight, a white beacon of light at the south end of the common. Its bell started ringing. Nine o'clock. When I'd first moved here, the bells marking the hours drove me nuts, but now they added a nice rhythm to my life. I craned my head to look across the street from the common. I could see lights on at Paint and Wine, my friend Carol's shop. I decided to swing by to see what she was up to. That was such a lie. I just didn't want to be alone yet. I trotted back down the stairs, out onto the sidewalk, and into the humid night air.

The door was locked when I got there, but there were still lights on in the back of the store, where Carol painted for pleasure. I rapped hard on the glass window. I didn't want to walk down the dark alley behind the store to knock on the back door. Moments later, Carol spotted me, nose pressed against the glass, and came to let me in.

Carol looked like Artist Barbie tonight, with a paint brush in her hand. She was tall, thin, and always looked stylish, even when she was in her store alone painting. Tonight, she had on wedge-heeled sandals and a black linen sheath.

"Come to the back with me. I'm painting tonight," Carol said after giving me a quick hug.

"As if the paint brush in your hand didn't give that away," I said.

Carol laughed. We walked through the front part of her store, with its long tables and stools where she held classes for groups who wanted to learn to paint or just to come have fun with their friends. This summer, she'd started teaching kids how to paint in the mornings when the store was slow, because most groups wanted to come when they could drink wine and paint.

Carol sat on a stool with a blue cushion on it. Before her was a large canvas with an impressionist-style harbor scene with lobster boats, fishermen and -women. A motorboat was stranded on the mud flats at low tide. It was a working harbor, not the one the tourists paid attention to. No tours, ice cream stands, or sailboats moored here.

"I love it," I said. I sat behind her on a chaise longue, adjusting a few of the many plump pillows on it. Carol and I had met not long after I'd met CJ. Like CJ, her husband, Brad, had been stationed at the Defense Language Institute in Monterey. Our friendship had spanned twenty years, many moves, and long separations until we were all stationed here a few years ago.

"We went to Rockport a couple of weeks ago. Brad's mom came up for a few days and we had a romantic getaway. The house we rented overlooked this harbor."

That made me realize I hadn't hung out with Carol for a couple of weeks. It wasn't like I'd been avoiding her and her happy family. Who wouldn't want a loving husband with three boisterous children, twin nine-year-old boys and her seven-year-old daughter? *Me*, my subconscious shouted. But summer is my busiest time of year, I told it.

"I've been trying to give you some space," Carol said. "But it hurts when you withdraw like you have."

She said all that with her back to me. She dabbed some blue paint onto the canvas filling in the sky.

Okay, so maybe I *had* been avoiding them. "I've been busy." It sounded lame even to me. "You're right, though. It's just hard to see everyone so happy when I still feel so miserable."

Carol turned around to face me. "I'm sorry you're miserable."

I waved my hand at her, trying to wave away her sympathy. "I knew I made the right decision regarding CJ. You know how hard we tried to reconcile." Carol nodded. "But then he took that job in Florida without talking to me about it."

"That was terrible," Carol said.

"But I'd been planning for our life here. I hadn't talked to him about that either. Not that he gave me the chance. I've second-guessed myself plenty of times since then." Especially late at night when there wasn't anyone to talk to.

"You said everyone is happy. Who is everyone?"

"You, Stella, the DiNapolis."

"You know Brad and I have had our ups and downs."

"But you managed to keep it together, unlike CJ and me."

"You need to quit beating yourself up about that."

"It's hard not to."

"Did you ever think that CJ made selfish decisions? That he was more concerned about him than you?" Carol continued to paint, adding more splashes of bright blue to the sky.

"I—" I hadn't thought of it that way. I'd been blaming myself since he left. "It just seems as if we should have been able to work it out. We'd been married twenty years. Now it's all wasted."

"So meeting me was a waste? Ending up here was a waste?"

Carol didn't say it in a mean way, but in a way that made me think. Her next brushstroke was sure and strong. I stretched my legs out on the chaise longue. I wished I felt the confidence with which Carol was painting. That I knew what needed to happen next in my life the way she knew which color went where. "I guess *wasted* is the wrong word. I wouldn't take back most of what happened. We loved each other. We just couldn't manage to keep loving each other."

"I never thought you guys loving each other was the problem."

I thought for a moment. "You might be right."

Carol put down her paintbrush. "Let's have a glass of wine." She went to a small fridge tucked in one corner of the room. I shivered for a moment, thinking of the man who'd died back here last fall. It didn't bother Carol. She had redecorated and had someone come and do a cleansing, complete with a sage burning.

Carol poured two glasses of wine. She tucked the bottle under her arm and carried the glasses over. "It's not a failure to realize something isn't working any longer and to move on. I want you both to be happy, and neither of you have been for the past year and a half."

Brad and CJ were almost as good friends as Carol and me. Who knows what she'd heard from CJ's side of things. It made me sad that he'd been so unhappy too, and that I'd been the cause. I moved my legs so Carol could sit down on the other end of the chaise. Carol handed me the bottle of wine. I looked at the label. It was a bottle of Meritage from a winery in Virginia called Paradise Springs.

I took a sip. "I don't want to turn your store into Paint and Whine again." It had been my nickname for the place right after CJ and I split up the first time.

"It's not whining. It's dealing with all of that stuff

you've bottled up. You can work twenty-four hours a day. But that wouldn't make all of the thoughts swirling through your head go away."

I took another drink, let the fruity goodness swirl through me. "You're right. It's easier to ignore it all than face it." I put down my glass. "I'll do better."

Carol nodded. "Did you hear there was another murder in town?"

I froze. I guess my involvement hadn't gone public yet.

"What?" Carol asked. She put down her wineglass too. "Don't tell me you're somehow mixed up in it?"

I nodded. "I am. Can you believe it?"

"Saying *yes, I can*, probably isn't a good thing."

I managed to laugh, which was way better than crying. I felt if I started, I might actually cry me a river. I needed to go home and get some sleep.

"I know better than to ask you what happened at this point. But are you okay?"

"It's been a long couple of days. When I saw the store still looked open, I buzzed right over. I needed a friend." *Don't cry. Don't cry. Don't cry.* I took another drink of wine. "I've barely even been home since it all happened."

Carol's phone buzzed. She looked down at it and frowned. "You aren't going to like this." She passed her phone to me.

Brad had sent her a link from an online paper. "Local Woman Involved in Murder." I clicked the link and saw that Kay's name had been released, and that I was mentioned as having discovered her body. I was relieved to see no mention had been made of the missing manuscripts or the limited-edition book. I handed Carol her phone back.

"It's a crazy story. One that I can't fill you in on right now." Weariness crept over me like an incoming sea fog. We finished our wine, chatting distractedly about families in the Air Force we both knew. Who was moving where, who'd been passed over for a promotion, how the new thrift-shop manager on Fitch was working out.

I washed out our wineglasses. "Thanks for listening."

"Thanks for stopping by. I've missed you and nights like this."

Minutes later I headed up the steps to the front porch of my apartment eager to sleep in my own bed. I was tired enough that I felt like I might actually sleep tonight. As I reached for the doorknob, a car door slammed behind me.

Chapter Twenty

"Miss Winston? Sarah?"

I turned around but didn't recognize the woman standing at the bottom of the steps. I didn't reply.

"I'm with the *Ellington Standard* and just have a couple of questions for you."

"No," I said. I turned back and opened the screen door.

"Don't you want your side of the story told?" she called.

There was no *my side*. I stepped into the foyer. As I closed the door, a big flash blinded me for a moment. Great. She had a photographer with her. I closed the wooden door but didn't lock it. Stella might be out, and so could Ryne. None of us had keys for this door, but I wondered if we should start carrying them.

I trudged up the stairs. The curtains in my living room blew gently, reaching toward me like white hands on either side of the window. I crossed the room and looked out. The reporter was talking on her phone. The photographer looked up and spotted me. As he raised his camera, I hastily closed the curtains and retreated to my bedroom. As I closed the curtains

in there, the photographer snapped another photo. I
wanted to flip him off but resisted and yanked the
curtains closed.

Banging on the door woke me up Thursday morning. I bolted out of bed, surprised to see light flooding
the room. I glanced at my phone. It was already eight
o'clock. I couldn't imagine what disaster could precip-
itate such vigorous knocking on the door. Then I worried about why I assumed it was a disaster. Maybe it
was flowers or donuts and coffee or a big box of choco-
lates. But then I heard Awesome's voice.

"Sarah? Are you there?" he asked.

I yelled back, "Coming." I hastily pulled on a pair of
shorts and a blue tank top as I hustled to the door. I
peeked through the peephole just to make sure it was
Awesome. When I threw it open, Stella and Awesome
stood there, then hurried me into the living room.
Tux, Stella's adorable black-and-white cat followed
them in. Stella had adopted Tux last fall. He stayed
near my ankles, as if he knew something was wrong.

"What the heck is going on?" I asked. I ran a hand
through my blond hair, which was probably a tangled mess.

"Why didn't you answer your phone?" Stella asked.
"I was worried."

"I started getting calls from random numbers last
night. Some of them were reporters, so I put my
phone on Do Not Disturb." I looked back and forth
between them so quickly my eyeballs hurt. "Is Miss
Belle okay?"

"Yes," Awesome said. "It's the reporters." He gestured toward the window.

I walked over and slid to the side, using a finger to

hook back the curtain. The sidewalk was empty, as was the street. I let the curtain fall back into place, relieved. "There's no one out there."

Stella and Awesome hustled over to the window, looked out, and shrugged.

"They must have given up," Stella said. "Nathan has been chasing them off the porch all morning."

I sank onto the couch, still weary. Tux jumped up beside me. I stroked his fur. His purr sounded like a sleek engine. "Any news on who killed Kay or why?"

Awesome was shaking his head before I'd even finished the question. I wasn't sure if it was a no, I'm not going to tell you, or no, we don't have any news. "No. But there is something else. Word of the manuscripts has leaked out."

"How? I thought the police were trying to keep it a secret."

Awesome nodded. "It's not in the reports. Maybe it was mentioned over a mic or scanner. But it's all over the international news. It's probably going to bring more reporters to town. This morning it was all local and regional people. It might get worse."

I shrugged. "It's not like I know anything about them. I only saw them briefly."

"But you held them. You read a bit. People are going to want to talk to you." Awesome watched me, waiting for some sort of reaction.

Rats. I hadn't thought of that. Miss Belle, Kay, and I were the only ones who'd seen them since 1922, as far as we knew. "I'll lay low as much as possible."

"I could drive you," Stella said. She picked up Tux, who meowed in protest.

"I'll be fine." I shooed them toward the door. "I need to get ready for the day."

* * *

I'll admit I peeked out my curtains before heading to my Suburban. I'd changed into a black knit tank dress and black flats. As I went down the steps, Ryne was coming up.

He held a bag from Dunkin's. "Donut?"

"Yes, please."

Ryne held the bag open, and I took one sprinkled with sugar and bit in. It almost melted in my mouth.

"Yum. This is so good. Thank you."

"I guess the news is out," he said as I continue to eat.

I shoved the last bite in, chewed, and swallowed. "Did you see it in the paper?"

"No. There were a couple of reporters lollygagging on the porch."

I frowned. "Do you know who they are?"

"I didn't recognize them."

Maybe that was a good thing. "How many of them are out there?"

"Just a couple. But no worries. I chased them off."

"Thank you."

"Stay safe out there."

I nodded as I went down the stairs. As a precaution, I stopped on the porch and scanned for reporters. The sun shone through hazy, late-July air. It sat on my shoulders like an extra burden. A couple ran past in shorts and tanks. They veered toward the town common. Even the Congregational Church seemed to slump a bit in the heat.

I trotted down the steps, headed left, noting that Stella and Awesome's cars were gone. Just as I opened the Suburban's door I heard someone behind me.

"Ms. Winston, do you have a comment about the missing Hemingway manuscripts?" A photographer shot video while a reporter shoved a microphone toward me.

I had a comment, all right, but it wasn't appropriate

for the public airways, maybe not even late-night cable shows. Other reporters rushed toward us. I think they literally had been hiding in the bushes. I hopped in my car, slammed the door, and clicked the locks, but I couldn't back out because a photographer stood behind the truck. I started it anyway. People hammered on the windows, tried the doors, and yelled questions.

On the one hand, I got it. Finding Hemingway manuscripts was a big deal. But for the love of all that was holy, someone had died. Show some respect. I put the Suburban in reverse. That didn't deter anyone. No one moved. I revved the engine. Nothing. My heart started to hammer, and with shaky hands, I reached for my cell phone. Where was Awesome when I needed him?

I started to dial the nonemergency police number when I heard the whoop-whoop of a siren. A police SUV parked across the back of the drive. Pellner stepped out and started moving everyone across the street to the town common.

"This is private property, folks. You're trespassing." Pellner said it over and over. He wasn't that tall, but his presence was commanding. Even with his deep dimples, he managed to look menacing. I'd had that look turned on me before, and it wasn't fun.

I watched in the rearview mirror as the reporters and photographers reluctantly retreated. When he was done, Pellner came and stood by the window.

I buzzed it down. "How did you happen to be nearby?"

"Awesome was worried. We've been swinging by more often than normal this morning. Although to tell you the truth, since you moved into town, there's been a lot more activity on Oak Street."

It wasn't really my fault. Maybe once. But I had

no comment on that for him. "Thank you. I need to get going."

"Why don't you let me take you wherever it is you have to go?"

I shook my head. A bit violently. "I have a lot to do." I gestured toward the reporters. "And it looks like you might have your hands full."

Even from here, we could hear the whirs and clicks of cameras and reporters doing updates for the eleven a.m. news.

Pellner frowned but nodded. "I'll back down the street. You back out and I'll follow you. At the end of the street, I'll block the road and you can skedaddle."

"Skedaddle? You New Englanders never cease to amaze me." I started to roll up the window but paused. "What's it like over at Miss Belle's house?"

"So far, so good. We're keeping a close eye on the situation."

"Any update on Kay's killer?"

"Have a good day. Call my cell or Awesome's if you need help." He turned and trotted down to his vehicle.

When he pulled back, I hit Reverse, wheeled out into the street, and took off. The journalists scrambled like ants fleeing a hill. No one stepped out in front of me. At the end of the street, I checked my rearview. Pellner's car slanted across the already narrow street. I headed the opposite direction from Miss Belle's house, just in case someone managed to run to a car parked on some other street.

Chapter Twenty-One

I whipped out my cell phone and called James. "Can you sponsor me on base?" I asked.

"Sure. For how long?"

"Long enough for me to drive in one gate and out the other." Reporters wouldn't have access to the base unless one of them happened to be retired military. It seemed unlikely.

"I'll meet you at the Visitors Center. What's going on?"

He deserved an explanation of my unusual request, so I filled him in. After I hung up, I drove through Bedford, a bit of Concord, and swung back around to the base. James was there, and we quickly filled out the paperwork. He put my destination as the base thrift shop. I would drive right by it on my way to the other side of the base so it didn't seem like a complete fabrication.

Fifteen minutes later, I popped out the other gate, which was in Lexington. I drove past Gilgannon's Irish Pub. Stella loved to go to karaoke there and often dragged a reluctant me along. So far, Awesome had refused to go. Even though I'd begged and tried bribing him. If he went, I wouldn't have to. I continued down the road, cutting through bits of Bedford and Ellington until I felt comfortable enough to head to Miss Belle's.

I made it to her house about nine forty-five, parked, and was heading to the front door when a big man stepped out in front of me.

"What da you think you're doing?" he asked. He wore a T-shirt that stretched across massive shoulders and a large belly. His jeans and thick dark hair were rumpled. I backed up as he stepped toward me. If he was a cop, I didn't recognize him. If he was a reporter, he needed to work on his people skills.

I pulled my cell phone out of my pocket, worrying I was going to have to call Pellner already.

The front door swung open and Frieda stepped out. "She's okay," she told the man.

Then I remembered her son-in-law was going to help out with security. I was surprised he was still here.

He nodded and lumbered off toward the side of the house.

"How's Miss Belle?" I asked as I trotted up the steps and into the house.

"Resilient." Frieda put a hand on my arm and pulled me over to a corner near a coat closet in the foyer. "You don't think she's going to want me to wear one of those silly maid's dresses, do you?"

The image of Frieda dressed like Kay almost made me burst out laughing. "I don't think she will. Was there any trouble last night?"

"No. Quiet as could be."

I hoped that was a good thing and not a gathering storm waiting on the horizon. We walked down to Miss Belle's study but didn't see her.

"Miss Belle?" I called.

We heard a shuffling sound. Miss Belle's rear end

backed out from under her desk. Next, her head popped up over the edge of her desk. As she stood, she swiped her hands against each other. Frieda and I exchanged a glance.

"Well, that book has got to be around here somewhere, right? I'm in no-stone-unturned mode."

"What about Sebastian's desk?" I asked. "Have you done the same with that?"

"I haven't," Miss Belle said. "Shall we?"

We trooped down the hall and into his study. His desk was massive. "I'll climb under this time," I said. I knew Frieda worked hard cleaning houses and probably was on her knees scrubbing things more than anyone should be. And Miss Belle had looked a bit stiff as she'd pushed herself up off the floor of her study.

I pushed the office chair out of the way. My heartbeat seemed to accelerate to supersonic speed in anticipation. I lay down on my back and scooted under the desk.

"Do you need a flashlight?" Miss Belle asked.

"Yes, please." It was darker under here than I anticipated, and I'd left my phone in my purse in Miss Belle's study. Frieda's head popped into view, and she handed me a large silver flashlight. It only took seconds to ascertain there wasn't a book hidden under here. I did see a bit of paper or cardboard stuck between the bottom of the large desk drawer and the back of the desk. I gave it a gentle tug. It came loose, along with several other pieces of paper.

I scooted back out, clutching the bits of paper, and stood up. I put them on the desk.

"These were hidden under there." They turned out to be vintage postcards, one from the New York World's Fair in the thirties, others from Paris, Hollywood, and

Washington, DC. I loved the graphic images, the bright colors, the heavy paper.

"Another thing Sebastian liked to collect," Miss Belle said. "Another time I'll have to have you sort through them, Sarah. They're tucked all over the place. Some in albums and some in shoeboxes."

I flipped over to the backs to see if there were messages, addresses, or postmarks, but they were all blank. For the most part, vintage postcards weren't worth more than five dollars. But the occasional one would have a rare stamp. Frieda and Miss Belle started going through drawers on either side of me. I drifted around the room, looking at all the books. There were so many, it seemed as if something could have been missed.

"Oh," Miss Belle said. She held a piece of paper in her hand.

"What?" I asked.

Miss Belle shook her head. "A letter Sebastian wrote me two days after we met." She smiled. "We're proof there *is* such a thing as love at first sight."

Frieda snorted.

I'd thought the same thing about CJ and me. "You made it last too," I said.

"Yes. It was hard work and a lot of compromise," Miss Belle said.

Even then, things didn't always end up the way you hoped and dreamed they would. I felt some twinges of guilt. Maybe I should have tried harder with CJ. Maybe I should have compromised more. If I had, I'd be living in Florida right now instead of here. But maybe, for once, CJ should have compromised more. He wasn't blameless in this situation either.

At eleven thirty, I explained that I had to leave. "I'm meeting a friend about a fund-raiser we're doing this weekend on the town common."

"Who is it for?" Miss Belle asked.

"Sergeant Eric Hunt. We're trying to raise funds to bring back a dog he adopted while he was in Afghanistan." I paused. "Eric has had a difficult time since he came home."

"Maybe I can find something to donate. I'd do books, but they're already promised to the library."

"No worries. The library is a good cause too." I said my goodbyes and took off to meet James at DiNapoli's.

I decided I'd park at home and then walk over to DiNapoli's. When I started to turn down Oak Street, I was stunned to see a TV truck parked out front and a few reporters encamped on the porch. There seemed to be some other people milling about too. I continued on down Great Road to the next light. I took a left, followed by two more, and parked in the alley behind DiNapoli's. The screen door was open, so I went in the back way, something I didn't normally do.

Angelo spotted me immediately.

"Everything okay, kid?" he asked.

"There are a bunch of reporters over by my apartment. I parked out back but can move if you need me too."

Angelo had a big meat cleaver in his hand. He shook it. "Need me to go over there?"

I smiled. My defender. "No. But thank you. I'm sure they'll get bored soon and move on."

"I'll fix you the best sandwich you ever had," he said a bit fiercely. Angelo meant *messenger of god* in Italian. The name suited him, and I think he sometimes thought he could fix all my problems by feeding me.

"But I thought the last time I had your roast beef sandwich you said it was the best sandwich I'd ever eat."

"It was the best *roast beef* you ever had." He paused

and had a slight frown. "Until I make you another one. But this will be the best *Italian* sandwich you ever had."

"I'm sure it will. It sounds delicious."

Fifteen minutes later, I sat across from James with most of a large crusty roll full of chopped salami, ham, and several different cheeses in a delicious Italian dressing still sitting in front of me. A corn-and-black-bean salad was served on the side. From the couple of bites I'd taken, I knew it was the best Italian sandwich I'd ever had. As with all Angelo's sandwiches, it was gigantic and would provide at least one, if not two, other meals. But seeing the reporters at my apartment had ruined my appetite.

James leaned forward. "How's it going with the sale for Eric?"

With all that had been going on with Miss Belle, I hadn't given much thought to the sale since the last time James and I had talked about it. Fortunately, almost everything was in place already. "I still have a few listings to put online, but I think everything else is set to go."

James nodded. "The permits to use the town common are done?"

"Yes. The vendors are all lined up too." This sale wasn't going to be as big as New England's Largest Yard Sale, which I'd run last fall, or the one in the works for this fall. I tapped a note into my phone to double-check to make sure there were no last-minute cancellations or additions. There was one particular vendor coming from the Berkshires I was really excited about. It was a husband and wife who had a small antique business they ran out of their barn near Pittsfield. They found the coolest stuff and resold them at great prices. I'd met them a few weeks ago at the new flea market on the west side of Ellington. They'd had an oak bookcase that folded flat. I'd been kicking myself ever since that I hadn't bought it. The practical side of me knew I didn't have much room for it. But at two hundred dollars, it had been a great price, and I'm sure I could have talked them down a bit.

"Everyone was really excited to be able to help out. How's Eric doing? We didn't really talk about him the other day."

"The idea of the sale seems to have taken him off the brink of self-destruction." James frowned. "I just hope we can raise enough money to bring King home."

I nodded.

"How's the entertainment lineup going?" I asked. James and his PTSD group had volunteered to take care of that aspect of the event, which was running from nine a.m. until three p.m.

"Getting the group involved was a great idea. Some of them formed a band."

I must have wrinkled my nose, picturing the boys who lived next door to me growing up and trying to be like Bon Jovi with disastrous results.

James laughed. "I wish you could see your face. Don't worry, they're good. Scott Pellner's daughter is going to open with a few patriotic songs. Midday, we'll have rock, and we're ending with a blues singer who used to live in Bedford but moved to Nashville. He's going to be in the area and said he'd be happy to help out."

"That sounds great, James. I'm glad you took that on."

"It's been good for all of us."

"Do you think Eric will show up? He seemed reluctant the last time we spoke. A face to the cause will really help out," I said.

"He plans to be. Although he feels a little self-conscious. We're going to use the photos of King Eric showed you the other day. I had them blown up to posters we can place around."

"That's a great idea," I said. "Should we meet at the town common tomorrow morning to finalize everything?"

"Sure. Did you have a chance to talk to Tracy?" James asked.

"I did, for a little while." I didn't want to give away any confidences we'd shared. "Being a military spouse can be difficult. It's never about you and your wishes."

"Excuse me, ma'am?"

I looked up at a man who stood beside our table. He had on a summer-weight tweed jacket with brown elbow patches, a white shirt with a bow tie, and heavy-framed dark glasses. He wore a tweed hat with the sides folded up. He looked out of place here, even though he was a nicely dressed man with waxed eyebrows and manicured nails.

"Are you Ms. Winston?"

I nodded reluctantly. "If you're a reporter, I have no comment."

"Oh, no, nothing like that." He pulled out the chair next to me and sat, casting a wary look at James, who, in his uniform, looked tough and muscular. "I'm a literary treasure hunter."

Chapter Twenty-Two

I stared at him for a moment. "A what?" I must have misheard him.

"I track down literary treasures, everything from rarities to oddities. Some have been stolen, some just lost. I seek them out with the relentlessness of a blood-hound. As soon as I heard about the lost Hemingway manuscripts, I flew in from Illinois."

I glanced over at James, who looked as mystified as I felt.

The man pulled a card from his pocket and handed it to me. It said *Trevor Hunter*, and beneath his name, it actually said *Literary Treasure Hunter*, followed by a phone number, email address, and Twitter handle.

"You're on Twitter?" I asked. I'm pretty sure I didn't disguise my incredulousness.

"It's where I get some of my best tips. My last name is Hunter. I was born to do this and I'm good at it. Better than the others who are going to show up."

"Others?" My face felt a little flushed. I didn't like where this was going.

"Yes. We're an international organization."

I squinted at him. "How come I've never heard of you?"

"We keep a low profile, doing a service to the world without expecting thanks or fame."

I looked over at James. He'd leaned back in his chair and had his hand resting on his mouth. I'm pretty sure it was to hide a grin.

"But I got to you first? Right?" Trevor asked. "Don't tell me Bull Hardwick found you."

"I've never heard of anyone named Bull Hardwick."

"Oh, good. You can't trust him. I blocked him on my Twitter account, so he shouldn't be able to see who my tipsters are. I can help you."

"Help me what?" He didn't look as if he could track down a flea, much less a murderer.

"Show the manuscripts to the world. It would be selfish to keep them to yourself."

James scooted his chair back a bit. I did the same thing.

"I don't have them. They were stolen."

"Listen. No one would let them out of their sight once they had them. No one." His voice had risen.

I looked around and saw one of the reporters who'd been outside my house this morning holding up her cell phone, taping this.

Trevor leaned in. "I just want to help you." He grabbed my arm. I yanked it away and stood so abruptly, my chair fell over. Memories of my stalker flooded back through me, and I froze. James moved in one swift motion and had Trevor by the collar, propelling him to the door. Angelo appeared by the reporter, blocking her view of me.

Trevor looked back at me. "Tweet me. I can help."

James escorted him out and made sure the reporter was out too.

Angelo locked the door. "Nothing to see here, folks. I'll let you out as you need to go." The people still in the restaurant were a mix of locals and military, just trying to eat their lunch.

"You'd better head out while you can," Angelo said, tilting his head toward the window.

There were more people dressed in tweed standing around. Trevor hadn't been kidding about others being here. Some of them were talking to Trevor. They seemed to smell a story, or maybe it was the aroma of Angelo's marinara sauce that had drawn them over.

"They'll see me go out the back," I said, gesturing to the growing crowd.

Rosalie came over. She clapped her hands. "Listen up. Would everyone please move to the windows? We'll block them, so the people gathered outside can't see Sarah go out the back."

"I'll walk you to your car," James said. "Just in case someone is already out there."

A couple of other military people said they would too.

No one grumbled about helping out. They seemed to enjoy thwarting those outside. Seconds later, they stood in groups, blocking the windows.

"Thank you. All of you. So much," I said to the crowd. I heard some *thanks* and *we take care of our own* comments as I walked toward the rear. My eyes filled with tears at the acceptance. These people had my back. It was why I loved living here.

Angelo held the back door open for me. "Go. Before they figure it out."

Twenty minutes later, I sat in my Suburban in the parking lot behind the hockey rink on the west side of Ellington. An out-of-the-way place where no one should be looking for me. I'd done my new normal of driving a circuitous route around town after thanking James and the other military folks who'd escorted me out to my car. In my rearview mirror as I'd pulled away, I'd seen them blocking the alley when a group of people dressed in tweed swarmed around the corner. I sent a quick thank-you text to James. He wrote back telling me to get hold of him if I needed further help.

I rolled down the windows to let some air in my already warm Suburban. The breeze coming in felt like the heat from flames on a grill, but I didn't want to keep the car running. I used my phone to post some ads on various sites to promote the fund-raising event for Eric. Then I typed *literary treasure hunters* into a search engine. What I was really hoping was nothing would pop up. No such luck. Literary treasure hunters were a thing, not unlike people who looked for stolen art. There was even an actual League of Literary Treasure Hunters. I looked through their list of members and found Trevor, but there was no sign of anyone named Bull Hardwick. I'd never seen so many photos of men and women dressed in tweed and bow ties. Sadly, not one of them looked like Indiana Jones. No whips, leather hats, or rugged good looks in this bunch.

I clicked the About statement. Their founder had been a fan of tweed and bow ties, which, after his death, the group had adopted. I read their Mission Statement: To scour the world for lost and stolen literary treasures. Then I noticed an urgent Alert button flashing on the upper-right corner of the website, so I clicked it. There was the story of the lost manuscripts and a picture of me. I sank down in the seat as I closed the website. What now?

Frieda called. "Don't come back. We've been overrun."

"What do you mean?" I gripped my phone. "Is Miss Belle okay? Has she been arrested?"

"Miss Belle's fine, and no, she hasn't been arrested. Although we could use some cops around here."

"Where are you?" I asked.

"The back deck."

I heard a thunk, as if Frieda had dropped her phone. Then the distant sound of her voice.

"Get out of here. Don't make me use this."

A few seconds later, she got back on the line. "Sorry about that. These weirdos in tweed have swarmed the place. Fortunately, most of them can be scared off with a mop. Bunch of wimps."

"They're literary treasure hunters."

"I don't care who they are. They're disturbing Miss Belle and she has enough going on."

"Thank you, Frieda. You've gone above any call of duty. I'll come over in a little while."

"I don't think that's a good idea."

"Why?" I asked. Some sweat trickled down my back.

"No offense, but you'll just attract more of these wackos and reporters. Haven't you seen the news?"

"I haven't."

"Take a look. You'll understand. I'll call you when things calm down."

I did a quick search and found all kinds of stories: stories about me. Some factual and some fringe. The fringe ones accused Roger, Miss Belle, and me of killing Kay, who they reported was trying to protect the manuscripts. Others said I'd stolen them and planned to sell them on the black market. There were photos of me looking angrily at the reporters this morning. Making the crazy stories a bit more believable. My mood sunk faster than a stone in a well.

A car door slamming made me look up. I hoped it was someone coming to skate but realized quickly the man standing by the beat-up gray sedan was looking right at me. How had this man found me? It wasn't as if this was somewhere I usually hung out. The guy was massive: Hercules come to life. His muscles bulged in his cargo shorts and T-shirt. His thick neck was almost nonexistent between his massive shoulders and shaved head. He wasn't wearing any tweed and he looked angry, like a bull going after a matador. Bull? Was this the Bull Hardwick Trevor had warned me about?

I started the car, shoved it into Drive, and peeled out, not wanting to find out what the heck his problem was. I heard a roar that sounded like a monster and then a thunk that rocked my car. I looked in my rearview mirror, startled to see the man clinging to the back of my Suburban. Out of instinct, I slammed on my brakes. It shook him off. I paused long enough to see him get up. I swear, he swiped his feet like a bull and charged toward the car. I tore off again, sliding around his car and bumping down the driveway.

I careened onto the street and took off.

Chapter Twenty-Three

I pulled into Sleepy Hollow Cemetery in Concord at one o'clock. I parked and walked toward my favorite spot, Authors Ridge. It's where Louisa May Alcott, Henry Thoreau, Ralph Waldo Emerson, and Nathanial Hawthorne were buried. All within feet of each other. It was one of my favorite thinking places. And Lord knows I needed a thinking spot right now. Trees towered over the spot as I climbed the hill to their graves. The shade provided a bit of relief from the heat. My knees shook a little after my encounter with Bull.

The name suited him for a number of reasons; not only his size but his personality seemed to fit. Who named their kid Bull? I crested the hill near Thoreau's grave before I realized my mistake. There were clusters of people all over the place. Some in tweed, some in bow ties, some in knee-length tweed shorts and knee-high socks. What was I thinking? Of course literary treasure hunters would stop here while they were in town.

While every part of me screamed *run*, I listened

to the voice that said *blend in.* Maybe they wouldn't recognize me. I had on big sunglasses, and the photo of me on their website wasn't that great. Although somehow both Trevor and Bull had tracked me down. I kept my head down and looked at Thoreau's modest grave stone. People had left rocks, pens, pencils, and notes around the flat stone that simply said Thoreau. I chanted *don't notice me* in my head.

I worked my way toward Louisa's family plot. Hoping I looked like a mourner in my black dress, and that I didn't stand out too much. My plan was to continue on beyond the Alcotts' plot and then cut through the cemetery and eventually back to my car. All went well until I plowed into someone.

"Excuse me," I said. "Lovely day." I crossed my fingers, hoping my casual act would fool her.

The woman looked perplexed. She wore wire-rimmed glasses and a large khaki hat that looked like something a zookeeper would wear. She blinked a couple of times. "I know you. One of the conventions?"

Oh, dear God, they had conventions? I nodded. "You look familiar to me too. Last year's?"

Her brow wrinkled, then smoothed. "In Maine?" she asked.

I smiled. "Yes, that must be it."

"The convention wasn't in Maine last year, it was in Indianapolis. You're Sarah—"

I didn't wait for her to finish before I took off. I dodged around gravestones, silently apologizing to the folks whose graves I passed so irreverently. Shouts sounded behind me, but I had a decent lead until I tripped over a root. I somersaulted down the hill, stopping just before my head slammed into a marble monument with an angel on top. I pushed myself up and hid behind the monument to catch my breath and assess the damage. None of it seemed permanent, just some cuts and scrapes. My dress had some lovely new grass stains, but they didn't show much on the black knit. The good news was somehow, I'd seemed to shake those chasing me. I hurried to my car and drove off once again for destinations unknown.

I realized I was spending the afternoon on the run, much as Roger had yesterday. At least so far, no one had tried to break my fingers or hold a gun to my head. Where was that gunman? The crazy literary treasure hunters weren't the only ones after the manuscripts. And it was only a matter of time until they found out about the limited-edition Hemingway book. If I wanted any peace in my life, I needed to find out what had happened to both.

I checked my rearview mirror constantly as I drove. I parked on a side street in West Concord. This street seemed to be as far from any literary spots as I could get for the moment. At least when the treasure hunters realized they weren't going to get any information from me, they could visit Walden Pond, Orchard House, and the Old Manse, among many other literary sites in the area. Their trip wouldn't be a complete waste. I called Stella.

"Is it clear to come home?" I asked when she answered.

"No." Stella almost shouted it. "It looks like most of the reporters are gone, but there's a bunch of odd-looking people outside."

"Are they wearing tweed? Hats?"

"Yes. How did you know?" Stella asked.

I quickly explained my encounters with the League

of Literary Treasure Hunters. "They seem to fancy themselves the book world's answer to Indiana Jones."

"I wouldn't mind if some Harrison Ford–type showed up."

"Stella! I thought you were happy with Awesome."

"I am. But you know, whips and leather. Be still, my heart."

"I really don't want to hear this," I said. "I'm sorry the house is surrounded."

"Never a dull moment with you, Sarah. But it's fine. As long as you don't show up, they're bound to get bored and leave eventually."

We hung up, and I wondered when that eventually would be.

I looked Trevor Hunter up on Twitter. He'd already sent me his phone number via a direct message, along with several apologies about coming on too strong. He explained that his passion for finding treasures occasionally made everything come out wrong, and that he didn't mean to scare me. I decided to call him. Maybe Trevor could call off his group of treasure hunters. Send them in another direction and give me more information about Bull. I blocked my number before dialing because I certainly didn't want someone like him having my phone number.

"I think I ran into your friend Bull," I said when Trevor picked up. I described what he looked like.

"That's him. What'd he do?"

I told him about the incident at the hockey rink. "Who is this guy anyway?"

"He used to be a member of the League of Literary Treasure Hunters. But he's a little crazy."

"Yeah, I noticed that when he jumped on the back of my Suburban."

"He was expelled from the group."

"Why?"

"Well . . ." Trevor paused.

I listened to him breathing in and out over the phone. "Well, what?"

"We think he has found rarities with the help of the group and sold them on the dark web. It goes against every principle we have."

"Have you told anyone about this?" I asked. "Anyone official, like the police?" I felt like I needed to clarify, because all these people seemed a little off to me.

"Interpol."

Gobsmacked didn't begin to describe what I was feeling. This all seemed so ridiculous, I had a terrible urge to giggle but didn't want Trevor to hear me. I managed a choking sound instead.

"I know, it's awful," Trevor said, apparently taking the noise I'd just made as some sort of disgust. "My best advice is to avoid him at all costs."

"I will," I said.

"And really, if there's any way I can help you, just let me know."

"There is one more thing."

"What? How can I be of service? I'll do anything. And I want to apologize again for scaring you."

Trevor was really over the top. "Can you call off the other members? I've been chased, and they're camped outside my house."

"I'll see what I can do, but don't hold your breath. We're an independent bunch. Probably half of them just want to talk to the person who held the lost manuscripts in their hand. You've seen words few have had the privilege to see."

"Do your best. Please."

My stomach rumbled at two. It seemed I'd eaten very little yesterday, and I'd hardly eaten anything at DiNapoli's because of Trevor showing up. I had a craving for a fluffernutter, the state sandwich of Massachusetts, with its white bread, peanut butter, and Marshmallow Fluff. The salty goodness, the sweet Fluff, sounded like perfection. Because making one wasn't possible, I drove to West Concord Seafood. I hadn't been there in a while. I peeked in the big plate-glass window. There were a couple of customers, but they were in normal summer clothes, not tweed, so I felt safe walking in. It wasn't a fancy shop, but they had a long counter of fresh seafood and, beyond that, a window to order food. I scanned the menu. Everything sounded delicious, but I stuck with my favorite, their lobster roll.

They piled the lobster high on a hamburger-type bun instead of the more traditional split-top hotdog bun. They mixed it with a touch of mayonnaise, but not too much, and there were no other fillers like celery or lettuce. I felt exposed in the shop, so I took my order, which included a side of fries, to go and found another side street to park on. I cracked the windows open but kept the doors locked. Bull had scared me. The houses were modest here, and hopefully, no one would mind if I was on the street for a bit.

After I ate, I decided to close my eyes for a minute to try to strategize. I'd read an article recently saying I was supposed to envision the future I wanted and then it would come to me. So I closed my eyes and pictured myself in my apartment, leafing through a magazine with the Red Sox on the TV. I had a glass of wine and there was a knock on the door. Then another, louder knock, right by my head.

I jerked up and realized I'd fallen asleep. A glance at the clock told me it was three.

A cop stood outside my Suburban. His face was creased with concern. I was sweating and drooling. I swiped at my mouth as I rolled down my window.

"Is there a problem, Officer?" I didn't know any cops in Concord. Not that knowing any in Ellington had ever helped me out that much. I kept my hands where he could see them. Something CJ had drilled into my head.

"We got a call to do a welfare check."

"I'm fine. Thanks."

"Stay here for just a minute."

I watched in my side view mirror as he trotted back to his car. I knew he'd run my plates. He might even check the National Crime Index computer database to check for warrants, or to see if I'd been reported missing. I adjusted my rearview mirror so I could see how I looked. My mascara was smeared, as was my lipstick. I looked like Bette Davis in *Baby Jane*. No wonder he was worried.

He came back over to me. "Please step out of the car."

I did as he asked without protest, even though inside I was yelling *why, why, why*.

"Have you been drinking?"

"No. Why would you even ask that? I just fell asleep." The officer made me go through all the drunk-driving field tests. My balance wasn't that great on any given day, but I managed to pass with flying colors, and no breathalyzer was involved. I thought about adding a twirl to the end of my walk but decided it might not be prudent. This cop seemed seriously lacking in the humor department.

"Do you make a habit of sleeping in your car? It's dangerous on hot days."

"No, and I had the windows cracked." I heard a car rattling toward us. As if my day couldn't get any worse, it was Bull. How the heck did he find me? Ugh, he probably had some kind of police scanner app and picked something up.

After showing the officer my license and registration, he said I could go. He added a quick warning about vagrancy and trespassing. I just nodded, glancing back at where Bull had pulled up to the curb half a block back.

"Is there a problem with the car back there?" the officer asked.

He might not be humorous, but at least he was observant.

"I think that man is following me."

The officer studied me for a moment. The look in his eyes changed. "You the Sarah Winston that's been in the news the past couple of days? Used to be married to Chief Chuck Hooker in Ellington?"

I hated the nickname Chuck but let it pass. "That would be me." I hoped this bit of information would garner some help.

"I hope my ex never creates as many problems as you did for Chuck."

Great; my reputation preceded me, and not in the way I hoped. "I hope she doesn't either. Would it be possible for you to block the street long enough for me to get a head start on him?" I glanced back at Bull. He had a newspaper out, as if he wasn't even watching us. I hoped he got the welfare check next.

"Sure. Then I'll have a little chat with him about how we do things in this neck of the woods. It doesn't include following women around."

I thanked him and waited until he climbed back into his car. He moved it diagonally across the road, effectively blocking it. For the second time in one day, a police officer had blocked a road for me. I headed off at a sedate pace, trying to figure out where to go next.

Chapter Twenty-Four

I called Ryne to see if I could hang out at his uncle's antique store for a while. I was parked at a Dunkin's in Lexington.

"Not a good idea today."

"Why not?"

"A bunch of people came in here asking about you. If I knew you, if you shopped here, that kind of thing."

"What were they wearing?"

"That's kind of a creepy question, isn't it?" His tone was joking.

I shook my head, not that Ryne could see me. "Tweed? Hats?"

"Yes. Do you have some kind of strange fan club now?"

"Hardly. They call themselves literary treasure hunters. I'm starting to think it's some kind of weird cult."

"Like Trekkies?" Ryne asked.

I laughed. "Kind of, but maybe weirder. I've been running from them or reporters almost all day."

"Sorry I can't help you out. Why are they chasing you?"

"It's not me they're after but the Hemingway manuscripts. Some of them have the crazy idea that I still have them."

"Oh, geez. I'm sorry."

"Me too."

I went into the Dunkin's and ordered an iced coffee with extra sugar and cream. Before I'd gone in I'd taken the precaution of tucking my blond hair up under an old Red Sox cap. One that I thought might have been CJ's, but it was mine now. I also left on my pair of large sunglasses. I tried to look as little like me as possible. But I felt a little foolish as I headed to a table in a back corner.

I looked out the window, scanning the parking lot for signs of Bull or people in tweed. My Suburban stood out like a big woolly mammoth out there. Easy to spot. The elephant in the parking lot. I might as well have a big neon arrow pointing down with an announcement that said, *Here's Sarah.*

After scooting across the hard-plastic seat, I checked the news on my phone and quickly scanned articles. The only good news was, no one knew about the rare edition of Hemingway's book. Yet anyway.

I reviewed my options. I couldn't go home. I couldn't go to Miss Belle's. I couldn't go to Ryne's uncle's antique shop. I couldn't even go to the DiNapolis. They had family in town, so staying with them was out. Carol had kids to worry about, so I couldn't risk bringing trouble to her house. Checking into a hotel or motel anywhere nearby seemed dicey; all the treasure hunters had to be staying somewhere. Boston and any place near the water was too expensive for my budget.

My closest friends from the base had all moved away or had kids. I thought about calling Mike Titone but dismissed the thought quickly. Although he seemingly had a good side, I knew the bad side was there too. Favors came at a cost, and a place to stay was big.

Bull had managed to track me down twice. How

had he and the literary treasure hunters so efficiently sussed out my life? It was as if someone had told them every place I went and everyone I talked to. Who would do that? I looked at my phone again. Ugh. Social media. I was on Instagram, Twitter, Snapchat, and Facebook. I was always posting pictures of places I loved around here. I checked my Instagram. Yep, there was a picture of me at West Concord Seafood from a few months ago. That meant I was going to have to avoid every place I loved. A tear rolled down my face. More followed. I grabbed a napkin, dabbed at the tears, and blew my nose. How long would it be before things reversed and my life went back to normal? I was alone and hunted.

I slunk back to my car and sidled in. I decided to call Awesome. Maybe small police departments had safe houses where they could stash someone. As unlikely as that seemed, it also seemed like my only hope right now.

"Does the Ellington PD have a safe house?" I asked when Awesome answered.

"No. Why?"

I swallowed once, twice. I didn't want to cry. I drew in a deep breath and let it out as silently as possible while I blinked my eyes rapidly in an attempt to chase away lurking tears. "I don't know where to go." It came out less shaky than I would have imagined, but not as confident as I would have liked. At least I didn't sob. "The literary treasure hunters seem to be everywhere."

"Ah," Awesome said. "There's probably a lot of press around too. I'd suggest my place, but I've already chased off a couple of those twits in tweed."

It wasn't very reassuring. "They found you too? How?"

"It must have been when I left Stella's. I've been lulled into a sense of peace living here."

"I'm sorry."

"Don't worry about it. Let me see what I can do," Awesome said. "I'll call you back. Just try to lay low until then."

I agreed, but easier said than done. I just sat in my Suburban waiting, for Bull to show up, for Awesome to call back, for someone to find out who killed Kay, and for the manuscripts to show back up proving that I wasn't a liar. Bull didn't show up, and Awesome finally called back an hour later. I think I'd dozed off again and was grateful Dunkin's hadn't called the cops on me for loitering, trespassing, or another welfare check.

"Meet me at the place we get the food for our guests at the jail. Then you can follow me to the site."

"Will do," I said before I hung up. They got the food for the jail at McDonald's in Bedford. *The site*; that sounded secure. It did worry me just a bit that he didn't want to give away the location over the phone. It meant he and/or the police department must be worried too. That didn't seem like a good thing to me.

Fifteen minutes later, I was following Awesome around Bedford. There was an old Nike missile site west of Bedford that Harvard owned now. Maybe there was some kind of living space there. But no, we drove right by it and turned back in toward town. In my tired, overwhelmed state, it didn't dawn on me where we were headed until we were only a block away. I slammed on my brakes. Someone behind me laid on their horn. I pulled over to the curb and got a less than friendly one-finger wave from them. But I didn't judge them harshly because I probably deserved it.

Awesome pulled over ahead, rolled down his window, and motioned me to follow. I tapped the steering wheel, again at a loss for what to do. We were almost to Seth's house. Why in the world would Awesome be taking me there? Seth was out of town. I figured there was only one way to find out, so I eased off the brake and pressed the gas. Minutes later, I parked across the street from Seth's.

Awesome was parked in front of me. I was out and by his door before he turned off his engine. He unfolded himself from the car. I looked up at him.

"What the hell are we doing here?" I asked.

"Seth's out of town and you need a place to stay." Awesome motioned me toward Seth's garage. He punched in a code, and the door rose. "Park in here. There's a spare house key in his top desk drawer."

I stood there staring at him.

"Go on. Your car sticks out like a sore thumb."

I got back in my car and drummed my fingers on the steering wheel. I could take off, but I really needed some place to stay. Seth's house was a modest Colonial, white with a bright red door. By the time I'd parked the Suburban in the garage, Awesome had gone through the door that connected the garage to a mudroom, then a hall. I found Awesome standing in the kitchen.

"Here's the key." He set it on the counter when I didn't reach for it.

"So, I'm just going to be a prisoner here until this all calms down?" I knew I was being overly dramatic, but I felt the push, pull, of all my emotions over the last few days gathering in my stomach. I hoped I could keep them from spewing out.

Awesome shook his head. "I thought you and Seth were cool with each other."

"We're not anything to each other. A couple of acquaintances." Talk about downplaying a relationship. I didn't know how much Awesome knew and wasn't about to tell him, even though Stella might have. I thought about Seth saying he wanted to take me out to dinner. It made being here even more awkward.

"Someone is going to drop a car off for you to use."

"Who?"

"I'm not sure. But we all agreed it would be better for you to have something other than the white monster for you to drive around in. Trust me, no one thinks you're going to sit around and wait this out."

A little chuckle slipped out. Awesome looked relieved, as if he thought I was a pressure cooker about to blow.

"Thanks," I said. "This will work for a couple of days, until I can figure out something else."

"Stella said she could bring you a wig from the *Phantom* wardrobe."

I could just picture me running around town in some elaborate wig with ringlets. "Thanks, but last time we tried wearing wigs, it didn't go so well." I smiled at the memory. We'd tried to be incognito at a restaurant and had failed miserably.

"I'm going to head out. Call if you need something. Call Stella. She's worried about you."

I nodded. "Will do."

After Awesome left at four, I wandered into the living room I'd decorated for Seth. I plopped down on the couch, a garage sale find, and hugged one of the throw pillows I'd picked out. It was so quiet, I could hear the hum of the refrigerator. The word *trespasser* came to mind. I shouldn't be here. I got up and roamed restlessly. The guest room was full of furniture from his last place, which some decorator had picked out. It was all sleek lines and chrome. It seemed too modern for this house. I peeked in the door of his office staring at the desk that brought back memories that made me blush.

I hustled down the stairs to run from the past. We'd set up the basement as a man cave, with its large TV, sports memorabilia, and bar. The vintage poster of Fenway, home of the Red Sox, I'd found and had framed, still hung in a prominent spot on the wall. I gave myself a little pat on the back for how great the room looked. I hoped Seth was enjoying it. I trotted back up the stairs to the main floor and hesitated at the stairs to the former attic. Whoever had owned the house before Seth had turned it into a master suite. It was the one room I'd never finished when I'd been decorating. But curiosity got the better of me and I headed up the stairs. I went slowly so my first view was of the wood floors, the legs of the bed, and then the whole room. Bed neatly made, a Robert Crais novel on the nightstand, curtains drawn against the August sun or the prying eyes of neighbors. The whole house was extraordinarily neat and clean for a bachelor living alone.

At the top of the stairs I turned to the right, an empty space where I'd envisioned a cozy reading area. The shelves full of books and comfy, overstuffed chairs were still only in my imagination. Beyond it was the large master bath with requisite giant tub and separate multi-head shower. I started to blush again, imagining what could go on up here. Maybe our chance at something had come and gone. Maybe I should say no to his offer of dinner.

Then I fled back to the living room and fanned myself. I needed a plan. I didn't want to stay here. Car doors slammed, and I peeked out the living room window. Oh, no.

Chapter Twenty-Five

A black SUV with dark-tinted windows sat at the curb. Mike Titone stood beside it with his driver, Joey. Was Mike here to see Seth? I craned my neck. A nondescript white four-door sedan sat in the driveway. Mike's brother, Francesco, stood by it. This must be the car Awesome had mentioned. Did he really not know who was lending it to me, or did he think I'd refuse if I did? I let the curtain drop back into place and debated whether to go out or not. A firm knock sounded on the front door. Hiding didn't seem like an option. Mike obviously knew I was here, and I really did need the car.

I opened the door. Mike strode in, followed by Francesco. Joey stood on the sidewalk, hands folded, watching the street.

"Joey is going to scare the neighbors," I said.

Mike glanced back. "Joey, come in."

I gave Francesco a quick hug. He was taller than Mike and had a mustache that reminded me of Tom Selleck. His eyes were the same glacial blue as Mike's, but a bit warmer. I looked warily at Mike. "What's this favor going to cost me?" The last favor had come at a steep price.

"This one's not on you. Someone else asked, and I'm helping that person out." Mike had icy blue eyes that were as direct as laser beams.

I managed not to squirm. "Who?" I thought about Awesome again. How had he become involved with Mike? Or was it Seth, which meant I owed him even more than just staying in his house.

Francesco handed me the keys.

"Doesn't matter," Mike said. "It looks old but has a V8 engine and a few other toys should you need them."

"So I'm about to become 007?"

"Hardly. Just take care of yourself. I heard you're in a mess."

The *again* was implied. Or my guilty conscience or lack of sleep put it there. "What kind of toys? Does it spurt out oil slicks and have rotating license plates? Rockets to launch?"

"You've been watching too many movies. It has heated and air-conditioned seats. I thought you might like that in this heat."

I was a little disappointed. But hey, air-conditioned seats sounded pretty nice.

"It also has a hidden dashcam that runs on a three-minute loop. If you need to record and save something, there's a button by the radio dial. It has a sensor that automatically records and saves if you get in an accident."

"I hope I won't need that feature. Thanks." I at least needed to be gracious. "I appreciate having a car to use."

"One of these guys could stay here with you." He jerked his head toward Joey and his brother.

A mob babysitter? No, thanks. "I'll be fine."

Mike gave me a lingering look before he nodded.

He flicked his head toward the door, and they all left. After I closed and locked the door behind them, I felt another pity party starting up. I could sit here and wallow, or I could get out there and do something. I looked down at my grass-stained dress. It was also wrinkled and a little smelly from my earlier nap in West Concord. I took it off, turned it inside out, and cut the tags off. After I gave it a good shake or two, hoping the wrinkles would fall out, I slipped it back on. I checked to see how it looked in the hall bathroom. The dress only had two side seams. I hoped they looked like a fashion statement and not a dress turned inside out. No matter. I had things to do. So I snatched up the car keys and left.

The car had a fancy Bluetooth system, so I only had to do a few voice commands to call Carol. "I wanted to swing by to talk. Does that work for you?"

"I'm full up with customers right now. They chose a picture of Orchard House to paint."

The home where Louisa May Alcott wrote *Little Women* and most of her other books. "Are any of them wearing tweed or hats?"

"All of them. How did you know?"

"I'll explain later." I disconnected the call. I flipped on the switch for the air-conditioned seats. Air moved my dress and tickled my thighs. This I could get used to.

I pulled to the curb and Googled myself. Me this time, not the missing manuscripts. I should have thought of it earlier, when I'd realized how much of my life was on Instagram and Facebook. Story after story appeared. How I'd helped Carol when someone had been murdered in her store, a picture of me with the DiNapolis at a lasagna cook-off in June, an old police blotter from May when someone had broken into a neighbor's apartment. It was scarily easy to put the pieces of my life together. Add my own social media into that mix, and I was screwed. Out of an abundance of caution, I did a search of my name with Seth's. There didn't seem to be any stories linking us, at least not out in the public domain. Staying at his house for a couple of days should be okay.

I decided to drive to Boston and visit the Blackmore Agency. Starting with where Kay had intersected with Miss Belle seemed like a good idea. I hoped my dress looked good enough so I could pass myself off as a perspective client.

I spotted a garage sale as I drove through Bedford and decided to stop. It was late in the day for a sale and a Thursday. I wondered how that was working out for the seller. Maybe I could find something to dress up my outfit and a good bargain at the same time. Or even a new dress to wear. Things were neatly displayed, and I headed over to the rack of clothes. There were only ten dresses out, all good-quality, but unfortunately none of them were in my size. They had cute labels on them. One said, "Talbots dress only worn once." It did look brand-new. Another said, "feel me I'm soft." Of course I had to touch the material.

As I turned from the rack, a woman with curly red hair came out of her house and hung up two more dresses. Smart move; if you jammed everything on racks at once it often discouraged people from going through things. Clothes could be hard to sell, and selecting a few good pieces and pricing them higher could make you more money.

"Can I help you with anything?" she asked.

"I was looking for something to dress up my outfit."

She ran her eyes over my inside-out dress but didn't turn up her nose. "How about a scarf?"

"That's a great idea." I wasn't really a scarf person, but there was a time and a place for everything.

She led me over to a table with scarves and vintage jewelry. I wished she didn't have the jewelry. It was a recent weakness of mine. I sorted through the scarves, piling possibilities to one side. When I hit the bottom, I'd set three scarves aside.

The woman pulled one from my pile. "This is a vintage Elsa Schiaparelli."

"I'm not familiar with her."

"She was an Italian designer whose rival was Coco Chanel. In the sixties, she designed mod scarves."

The scarf was hot pink, black, and white in a bold graphic design that would go perfectly with my outfit. "How much do you want for it?" I asked.

"I have it marked ten. It's silk."

Ten seemed high, even if it was silk and from a famous designer. This was, after all, a garage sale. Because she said it was marked ten, I assumed there was room to negotiate. "Will you take five?"

"Sure," she said.

I took five ones out of my purse. I glanced over the jewelry and spotted a big bangle bracelet in a gold tone that was intertwined rectangles of various sizes. "The bracelet too, please." We settled at five dollars for it too. "Thank you," I said. I hung the scarf around my neck.

"Do you want me to tie the scarf for you?" she asked.

"Yes, please. I'm hopeless at it and would have just let it hang."

She draped the scarf around my neck and did some fancy knotting. "Here's a mirror so you can take a look." She handed me a vintage Bakelite mirror. "The mirror is for sale too."

I laughed. "You're a good saleswoman, but I'd better stop before I'm shoving everything you have in my car." I looked in the mirror at the scarf. "It looks fabulous. Thank you."

"You're welcome."

"It's late in the day for a garage sale."

"I'm not a morning person, so I've been doing some from four to seven in the evening."

"Interesting."

"Turns out there are a lot of people who aren't morning people."

"Thanks again," I said.

"Have a good evening."

Geez, I hoped to.

I pressed the accelerator to merge onto the 95, and the car shot forward. Wowsa. That was impressive. That must be the advantage of a V8. I'd had no idea what Mike had meant when he mentioned it. I hadn't wanted to admit my ignorance about cars.

Forty-five minutes later, I paid an exorbitant amount to park in a lot a couple of blocks from the Blackmore Agency. Before I got out of the car, I fluffed my blond hair and put on a fresh coat of lipstick. Hopefully, I looked like a confident woman in need of help and not a tired old hag who'd rolled down a hill that was definitely more along the lines of how I felt.

The agency was in a brownstone in the Back Bay area, another beautiful neighborhood in Boston. It was already five thirty, so I hoped someone was still there. I tugged on the fancy brass knob of the ornate walnut door, but it didn't open. I found a doorbell and rang. A few seconds later, a voice came out of an intercom I hadn't noticed.

"I'm Alicia Blackmore. May I help you?" The woman

sounded polished and smooth and maybe slightly annoyed by my presence.

"Yes. I've just moved to town and find myself in need of staff."

"We require an appointment and a reference."

Really? I obviously didn't know much about how rich people lived. Some people on base had help when they were posted overseas. Help was cheap in a lot of parts of the world. But most of us made do on our own. It wasn't like we were rolling in money.

"Oh, what a shame. Mrs. Anderson of Beacon Hill and Nantucket recommended you. But I'll just try the other agency she suggested." Anybody who was anyone in Boston had heard of Seth's family.

I heard a rustling noise.

"Because you're here, we'll see if we can juggle things to make time for you." The woman put just the right amount of irritation and solicitousness in her voice, making sure I knew my place.

I tried not to smile in case they had a hidden camera pointing down at me. Moments later, the door opened. A woman in an expensive aqua suit with big honking diamonds in her ears gestured me in. She glanced over my outfit without comment. Whew.

"I'm Alicia Blackmore. And you are . . . ?"

We stood in a foyer. A walnut staircase was to our right. Alicia turned to the left, and we entered what had once been the living room of the home. There was nothing so tacky as a desk or file cabinets in the space. We settled across from each other on twin rose velvet couches.

"I'm Sarah Spielberg. Of the California Spielbergs." I had no idea where that came from. Alicia's facial expression barely changed. Only the slight raising of her left eyebrow. I couldn't decide if she was impressed, had a BS meter, or too much Botox.

"How can we help you?" she asked.

"I'm looking for someone to help run my household so I can concentrate on my business."

"What duties did you have in mind?"

Very discreet. She didn't bother to inquire what kind of business I ran. "Someone capable of doing everything from greeting guests to cleaning. Maybe some light cooking." I thought that pretty much covered the bases of what Miss Belle had told me Kay had done for her. "And I'd prefer a woman."

"When would you need her to start?" Alicia asked. She crossed her ankles.

If one didn't know better, she could pull off being royalty. Maybe I needed to Google her. "As soon as possible." Alicia didn't seem like one to share tidbits of gossip, so I decided to take a direct approach and studied her reaction.

"A friend highly recommended Kay Kimble. She worked for a friend of a friend."

Alicia's mouth moved slightly, almost into a frown but not quite. I tried to decipher her reaction. Maybe she thought talking about murder was distasteful. Maybe she didn't want to admit someone from her agency had done something so unseeming as stealing and getting killed.

She leaned forward. "I can assure you that no one by that name has ever worked for me."

Chapter Twenty-Six

I sat back, stunned. What did I do now? Confess? Pretend to get an important call and leave? Maybe she was lying. My phone binged just then. It was an alert that there'd been an accident on the 93.

"I'm so sorry. I have to take this," I said as I stood. "Urgent business. I'll be back in touch." With that, I hustled out the door and down the street. I scanned the parking lot for my car but couldn't see it. Then I remembered the Suburban was parked back at Seth's house. I finally figured out which white sedan—who knew there were so many?—was mine and headed back toward Ellington, avoiding the 93.

I called Miss Belle, but Frieda answered the phone. Her voice was artificially high, as if she thought she sounded more businesslike. It made me smile.

"I need to talk to Miss Belle," I said.

"She's resting right now."

"How's it going over there? Are you still surrounded?"

"Na. Most people have drifted off because nothing's going on."

"Okay. Then I'm going to stop by. I'm in a different

car." I described it to her. "Let any of the people helping with security know so they won't stop me."

"Won't they recognize you?"

"I'll try a baseball cap and sunglasses to hide my face. Wish me luck." I disconnected.

Forty-five minutes later, I sat in Miss Belle's study. The door was closed, and Miss Belle looked at me wearily from behind her desk.

"Kay didn't work for the Blackmore Agency?" Miss Belle asked. She put a shaky hand to her mouth.

"That's what the woman I spoke to said. She introduced herself as Alicia Blackmore." I worried for Miss Belle. She'd been through a lot these last few days, and while she was a strong woman, all these blows seemed to be taking a toll.

"But that's who Rena called."

"Do you still have the number she called?"

"I'm not sure. I'll look." She started scrounging around in the drawers of her desk. Miss Belle pulled out an old-fashioned Rolodex filled with typed and handwritten cards containing all the contact information I stored on my cell phone. I remembered how I loved to play with one my grandmother had. She plucked a card out of the mix. "Here's the card Rena stuck in here for them."

I leaned over the desk and took it from her. The card was heavy stock with raised lettering. I compared the number to the one I called. It was the same.

"What?" Miss Belle asked.

"It's the same number. Maybe Alicia lied to me."

"Oh, dear."

"Have you heard anything from Roger?" I asked.

Miss Belle nodded her head. "Yes. I called when he

didn't arrive by ten. He said he's busy. Reporters and those treasure-hunting people have descended on him too."

"Oh, boy." I stood. "I'm going to head out." For some reason I didn't want to say where I was staying.

Miss Belle nodded. "Take care, dear."

I sat on the edge of Seth's couch like a doe about to bolt. This was ridiculous. I leaned back and tried to settle in. I realized with all my running away from the literary treasure hunters, I'd forgotten to follow up with Rena. I did a quick search and found a phone number for her. I dialed and was surprised to get right through. I quickly explained who I was and that I was helping Miss Belle with a book sale.

"How is she?" Rena asked.

I wasn't quite sure how much to explain to her, but then decided to plunge in to the story. It would be easy enough for Rena to look it up online. In fact, now that I thought about it, I'm surprised she didn't already know the whole story. Surely she must still have friends in Massachusetts who would have heard and alerted her.

"I'm sorry all this happened to Miss Belle. She's a dear. But why are you calling me? I'm not interested in going back to work for her."

"It seemed you left her abruptly."

"I gave her two weeks' notice. And again, I don't see how this is any of your business."

Hedging around the issue didn't seem to be working. She was either going to talk or hang up. "It just seems like a lot of odd things started happening not long after you left. Did you come in to money right before you quit?" I expected to either get shouted at or hung up on.

"Yes. An inheritance that, along with my savings and social security, made it possible for me to move."

What a coincidence that Rena inherited money that allowed her to retire and move to Florida.

"I can tell by your silence you're skeptical," Rena said.

I did a few quick calculations in my head. Some kind of inheritance would be a small drop in the bucket compared to the worth of the manuscripts and the limited-edition book. "It's the timing."

"I can send you a link to the obituary of my great-aunt if you want."

"No. I'm sorry if I seem overly suspicious. I'm just worried about the toll this is taking on Miss Belle." I could look up the obituary on my own. "How did you end up in Key West?"

Rena made a harrumphing noise. "My sister has lived here for twenty years. She had an empty apartment over her garage, and there's no ice or snow in the winter. Is that good enough for you?"

Another theory bites the dust. "Does she have any other empty apartments, because now I want to move down there too?" I hoped by lightening the mood, I could get a little bit more information out of her.

Rena laughed. "Sorry, but you're on your own. Please tell Miss Belle I'll be in touch. I'm sorry for her troubles."

"Before you go, I have a couple of other questions."

Rena sighed but didn't hang up.

"Did you help Miss Belle find your replacement?"

"I checked with a couple of friends, but no one was interested."

She didn't really answer my question. "Miss Belle said her mother-in-law recommended the Blackmore

Agency to find a replacement for you. But that you made the call."

Rena snorted. "It was really Mrs. Winthrop Granville's companion Ruth who made the recommendation. That's where Ruth originally worked. I did call. What choice did I have?"

So she didn't like Ruth, but made the call anyway. All of this was making me very uneasy. "Do you have any thoughts on a possible replacement for Kay?" Not that I would suggest them to Miss Belle, but I was curious to see what she'd say.

"Anyone not recommended by Ruth."

"Why?"

"There's just something off about that woman."

"Okay, thanks." I hung up and stared at my phone. Ruth had seemed cold to me, but then, so did a lot of New Englanders. But maybe it was something more.

I tried calling Roger to see how he was doing. He didn't pick up. It all made me feel more isolated and alone. I couldn't just sit here feeling sorry for myself, so I stood and headed to the kitchen. I'd stopped and bought stuff to make fluffernutters on the way home, along with a bag of chips and cookies. At least making a sandwich and eating would give me something to do while I figured out my next move.

I was halfway down the hall when there was a knock on the front door. I reversed directions, went into the living room, and peeked out the window. For the second time in a matter of hours, I couldn't believe my eyes.

Chapter Twenty-Seven

Luke, my younger brother, stood there with a brown leather backpack slung over his shoulder. I raced to the front door and threw it open. "What are you doing here?" I asked as I pulled him in and closed the door. "Seth's not here." Why would Luke be visiting Seth? Then I realized he didn't look surprised to see me. "You knew I was here. How?"

"I've been to the police station. I wanted to straighten things out with them after what happened last May."

I just stared at him. We'd been estranged for almost twenty years. He'd dropped in and out of my life so fast in May, I'd started to wonder if I'd dreamed the whole thing. But here he was. Gazing down at me. His brown hair was shorter, he had a neatly trimmed beard, and he didn't look as defeated as he had.

"How'd that go?" Even though I was mad that he'd left so abruptly in May, I didn't want him to be in trouble. Yeesh, I was still trying to take care of him as I did when we were little.

"That Pellner guy is one hard-assed cop. But when it came right down to it, I think it was more because I hurt you than because I broke any laws."

"Oh." The thought of Pellner defending me was an unusual one.

"He described in detail your reaction to the news I wasn't around." Luke put a hand on my shoulder. "I'm sorry I did that to you."

"You can't just pop in and out of my life. It hurts too much." And I'd had enough hurt, more than enough, the last few months to last a long time.

"I'm sorry. You're right."

I led him into the living room, still feeling awkward about being here. Luke sat on the couch. I sat in the chair I'd bought for Seth and had reupholstered. When I realized I was perched on the edge, I slid back. It was like my body was telling my mind not to get comfortable here.

"Why are you here?" I asked.

"For you. You're all over the news."

"Ugh. I saw some of the stories."

"You might want to check again," Luke said.

I grabbed my phone and searched my name for what seemed like the millionth time today. It had gotten worse since the last time I'd looked. There were stories in the local and regional newspapers. Holy crap! There was an article in *The New York Times* about the missing Hemingway stories. And the murder. And me. I was just one story away from being a guest on *60 Minutes* or, worse, a guest of the Massachusetts prison system, the way some of these stories were spun.

I held up my phone. "You can wave a magic wand and make this all go away?"

Luke was a reporter. Maybe he knew people who knew people.

"No. I wish I could, but I can't do that."

My stomach rumbled. "I'm hungry. Want a fluffernutter?" I headed to the kitchen and took the ingredients out of a bag I'd left on Seth's counter. I found a knife and a couple of plates. Ratios were important here. Too much peanut butter or too much Fluff threw off the whole thing. I spread pieces of white bread with peanut butter and with Fluff, and then cut the bread diagonally.

When I turned, Luke was sitting at Seth's dining room table looking perplexed. I held up a plate. "Do you want one?"

"Sure," he said.

I brought the sandwiches, chips, and cookies to the table. We munched in silence, washing the sandwiches down with glasses of water. I hadn't thought of getting anything else to drink and didn't want to use anything that wasn't mine.

I looked at Luke. "You look worried," I said when we finished.

"I don't like to see my big sister in the headlines."

"So what can I do about it?"

Luke ducked his head, as he had when we were little and he hadn't wanted to give up bad news. But this time he looked back up. "Not much. Have you talked to Mom and Dad? They're bound to see this."

I shook my head. "I didn't even think about them. It's been crazy here. I'll send them a quick text." I typed away for a few minutes, reassuring my mom I was okay and didn't need to come home. I knew her first reaction would be to tell me to move back home to California. "Can you think of anything else?" I asked.

Luke leaned forward and clasped his hands together. "I can get out your side of the story."

I liked that idea. "How?"

"I'll interview you. Write a piece and submit it to the *Globe*."

He meant the *Boston Globe*. I knew he'd written for them in the past. "Interview me? You want me to spill my guts? Have my life splashed all over the place?"

"It already is splashed all over the place. But not from your viewpoint."

I narrowed my eyes as a mean thought crossed my mind. "This would help you out. Your career. Is that why you're really here?"

Luke leaned away from me. He looked hurt. "I can see why you'd say that. I was here, got your help, and left without telling you, when I promised I wouldn't do that." He leaned back in and took my hand. "But that's not why I'm here now."

Luke had always gotten to me with his eyes when we were growing up. He was just ten months younger than me, and we'd always been close. Maybe too close; maybe that's part of the reason why the rift between us had become a deep gorge.

"I'll think about it," I said, pulling my hand away. "Where are you staying?"

Luke shrugged.

"Stay here." Not only was I invading Seth's space, but now I was inviting guests without his permission. But maybe being here wouldn't be so awkward with Luke around.

"Are you sure?"

"Yes." It would give us a chance to talk. We'd been under a lot of stress when we were together in May. Maybe we could start to have some kind of normal relationship again.

"Why don't you tell me your thoughts on what's been going on?"

I looked at him, trying to figure out his true motive.

"Completely off the record. I know you're good at making connections, so maybe talking it out will help you."

I nodded. "Okay. So you know the basic story."

"Yes. You found some valuable manuscripts, a woman

stole them, ended up dead, and now the manuscripts are missing. What's your theory?"

"I think Kay was in the house looking for a missing limited-edition copy of *The Sun Also Rises*. If she was looking for the short stories, she would have found them."

"What? That hasn't made the news. Tell me about it."

I filled him in.

"How did she find out about it in the first place and get herself hired?"

"I've been wondering that too. Either Miss Belle's former housekeeper was in on it or someone paid her to leave, setting up the opportunity to get Kay in place."

"That seems pretty risky. Miss Belle could have hired someone else."

"I've thought about that too. But it worked."

"It did."

"I think stealing the manuscripts had to be a crime of opportunity. When I found the manuscripts and took them down to Miss Belle, Kay must have overheard us talking about them." I explained how I'd gone back upstairs to work and after a couple of hours had heard Miss Belle cry out, and then the rest of what had happened that morning and Roger's story of his day.

"Wow," Luke said. "So how many people do you think were involved?"

"At the very least Kay, the person who killed her, and the person who found the overnight case."

"Who may or may not be the person who killed her," Luke said.

"Right. And the person who was after Roger."

"Do you think they're all working together?"

"I'm not sure." I took another drink of water. "I keep asking myself why Kay hid the suitcase in the woods."

"Have you answered yourself?" Luke grinned.

"What if between the time she heard Belle and I talking about the manuscripts and contacted whoever wanted the book she realized how valuable the manuscripts were? She called Roger that morning and asked him to meet her. Maybe to see if he'd help, but she never showed up."

"So she scrapped the Roger plan and decided to get more money out of whoever she was meeting," Luke said.

"Exactly. And they didn't like it."

"How did she die?"

"A limb was shot off a tree and it killed her."

"That's a lucky shot," Luke said.

"Or a really bad one, if the person was just trying to scare her in to telling where the overnight case was." I swirled the water in my glass. "I keep thinking she called someone she trusted and told them where the overnight case was, just in case things didn't work out with whoever she was supposed to meet in the woods."

"Whoever took it could be long gone." Luke tapped his hands on the table for a moment.

"I know. It's all my fault that the missing Hemingway manuscripts are missing again."

"It's not your fault. It's Kay's fault." Luke stood. "I'm going to go over to Ellington and mingle with the locals."

"You make them sound like some kind of strange tribe you need to study."

Luke laughed. "I want to find out what I can, so I can prepare a strategy for making sure people know you're on the side of good."

I needed all the help I could get. "Have you ever heard of the League of Literary Treasure Hunters?" I asked.

"Come on, you're joking."

"I'm not." I filled him in on the details. He checked out their website.

"And these people are in town?"

"Swarms of them."

"Hmmm. They may be helpful too." He stood and gave me a kiss. "I'll see you later. Maybe I'll find out something that can help find the manuscripts. What are you going to do?"

"I don't have any idea."

After Luke left and I could hear the sound of the refrigerator again, I realized I'd go nuts just sitting here in another quiet house waiting for something to happen. I decided I'd drive back into Boston, even though it was almost eight, to call on Roger. Maybe I should pick up some hair dye and scissors, the way women always did in movies. I could have Luke help me dye my hair brown and then we could chop it short. But I just laughed at myself for being melodramatic as I climbed in the car. Not going to happen.

Thirty minutes later, I parked down the block from Roger's store. It was a little risky because it seemed the treasure hunters might come here with or without knowing about Roger's involvement. They loved rare books, and he sold them. I pulled my hair back into a loose bun and tucked it back under my baseball cap again. It wasn't much of a disguise, but the best I could do on short notice.

I slipped into the store, which was pretty busy. One woman was ringing stuff up, and a man was showing someone in tweed a book he'd taken out of a locked case. Oh, no. Maybe I *should* leave. But he was distracted so I headed toward the rear of the store. I remembered that Roger had mentioned an office and security system. I walked down a quiet hall, past the bathrooms. A door marked Employees Only was locked, and no one answered my knock. I went back out and started looking for security cameras.

The first one I spotted was in the Mystery section. I plucked a first-edition Agatha Christie off the shelf and opened it. But instead of looking down, I looked up at the camera. Trying to make sure Roger saw me, if indeed he was here. There was also one of those big, round mirrors in the corner, slanted down, that gave me a good view of the store. Someone was behind me. Someone who looked familiar. Bull.

Chapter Twenty-Eight

Before I could stop him, he'd yanked me into the hall with the bathrooms. It was quieter back here. And darker.

"We need to talk," he said with almost a growl.

"Let go of me." I jerked my arm, but he didn't release it.

Over his shoulder, I saw the office door open. Roger stuck out his head and put a finger to his lips. He slipped out of the door.

"So what do we need to talk about?" I asked as Roger crept toward us. "Why are you chasing me?"

"I can explain."

I heard a sizzle, and Bull let go of my hand and dropped to the ground with a puzzled expression. Roger stood there with a TASER in his hand.

He looked at it, then Bull. "It actually works."

Bull groaned.

"Come with me," Roger said.

He turned, and I hustled after him into the office. Roger locked the door. We slipped out a back door.

He leaned against the brick wall that formed the

back of his store in the alley, which was old, narrow, and dark. There were a couple of fire escapes on buildings, a few trash cans, and a smell I couldn't identify and probably didn't want to.

"Are you okay?" I asked. His face was pasty in the dim light.

He bent over and put his hands on his knees. "I Tased someone."

"It's okay. He's okay. Let's get out of here."

"Where? No place is safe." His voice had an edge of hysteria.

"My car is parked down the block." I started hurrying down the cobblestone alley, hoping I didn't twist an ankle. I didn't hear Roger following. I turned, and he stood in the middle of it. "Come on."

Roger finally started moving, and we trotted down the alley.

At the corner, we peeked left and right but didn't see anyone. We scuttled to the next corner and checked again. I found my car and pushed Roger ahead of me toward it.

Bull came charging out of the front of the store and spotted us just as I slid into the driver's seat. I cranked the engine, and the V8 roared to life. I hit the button that would start the Record mode for the dashcam as Bull ran to the curb. He'd seen us. I wondered if the hidden dashcam got a picture of him. Bull now knew the make and model of the car. Maybe he'd even gotten the license plate number. I didn't want to do it, but I had to call Mike.

I pulled up in front of a warehouse on the edge of the Charles River at eight forty-five. It was dank and seedy-looking. The building had no signage.

"Are you sure we should be here?" Roger asked. "The man you called didn't sound very happy when you broke the news to him about the car."

"I don't think we have any other choice."

"You could have just dropped me off, like I asked you to." Roger sounded like a whiny kid.

I wanted to smack my head on the steering wheel. We'd gone over and over this since we'd left the store. "We're probably safer together. Where else are you going to go? Crazy people are everywhere trying to find us."

"Yes, but I heard you call Mike Titone. Do you know what people call him? The Big Cheese. Do you know why? He's a mobster. You get on his bad side and you find a piece of cheese on your doorstep. Then you disappear. Forever."

"That's a rumor. Really, who would leave a piece of cheese on a doorstep when it could be traced back to them?" I gripped the steering wheel. "I think it's just an urban legend." I really, really hoped that was true. I pulled out my phone to call Mike and let him know we were here. Just then, a big garage door rolled open. There must be cameras out here somewhere that spotted us. I pulled into the building and the garage door eased down behind us with only a whisper of electric wheels turning.

I turned off the car and got out. There was a door just a few feet away in front of us. Other than that, the space was empty. Concrete floor, walls of dry wall, and a light bulb swinging above us on a string. I walked toward the door and realized I hadn't heard Roger get out of the car. I went back and opened his door. "Come on, let's go."

He shook his head. "I don't want to die."

I had to admit the space was creepy, but sitting in

the car accomplished nothing. "Okay, just sit here, then. I'm going through that door." I pointed. "Maybe these walls close in and crush cars. Maybe noxious gas is going to flood the space. You can wait here and find out."

I spun around.

"Wait, okay, I'm coming," Roger said. "I'd rather not die alone."

"No one's dying."

"I'll bet Kay thought that too. She's dead."

"Well, Kay was stupid. She stole something that wasn't hers. I just borrowed a car."

"From a mobster."

"Keep your voice down. Please." There could be microphones in here. I put my hand on the doorknob but hesitated. What if Roger was right? I shook my head. Mike wasn't going to literally kill us, but that didn't mean he'd be happy. I glanced back. The big garage door looked solid, and I didn't see any way to open it. No place to go but forward.

The door flew open before I turned the knob. Mike's brother, Francesco, stood there. Behind him, a dimly lit hall stretched toward another door. These walls were cement and not at all inviting.

"Hey, Sarah. Ran into a bit of a problem?" Francesco looked behind me and spotted Roger. "And you've brought a mystery man."

"This is Roger. He's in rare books."

Roger gave a quick nod, his face pastier than usual. I saw him stick his hand in his pocket. Oh, no! Did he still have his TASER? I hoped he had enough sense not to use it here.

"How's Mike?" I asked.

"Oh, he's in a mood. Follow me."

We headed down the hall. Roger was so close, I

could feel his somewhat-labored breath on the back of my neck. I turned toward him. "If you have your TASER, don't even think about using it here."

Roger blanched and took his hand out of his pocket. I'm not sure who he was more scared of at this point, me or Mike. Francesco opened a door, and we were in an enormous room filled with giant wheels of cheese.

"Your cheese warehouse?" I asked.

"Yeah. Where'd you think you were?" Francesco asked.

He probably didn't really need to hear an answer to that. "This is amazing." The air was cool and had a slightly musky scent from all the cheese. As we progressed through the space, we passed all sizes, shapes, and types of cheese. Oh, for a regular night with some crackers and a nice glass of wine. Preferably back at my apartment, with no press and no treasure hunters lurking around. Kay's murder solved and the manuscripts somewhere safe.

We went through another door and came out into an office space. The lighting in here was also dim. I was starting to wonder if Mike was having financial difficulties and this was a cost-cutting measure. Francesco knocked on a door with his knuckle. He opened it without waiting for anyone to yell, "Come in."

Mike sat behind a large desk with a laptop and stacks of papers. He had on reading glasses and looked like any other normal businessman. Mike smiled and came around the desk. He gave me a kiss on the cheek and shook Roger's hand when I introduced them. Roger's knees were shaking visibly. I looked at Francesco with my eyebrows raised. He grinned back. He had said Mike was in a mood, but apparently, it was a good one.

"Sit, sit," Mike said.

Roger perched nervously on the chair nearest the door. He had the word *bolt* written all over his expression. I chose a comfortable leather chair across the desk from Mike. He sat back behind the desk and his brother lounged against a bookcase to Mike's side.

"So, Sarah. You may possibly have broken a record for fastest return of a borrowed car," Mike said. But he grinned as he said it.

I shrugged. "I couldn't sit home and do nothing."

"I think I know you well enough now not to expect anything less."

I'm not sure that was a compliment. "If you can just drive me back to Seth's house, I'll pick up my Suburban and be out of your hair."

"I believe it was decided it would be best if you laid low for a while. Or at least weren't so recognizable as you move about."

"It doesn't seem I have a lot of choice."

Mike reached in a drawer. Out of the corner of my eye, I saw Roger stiffen. Mike seemed to notice too, and made no attempt to hide his grin. I think he enjoyed his reputation as a bad guy. He pulled his hand out of the drawer and held up a set of keys.

"I have another car for you." He dropped the keys into my outstretched hand.

"What are you the Oprah of the mob world? Cars for everyone," Roger said. He clapped his hands to his mouth with a horrified expression. He turned so pale I was afraid he was going to pass out.

"You're funny. That's cute," Mike said.

Roger bobbed his head up and down. "Lots of people say that." The bobbing got faster.

I'm pretty sure no one ever said that to Roger. I stifled a laugh.

Mike focused on me. "Since they'll now be looking for nondescript, I thought we'd go in another direction."

"That's very nice of you," I said, worrying what kind *another direction* meant to Mike. "Before we go, I have another favor to ask."

"Sure, what is it?" Mike said.

Wow, he really was in a good mood. I'd asked for a favor and he'd said yes without warning me about the cost of favors and owing him. "I recorded something with the dashcam and wondered if we could take a look at it."

"That's easy." Mike opened his laptop, tapped a few keys, and motioned me to come around. Francesco followed me, but Roger stayed right by the door.

Pretty soon, a scene started playing. There was a brief glimpse of Bull as we sped off.

"That's the part I want to see," I said. "The man we pass."

Mike tapped some more keys and brought up a still picture of Bull. It was hard to see him because he was at the very right edge of the shot.

"Can you zoom in at all?" I asked.

Mike managed to get the photo a little bigger. "How's that?"

"Better." The image was pretty clear. "Any chance you recognize him?" I asked. Roger perked up when I said that. My hope was that Mike might recognize him, know his friends, and we could shut him down. And by *we* I meant Mike or the police.

Mike and Francesco studied the picture.

"I got nothing," Francesco said.

"Doesn't look local to me either. A guy like that stands out," Mike said. "I can ask around."

"Thanks for taking a look," I said.

Mike stood and led us out of the office, down a corridor, and into a bigger garage than the one I'd parked in. The garage held some panel vans with Il Formaggio, Mike's cheese shop in the North End, painted on the side. There were three dark-black SUVs Mike seemed to prefer to be chauffeured around in. I wondered if he even knew how to drive.

We walked toward the panel vans. At least he'd get some free advertising in our neck of the woods when I was driving one of these. He walked right on by. On the other side of the third van sat a bright red Volkswagen Beetle. One of the newer models, only this one had darkly tinted windows.

"Like the last car, it has a bigger engine than a regular car. And from the sound of things, you'll need it." He flashed another grin. "But there's no dashcam or air-conditioned seats."

"Thanks, Mike. I owe you." I almost shuddered at the thought and the words. I already owed him for a favor last February. I hated piling on, but these were desperate times. Roger looked distressed at the thought. Or maybe it was just being here.

"Like I said before, you don't owe me. Someone else does."

I looked for the grin but didn't see one. That worried me.

Chapter Twenty-Nine

"Where to?" I asked Roger as we set off.

"So, now you care where I want to go?"

I didn't bother answering.

"I have a friend in Woburn who said I could stay with him."

I plugged the address Roger gave me into my phone. At least Woburn wasn't too far from Seth's house in Bedford.

"Do you know Trevor Hunter?" I asked.

I glanced over at Roger, who shook his head. "How about the League of Literary Treasure Hunters?"

"I've heard rumors about some internet group that fancies themselves saviors of rare books. Frankly, it's people like me who are the ones saving books. Why?"

"They're more than an internet group. Did you notice all those people in tweed at your store?"

"Yes."

"That's them."

"It doesn't seem to me that any legitimate rare book dealer would have anything to do with them."

I wondered if that were true. We didn't talk much for the rest of the trip to his friend's house. Twenty minutes later, I parked in Seth's driveway, because my Suburban was still safely tucked in his garage, and went back into his house. No reporters or treasure hunters were lurking. I'd driven around the block twice before I pulled into the drive.

I spotted Luke's brown leather backpack on the dining room table. The shower was running, and I could hear him singing. It made me smile. He'd always loved to sing. Like me, he could carry a tune, but that was about it. From the relaxed sound of his voice, he seemed to be adjusting to Seth's house way better than I was.

I slumped into a chair in the living room overwhelmed by all that had happened. A few minutes later, he came out with wet hair and a big smile when he saw me in the living room.

"Roosters going to land on your lip with that face," Luke said. Our grandmother used to tell us that whenever we frowned.

I stuck out my tongue at him, reverting to our youthful relationship.

"Why the long face and ten-year-old attitude?" Luke asked.

"It's been a horrible few days. I need to take a shower, but I don't have any clean clothes. I feel as if I've had this dress on for years. It probably smells like it too."

"Take a shower. Borrow something from whatever dude owns the place. I'm sure if he's loaning you his house, he wouldn't mind loaning you a T-shirt and some sweatpants."

I realized then that Luke knew nothing about Seth or why I felt so awkward being here. I wasn't in the mood to discuss it anyway. "I suppose that would work in the short term, but I can't go around in 'some dude's' clothes for long."

"Why don't you call one of your friends, have them pack a bag, and I'll go get it. No one will be the wiser."

"You'd do that?"

"Sure, if it will put a smile on my much-older sister's face."

"Much older? Ten months isn't much older." I threw a pillow at him. He dodged it without a problem and tossed it back at me.

"That's the fighting spirit I'm used to," he said.

I called Stella and asked if she could get a bag together for me. "Or better yet, have those crazy treasure hunters left?"

"Let me look out the window," Stella said.

I heard Tux meow in the background.

"Sorry, some of them are still out there. They seem to have set up camp on the common and have rotating shifts." Stella paused.

"Please tell me you're kidding," I said.

"I wish I was. There are tents. Grills. It's practically a tailgating party out there. I think some of the locals are joining in."

"Is that legal? Can they do that on the common?" Eric's fund-raiser was on Saturday. They needed to be out of there by then.

"I'll call my aunt."

Stella's aunt was the town manager. "Okay. Thanks for checking, and for packing a bag for me."

"No problem. I hope this ends soon so you can come home. I miss you."

I smiled at the *home*. Ellington was my home. Stella was family now. "I miss you too. Give Tux a cuddle for me."

"I will," Stella said. "And I look forward to meeting Luke."

* * *

I filled Seth's giant tub with steaming water after Luke took off. My apartment had a giant tub too, which was one of the reasons I'd rented it. Nothing like a good soak to get my mind settled back in order. I didn't do it as often as I liked, especially during garage-sale season. This was the time of year I made most of my money, so taking time to indulge myself didn't usually work out so well. I played some loud country tunes, which always made me feel better about my own life.

Before Luke left, I told him my plan and let him know that if the door to the upstairs was closed, it meant I was still in the tub. I eased into the tub and ran my hands back and forth across the water. This tub was so big, I could almost float. I closed my eyes and let my mind drift. In the morning, I'd get hold of Alicia Blackmore. I'd fess up to her why I'd really been there and figure out if she'd lied about knowing Kay Kimble.

I also needed to meet with James to work on the final touches for the fund-raiser. Not to mention I had to get back to Miss Belle's house to sort through books. Checking in with Eric's wife, Tracy, was another thing on my list of things to do.

A bone-deep weariness settled over me. Could I keep this up? I loved what I did, but could I truly support myself for the long term? CJ and I had split our savings when we'd broken up, but I was determined to leave that untouched. I was a big believer in having money tucked away in case life took an unexpected financial turn. Also, half of his military retirement pay was deposited in my account every month. I'd toyed with the idea of stopping it, but it was tough as a military spouse to have any kind of career. Even if you did something more portable, like teaching or nursing, it was impossible to work your way up because you moved before you could.

The spouses and kids gave up a lot, along with the men and women who were active duty. And then were called *dependents*, as if they were some kind of hangers-on instead of people supporting the active-duty spouse's mission. I thought again about Tracy. Keeping the home fires burning was a real thing and, at times, could be extremely difficult. People focused on veterans' issues while spouses, like Tracy, and kids could be an afterthought. I hoped Tracy would contact people who could help her.

I let out a sigh. For a supposedly relaxing bath, I was sure having a lot of deep, dark thoughts. I pulled the plug and stirred as the water swirled out of the tub. Seth's jumbo white towels were powder-puff soft. I wrapped one around me several times. It draped to my ankles. I heard a noise on the other side of the door and froze.

The door creaked open. Seth stood there, head down, talking on his phone, one hand on the doorknob.

Chapter Thirty

I stared in horror, grasping the towel more closely around me, even though he'd seen me in less. A lot less. Seth looked up and just stared at me.

"I've got to go," Seth said into the phone. He swiped it closed. "Sorry. I called out when I came in. When no one answered, I thought I was alone."

But he didn't move to leave. Lots of thoughts flitted through my mind: bathtub, shower, bed, Seth. The heat of a blush coursed its way up from my chest to my neck. *Way to look dignified, Sarah.* I tightened the towel around me again. In my imagination, when I'd thought about seeing Seth again, it hadn't happened like this, in his bathroom with his bed as a backdrop.

"I thought you were in the Berkshires for the trial."

"I had some business to take care of here. I'm heading back tonight."

"At ten? You won't get back there until midnight."

Seth shrugged. I felt the towel slip a little and grasped it to me.

"Could you give me a minute?" My clothes. I'd left them in Seth's bedroom, stuffed in a corner, hoping Luke would be back quickly with something clean.

"Go back downstairs?" My voice came out hesitant. Oh, dear, he'd think I wanted him to stay. I pointed. "Downstairs. My brother is going to be back soon." Whew, that was better.

"Your brother's in town?" Seth asked. They'd never met, but Luke had definitely been on Seth's radar.

Did he look disappointed there for a minute? "Yes." I nodded vigorously, flinging water droplets around. "He left a while ago to get me some clean clothes." I paused. "He'll be back any minute." Yes, the implication was that I didn't want Luke to find us together in the bathroom.

Seth grinned and nodded. "Okay, then." He backed out and closed the door behind him.

What the heck was he doing here? And why now? I shook a fist at the ceiling. *Why now?* In my head, I'd always looked stunningly beautiful when we saw each other. I'd be dressed in some fabulous dress with peep-toed shoes, and he'd be wowed. So maybe I'd done a little daydreaming about that dinner Seth had mentioned. Or he'd see me when I was on the stand, composed, smart, testifying against my stalker. My imaginings had never included me standing with straggly wet hair dripping down my back. I leaned my head against the bathroom door. Steps receded. Thank heavens for wooden floors. I cracked open the door, stuck my head out.

The top of Seth's head disappeared out of view, down the steps. I scurried over to my clothes, grabbed them off the floor, and scurried into the bathroom. I slipped my clingy, black knit dress over my head, seams in this time, and fanned my face with my hand. A few pieces of blond hair curled around my face from the steamy bath. My eyes looked really blue against the red blush.

I ran my wrists under some cold water. I needed to

go down before Seth came back up to make sure I didn't faint or something. Cool, composed, think of ice. *Be ice.* My feet were bare, as were my legs. I wish I had more layers to hide under; even shoes would help me feel less exposed. I'd left them downstairs someplace.

After a couple of deep breaths, I went downstairs, peeking in rooms as I went past. The bedroom, bathroom, and office were all empty. At the end of the hall, I saw Seth's back. His broad shoulders, that pristine white shirt stretched over a powerful back and tucked into well-tailored pants. He was shaking hands with Luke. Luke looked over Seth's shoulder at me and smiled. "Look, Sarah, our host is here."

I stepped forward as Seth stepped back, turning to me. Our faces almost crashed together, his divine smell washing over me. Don't blush. *Do not blush.* We both stepped back a bit hastily. Luke looked from one to the other of us. I could tell his reporter self was on high alert. Maybe his brother side was too.

"You know each other," Luke said.

"Yes," we said in unison.

"We met in a bar," Seth said.

"We met over a body," I lied at the same time. Luke knew I'd stumbled over a few in the past year and a half. That would give me a good reason for knowing Seth.

"In Lowell," we both added.

"About a year and a half ago," I added for good measure. Seth nodded. Both watched me, each waiting for a cue from me.

"So, a year and a half ago in Lowell, you met over a body in a bar?" Luke asked.

"Yes," I said. There hadn't been a body, but I was hoping Luke would think we'd met in some kind of professional capacity. Not because I'd been out alone and lonely.

"Pretty much," Seth added.

"Seth's the DA. So we've run into each other over a few cases."

"Yeah. She's always causing trouble." Luke laughed, but neither Seth nor I joined in.

"Let's go into the living room," Seth said.

"Good idea," I said.

Seth stepped back so I could lead the way. I took the chair, so Luke and Seth had to share the couch.

"How about a glass of wine?" Seth asked.

"Great," I said, a little too fast and loud. Maybe alcohol would make this less awkward, if that was possible.

Seth left.

"What's with you two?" Luke asked.

"Nothing?" I didn't mean for it to come out as a question.

"Something."

"Ancient history and nothing I want to discuss with my brother."

"Did he hurt you?"

I didn't want Luke to go into protective brother mode. He'd started that when we were in grade school. If some boy even looked at me wrong, and God forbid they should ever say anything derogatory, they got what we at home called "the full Luke." For as gentle as Luke usually was, he had a temper.

"I hurt him," I said.

Luke nodded. We both fell quiet when we heard Seth coming back. He returned with an uncorked bottle of red wine in one hand and three glasses in the other. He put it all on the Louis Vuitton trunk, the family piece I'd turned into a coffee table for him.

"Would anyone rather have a beer? There's plenty of Sam in the basement fridge."

Sam was Samuel Adams beer, brewed in Boston. "Wine is fine," I said.

"A beer sounds good to me," Luke said. "I'll get it. Just point me in the right direction."

I had a feeling he did it to give Seth and me a moment alone. Seth poured the wine and brought me a glass.

"How are you? Really. You've had a lot going on since we met in my office."

I assumed he was talking about Kay and the missing manuscripts. "I'll be happy when Kay's murderer is found and life goes back to normal."

"It's not the only thing you've had going on." Seth sat back down on the couch, and we both took a sip of wine.

Was he referring to adjusting to life without CJ? "Right. The missing manuscripts. *And* the book." I didn't want to talk about anything personal. Luke would be back any second. There wasn't time for a long conversation now. "How's the case going?"

"I'm hoping your stalker is going to plead out so you won't have to testify."

My stalker. It still sounded so odd to me. It felt distant, as if it had happened to someone else. Just a story I'd read in the newspaper. "I'd rather not, but if I have to, I will."

"CJ's testimony was damning." Seth looked away as he said it.

I'd known CJ was going to have to testify, but I didn't know when. I tried to keep my face neutral, but my eyebrows popped up in surprise.

"He flew in and out the same day," Seth added.

I nodded. What CJ did wasn't any of my business anymore. But I was relieved to hear we wouldn't run into each other if I did have to testify. Part of the problem with our relationship had been blurred lines.

Even though we'd divorced, the lines between our old life and our new one kept blurring, like watercolors that spread across thick paper. We never managed to get it right either—when we were apart or when we were together.

Luke trumpeted his return by pounding up the steps. He popped back into the living room with a beer in each hand, Sam's Summer Ale. My favorite of the Samuel Adams beers.

"Need a glass?" Seth asked.

"Nope. The bottle is just fine with me. I'm a simple guy," Luke said.

I didn't know if that was some kind of dig at Seth. His life had been anything but simple growing up in a prestigious Boston family with a house on Beacon Hill and a compound on Nantucket. I'd always been surprised that Seth had settled in this modest house in Bedford instead of something big and fancy. And that he'd had me help him furnish it with secondhand finds. Luke had done some research into Seth the last time he'd been in town, but I never knew how much.

If it was a dig, Seth didn't seem offended. I remembered he'd once told me how hard he'd worked to prove to the world that his success was due to his own hard work and not his family's connections. Luke raised his bottle to him, and Seth responded by lifting his glass.

"Thanks for letting us stay here," I said.

"You're welcome. I didn't mean to disturb you, but I needed to pick up some things." Seth stood. "If you'll excuse me, I'll get what I need and be on my way."

Seth left the room and trotted up the stairs.

"That's the flimsiest excuse I've ever heard," Luke said. He took a long pull of his beer and then pointed his bottle at me. "He came to see you and didn't expect me to be here."

Could that be true? Seth came back ten minutes later with a suit bag folded over his arm. Luke looked at his phone.

"I have to take this," Luke said.

I suspected he didn't have a call but was trying to give Seth and me some more privacy. It was so embarrassing.

"I'll let you know if anything changes with the trial. If not, you're going to need to come to Pittsfield early next week."

"Are you sure you should go back tonight? Luke or I can sleep on the couch."

Seth gazed at me, then nodded. "I have an early morning meeting."

"Okay," I said. "Thank you. Safe travels."

"Thank you. I'm fighting for you, Sarah." He turned and left.

Fighting for me? Did he mean that as a lawyer or as a man? How did I want him to mean it?

Chapter Thirty-One

Luke came in the room, which, thankfully, distracted me.

"How was your call?" I asked, using finger quotes when I said the word *call*.

"The *Globe* wants your story."

"I've got nothing to say. No comment."

"Sarah, this is a great opportunity for you." Luke gave me that look again. The one that persuaded me to do almost anything for him when we were kids.

"Or you," I snapped at him. I rubbed a hand over my eyes. "Sorry. I'm exhausted and going to bed." I turned on my heel and made a grand exit. Then realized I didn't know where to sleep or where the things Luke had picked up for me were. I reversed direction.

"My bag?" I asked.

"Next to the dining-room table."

"Thanks for getting it for me."

"You're welcome. I'm taking the guest room in the hall."

That left me the couch or Seth's room. Luke stood up and gave me a big hug. I expected him to launch into a list of reasons why I should do the interview. It would have been his MO as a kid. Instead, he kissed me on top of the head and let me go. He had grown up. I knew so little of him still.

I grabbed my bag and reluctantly walked up the steps to Seth's room.

At eight Friday morning, I sat across from Alicia Blackmore, confessing that I'd pretended to be someone else yesterday. The look on her face had gone from polite interest to annoyance to distaste. It wasn't going at all as well as it had when I'd told Luke my plan on the way over here. He'd insisted on coming along because he was worried about me. I'd made him promise to wait in the car. I thought Alicia might be more forthcoming if it was just me in there.

"So you lied to me."

"Yes, and as I said, I'm sorry. I think the bigger issue is, someone seems to be pretending they worked for you." Not to mention someone had been murdered and I'd been chased all over the place. But I'd keep my mouth shut to try to gain Alicia's cooperation, to get her to tell me the truth about Kay. Maybe my honesty would make her admit she'd lied too.

She frowned, but this time it didn't seem so much at me but with me. Alicia studied me with keen eyes. "I can't decide if you're completely nuts and I should call the police or if you're telling the truth."

"I might sound nuts, but I'm telling the truth. Also, Miss Belle Winthrop Granville thinks her employee came from here. You don't want that to get out."

Alicia got up and paced around her office for a moment. "I don't understand how this happened. I double-checked my records after you left last night."

"This is going to sound bad, but do you have any

enemies? Someone who's mad at you, or a disgruntled employee or client?"

Alicia clicked her way back over to me and sat back down. "I can't believe we're having this conversation."

I shrugged. "Have the police or state troopers been by?"

Alicia pulled back. "No. I thoroughly vet my employees and my clients." She gave me a look that would wither steel. "I can't imagine either group would help with this—this fraud. Give me some time to sort this out. I'll figure out a way to find out who did this."

"Thank you. Let me know what you find out."

On the drive from Boston to Ellington, I told Luke what Alicia had told me.

"Do you trust her?"

"I'm not sure who to trust."

"I'll see if I can find out anything more about her agency," Luke said. "Drop me back at Seth's house and I'll get on it. What are you going to do?"

"I have to meet someone about the event tomorrow."

This morning at breakfast, I'd filled Luke in on the fund-raiser but hadn't told him about Tracy. I wouldn't without talking to her first. Luke had told me he hadn't learned much in town yesterday. He was going back to mingle with the treasure hunters because he wanted to find information to help me, and he wanted to do a story on them. But I guess digging into the Blackmore Agency now took priority.

I wanted the fund-raiser to be a success even in the midst of everything else that was going on. After dropping Luke off, I met James at the town common on the side farthest away from my apartment just after nine. The tents seemed to be gone, but I could see a group of tweed-wearing people milling about on the other side. Apparently, Trevor hadn't had much success getting them to leave.

I still had on the pink-flowered sundress I'd worn to see Alicia. As a precaution, because we were meeting out in the open, I'd tucked my hair up under a baseball cap and donned sunglasses again.

"Do you think we're going to pull this off?" James asked. He was in his uniform.

"Of course." I said it with a bit more confidence than I felt. But I chalked up the doubt to exhaustion. Even though I'd slept pretty well last night, my mind was a tornado of bits of information. I kept hoping they'd swirl together and reveal an answer. My bigger fear was that it would all just blow away before I could figure everything out. *Focus, Sarah.* I explained to James how I'd envisioned the day going.

"Any last-minute details I need to work out?" James asked.

"The base is going to let us borrow some tables and chairs?"

"Yes. A team will bring them over here early Saturday morning. Eric's fussing like an old woman about everything."

"Normally, that wouldn't be fun, but in Eric's case, I'm glad he's so involved."

James laughed. "It's better than seeing him alternate between anger and apathy." James paused. "It's just if we don't make enough, I'm not sure what that will do to him."

"If we don't make enough, we'll have another sale. Or find some other way to raise the money." I was determined this airman was going to be reunited with this dog. It would cost between four and five thousand to bring King home. I pictured King's sweet little face in the photo Eric had shown me. King might be Eric's only hope of surviving, of fighting back from the very dark place he'd landed. I didn't want him to become another statistic of veteran suicides.

We heard cheers from the other side of the town common.

"What's going on over there?" James asked.

I squinted. Stella stood on the steps, which was what had caused the shouting, apparently. We looked nothing alike; she had dark hair, green eyes, and Mediterranean skin. I guess anyone going in or out was cause for an uproar. Stella made a gesture that didn't look very friendly. She stomped down the remaining steps and hopped in her car. Things calmed back down after she took off.

"Who are all those people?" James asked.

"Remember Trevor from DiNapoli's yesterday?"

James nodded.

"It's more of his group." I quickly explained what I'd found out about them.

"They sound a little crazy."

"I can't argue with you there," I said. Another cheer went up. This time, Ryne stood on the steps, but he trotted down them over to the group. I could see him shaking hands and clapping people on the back. Of course Ryne would charm them. Maybe I should ask him to get them to leave.

"You'd think they'd get bored and take off," I said.

"How are you getting in and out?" James asked.

"I'm not. I'm staying with a . . . friend," I said. James looked curious, but I didn't want to talk about it. "Anyway, back to tomorrow. The VFW is going to do a pancake breakfast. And then the American Legion will cook burgers and hotdogs at noon. Both organizations will donate all the proceeds to the cause."

"That's great."

"Anything else you're worried about?" I asked.

James smiled. "Sorry to be a pest."

"Not at all. We both want this to go well. I appreciate how much work you've done."

We said our goodbyes, and I headed up the block away from Great Road to where I'd left the Volkswagen Beetle. I'd almost reached it when Bull popped out of nowhere on the sidewalk in front of me.

I screamed loud and long. James came tearing back over. He took one look at Bull and stepped between us. James was a lot smaller than Bull but strong.

"Get out of here," James said to me.

Bull tried to reach around him and grab my arm. James whacked it away. I took off across the street. I didn't want to go to the car because then I'd be at square one again with cars. I dodged between two cars parked on the other side of the street. I looked back to see the treasure hunters streaming across the town common in this direction.

"I just need to talk to you," Bull yelled after me.

I hesitated. What did he want to talk to me about? Then I remembered his weird and scary jump onto the back of my Suburban. That didn't seem like the behavior of someone who just wanted to talk to me. James took a step toward him. Bull put up his hands and backed away. The treasure hunters were getting closer, so I took off down the sidewalk and ran around the corner, out of sight.

Chapter Thirty-Two

I ran down the street, looking over my shoulder every few seconds. I found a giant oak tree to hide behind and ordered an Uber. Five minutes later—five long, excruciatingly slow minutes—a woman picked me up in a blue car that looked like a shoebox on wheels. As she found my destination on her app, I heard a car behind us. Bull.

"Go," I yelled. How did he keep on finding me?

The woman tossed her phone on the seat next to her and took off, tires squealing. It made me wonder how often this had happened to her. She drove toward Great Road and turned left in front of an oncoming U-Haul, whose driver honked and gave us the standard one-finger salute. I turned around and saw Bull turn the corner behind us.

"Where to?" the driver asked. "Your original destination"—she tipped her head to her phone still lying on the front passenger seat—"or somewhere else?"

I needed to lose Bull. "The flea market on the west side of town." The flea market was relatively new. It had sprung up at the site of an old consignment store.

It was only open a couple of days a week, and today was one of them. The woman wended her way through back roads, but I kept getting glimpses of Bull behind us. Trees, low slung stone walls, and Colonial houses flashed by.

"Do you do this often?" I asked.

The woman laughed. "I was married to a no-good piece of work who stalked me after our divorce. I became adept at evasion." She glanced at me in the rearview mirror. "You never know when your past will help you out."

"I don't know how he keeps finding me."

"The bad ones always seem to find a way."

That wasn't much comfort.

"I'll drop you at the east end," she said. "That's where most people park. That should hold your friend off for a bit while he tries to find a place to park."

"Yeah, well, he's no friend."

"Honey," she said, "I kind of figured that out right after you yelled *go* when he pulled up behind us."

"Thanks for this."

"How are you going to get away from the flea market?"

"I'll call someone," I said. Pellner, Awesome, or James. I should have thought of them in the first place but had panicked when I saw Bull.

"Tell you what, I have a friend who's an Uber driver too. Want me to give him a call? He looks like a mean son of a bitch but is really just a big old cuddle bug."

"That would be great."

"He drives a black pickup truck. It's got giant wheels because he also does monster truck competitions."

Figures. But whatever; a ride out of here was a ride out of here.

"I'll have him meet you at the west end of the flea."

She roared up to the flea market entrance. Even though you aren't supposed to tip Uber drivers, I tossed twenty-five dollars on the front passenger seat next to her phone. "Thank you."

"Give me a good rating," she called as I took off.

I nodded and gave her a thumbs-up as I ran.

The flea market consisted of one long, low-slung building with a bunch of booths with awnings on the west end. The air inside was cool, and I had to stop and blink a couple of times to adjust my eyes to the dimmer light. Then I realized I was still wearing my sunglasses. I stuffed them in my purse, along with my Red Sox hat. The floors were concrete and the walls cement block. It wasn't pretty on the outside, but the inside was full of fun for bargains hunters like me. Only not today. Today was about running from hunters.

The place was packed even at ten in the morning. The air was scented by the vendors who sold hotdogs, kettle corn, cotton candy, and drinks. I passed a booth with hats, did an about face, dodged around some browsers, and made it back to the booth. I bought a straw sunhat with a broad brim without even taking the time to bargain. Farther down, I stopped at a booth with all kinds of mirrors.

There was a walnut-framed mirror that surely used to have a bureau attached to it. One with roses etched around its border. Another with palm trees and flamingos painted on it. It looked like a Turner, but I didn't have time to stop to do a thorough investigation. I used a cheap full-length mirror with a thin black frame to look behind me. There was Bull's head sticking out above the crowd. His eyes were sweeping from one side to the other. He hadn't spotted me yet.

"Can I help you?"

I turned to the woman who spoke to me. "I'll take this mirror." I pointed to the cheap full-length one.

"Ten dollars."

"Five." I stuffed a five in her hand and picked up the lightweight mirror as soon as she nodded her consent. I worked my way to the edge of the crowd, holding up the mirror like a shield as I sidled along. While I wasn't moving as fast as before, anyone glancing at me would only see a reflection of themselves and the crowd.

I hurried by booths of Depression glass, cookware, and books. Books! I needed to find that darn copy of *The Sun Also Rises* and the manuscripts. Doing that would put an end to all this nonsense. The west-end exit was fifteen feet in front of me. I could see a huge monster truck idling outside. An equally large man stood beside it. I hoped to heck that was my ride.

I passed a vendor with bentwood chairs. I spotted a ball-and-stick rocker; at any other time I'd be pausing to see how much it cost.

"Hey. *Stop.*"

I knew without turning around it was Bull. I thrust the mirror into the unsuspecting arms of a passerby and took off running, dodging around people like a pinball bouncing around a game. I could hear Bull behind me saying, "Excuse me, coming through, excuse me." He was getting closer. The man by the monster truck saw me coming. He threw open the passenger door and dove across the seat to the driver's side.

"Wait," Bull yelled.

If frustration could be rated on a scale from one to ten, Bull's voice was near infinity. But waiting was something I didn't plan to do. I leaped up on to the running board of the truck. The driver grabbed my outstretched arm, hauling me in the rest of the way. He took off as I slammed the door closed. Bull came running out of the flea market as we tore off. I glimpsed him standing slumped shouldered in the side-view mirror.

I sent a quick text to Luke, telling him I didn't have anything new to report. If I told him about Bull, he'd probably lock me in a closet or barricade me in Seth's basement. As we got close to Belle's house, I bent down, pretending to go through my purse so no one could see me in the truck. My driver made no comment.

Frieda let me into the house at ten thirty. She had a dour look on her face. "We've got company." She tipped her head toward the living room. I could hear voices. "Again," she said.

I followed her to the living room. Miss Belle had a polite smile plastered on her face. Her mother-in-law and Ruth, maid/companion/nurse, whatever she was, sat there too.

"Miss Sarah Winston," Frieda announced in a grand tone, as if the queen were in attendance. "Of the Pacific Grove Winstons."

I glanced over at Frieda, my mouth twitching with suppressed laughter. She winked at me.

"Sarah, dear. How has your day been?" Miss Belle asked.

I didn't get a chance to answer.

"I'm afraid that woman"—Mrs. Granville Winthrop tilted her head toward Frieda as she left with a bow and a flourish—"isn't a suitable maid."

Miss Belle's hand tightened on the arm of her chair. It was the only discernible sign she was irritated. "Why not, Mother?"

"Well, look at how she's dressed." Mrs. Winthrop Granville moved a Murano glass paperweight from one position on the end table near her to another.

Frieda had been wearing a pair of clean black slacks and a spotless polo shirt. It was the most dressed up I'd ever seen her.

"And who bows like that? I think she's mocking us."

At least Mrs. Winthrop Granville had her wits about her this morning.

"It's fine, Mother. She's a hard worker."

Miss Winthrop Granville sniffed.

Ruth stood up. "Excuse me."

"Where are you off to?" Mrs. Winthrop Granville asked her in a grumpy voice. She picked up the paperweight and held it in her hand. She set it back down, aligning it with the edge of the end table.

"Just to powder my nose," Ruth said. "I'll be right back."

Really, the woman had to have the patience of all the saints combined. She said it without resentment, in a light tone. On the other hand, Rena had said she thought something was off about the woman.

I waited a few minutes and excused myself. Mrs. Winthrop Granville was droning on about a party she'd attended in 1955. I don't think she even noticed I'd left. I wanted a chance to talk to Ruth about the Blackmore Agency.

There was a powder room down the hall beyond the two studies. I hoped that was the one Ruth used. It was a big house, and if she went upstairs, I'd miss her completely. Fortunately, Ruth came out as I neared the powder room door. She smiled at me, looking more relaxed away from Mrs. Winthrop Granville. But the job had to be stressful.

"You're really wonderful with Mrs. Winthrop Granville," I said.

"Winnie's a dear."

"How did she come to be called Winnie?" I asked.

"It's some nickname from boarding school."

I tried to puzzle that out. She wouldn't have been a Winthrop until after she was married. But I didn't know her first name.

"How long have you been with her?"

"Twenty years. I'm fortunate in this economy. So many of my friends who are staff have been let go."

"Did you know Kay well?"

"Hardly at all. Why would you ask?"

"Miss Belle said her mother-in-law recommended the agency Kay worked for." I managed not to say *supposedly* worked for.

"She recommended the agency. Not Kay specifically." Ruth clasped her hands together. "I feel terrible that my recommendation might have caused this distress to Mrs. Winthrop Granville."

"Miss Belle?" I asked.

"No, Winnie. This has all been very upsetting for her."

"How long has she been having memory problems?"

Ruth looked down at the floor so long, I didn't think she was going to answer.

"It's been getting worse over the past year. The past six months." Ruth sighed. "I try to protect her. I don't want her to become fodder for gossip. I've insisted her social engagements be during the day because she's worse at night. And now, because of the robbery and murder."

I nodded. "I had a great-aunt who had a similar memory problem. It's difficult."

We turned to head back down the hall.

"Didn't you need to use the powder room?" Ruth

asked with a sharp tone. "Or were you just trying to get information out of me?"

She bustled past me. I stared back at her, mouth agape. Maybe Rena was right and there *was* something off about Ruth.

Chapter Thirty-Three

As I returned to the living room, I heard Mrs. Winthrop Granville's raised voice. "And what kind of name is Belle? Belle of the ball? 'Ding-Dong! The witch is dead.' Southern Belle. Some character out of a Disney movie? Which are you? I demand to know."

"Mother," Belle said.

"Don't you *mother* me. You took my beloved Sebastian away from me. Made him move all the way out here. How dare you. How dare you."

As I came around the corner, Mrs. Winthrop Granville started crying. Miss Belle's face was very white, as was Ruth.

"Could you please have our car pulled round?" Ruth asked Miss Belle. "I think Mrs. Winthrop Granville has had enough visiting for today."

"It's a ridiculous name. There are no Belles in Boston society," Mrs. Winthrop Granville said to Miss Belle's retreating back. "And what's your name?" She focused on me.

I looked at Ruth for guidance. If this was how Mrs. Winthrop Granville was during the day, Ruth must really be busy at night. She gave a small nod. "Sarah Winston, ma'am."

"That's a proper English name." She sighed deeply and closed her eyes.

After a minute, Miss Belle returned. "The car has been pulled up." She darted a nervous glance at her mother-in-law.

"Thank you, dear," Mrs. Winthrop Granville said, as if nothing had happened. She reached over and picked up the Murano crystal paperweight again. She weighed it in her hand as she stood up, then slipped it into her purse.

I looked over at Miss Belle, who shrugged. Ruth didn't seem to notice.

Ruth helped her out to the car with a small nod to us as they left. We stood on the porch watching them pull away.

"It's so sad to see her like this," Miss Belle said as we went back into the house. "Even though there wasn't a lot of love lost between us, she was a grand woman. Smart, well-educated. Wellesley, of course. I'm glad Sebastian isn't around to see this."

Miss Belle looked so sad, I wanted to hug her.

"I realized a few months ago that her being in her own house isn't feasible anymore, so we've quietly been moving things over here and having her furnishings appraised."

Moving her things here? I thought back to the day I found the manuscripts and Miss Belle's reaction to the overnight case. I'd assumed it was because she'd never seen it before.

"I'm afraid I lied to you, Sarah."

"You did. You told me you had no idea where the overnight case came from."

"I was scared. Worried about the legal implications for my mother-in-law."

"Did you lie about anything else?" Now I was wondering if I'd thrown my trust to the wrong people, helping someone guilty of murder. I looked out the door. Maybe I needed to get the heck out of here.

Miss Belle shook her head. "Nothing else. I promise. I hope you'll believe me."

I pondered everything I knew about Belle. She fidgeted while I thought. Something I'd never seen her do. "I understand why you didn't tell me right away. We barely knew each other."

"Thank you. I don't want my mother-in-law to go to a home. And while she won't be happy about moving here, it will be better, right?"

"Yes," I said. "It will be for her." I wasn't sure it would be for Miss Belle, but I admired her decision.

"Ruth will return the paperweight you saw her take," Miss Belle said. "Shall we get back to work? With all that's been going on, we still have the book sale to get ready for."

"There's still no sign of the missing book?"

"None. I just can't worry about it. Except for those crazy literary treasure hunters, things have been calm around here. Roger is even supposed to show up to work today."

"Great. I'll get to work, then." I climbed up to the attic but stopped in Kay's room. The telescope beckoned me, so I peered through it, scanning the woods. From what I could see, all seemed quiet.

I walked into the attic space and tackled a box containing books by Dorothy L. Sayers. Miss Belle had various volumes, plus collections of short stories. I took a quick peek inside *Whose Body?* the very first book Sayers published. It introduced the iconic character Lord Peter Wimsey. While the writing style was very different from today's standards, Lord Wimsey and his mother leaped off the pages. I had to remind myself on page five that I was here to work, not read.

Belle's books were all in excellent condition. They didn't smell and there wasn't any water damage. The covers were all pristine. The books should bring a good price even if they weren't first editions. It was slow going, because I had to check prices as I went. I'd checked sites like eBay but also book resellers. It gave me a better idea of how to settle on a price. Truth be told, I would have loved to curl up with one of them and escape my problems for a couple of hours. But I put that desire aside and pushed on.

At noon, I stood and stretched, leaning my neck first to one side and then the other. Unfortunately, I wasn't any closer to figuring out anything about Kay's death, the missing manuscripts, *The Sun Also Rises*, or the Blackmore Agency than I'd been an hour before. I looked around the room and spotted the trunk that held the scrapbooks I'd seen the other day. It would be fun to take a closer look at them and would clear my head from all the pricing.

I picked up the first scrapbook. It had a red leather cover with the word *scrapbook* stenciled in gold. The photos were all in black and white with scalloped edges. There were pictures of people drinking martinis at parties, sailing outings, and balls. The clothes screamed the fifties to me. It all looked very glamorous. A boy was in some of the photos, possibly Sebastian.

The next volume was from the forties. It had pictures of men dressed in uniforms and women in gowns. There were champagne toasts and sabers. The photos belied the horrors of World War II. After studying some of the photos, I realized I was looking at pictures of a younger Winnie. I flipped back through the other scrapbooks and watched her age. She must have put these together. The thirties scrapbook was slimmer but again filled with beautiful people in beautiful clothing. It reminded me how little reality any of us ever really showed the world, and made me wonder how Tracy was doing.

The twenties album was full of women in flapper dresses, beaded and beautiful. There were tickets for ships sailing to and from Europe. Photos in front of famous landmarks like the Coliseum, the Eiffel Tower, Windsor Castle, the Alps. Pictures of people skiing. One of the women looked a bit like Winnie, but it must have been her mother or grandmother. The wealth of the times was evident. I imagined their steamer trunks being packed and whisked from spot to spot in luxury cars driven by chauffeurs. Living as if they were in an episode of a BBC production.

The war was behind them, the stock market crash ahead, and the next world war off in an unsuspecting future. No wonder the twenties were roaring for the rich. I flipped to a page filled with train tickets. One was from Gare de Lyon to Lausanne, Switzerland. Another from Paris to Constantinople, which must have been a ride on the famed Orient Express. A third was from Vienna to Paris. Train travel all sounded so glamorous.

I started to turn the page when a bit of history tugged at my brain. The Gare de Lyon to Lausanne. I stared down at the ticket dated the first week of December in 1922. That was the route Hemingway's first wife, Hadley, took when she lost Hemingway's manuscripts.

Chapter Thirty-Four

I snapped a photo of the ticket with a shaking hand. Could that be how the manuscripts ended up here? Some relative of Sebastian's had stolen them and hung on to them all these years? I thought about Mrs. Winthrop Granville taking the Murano paperweight. I typed in *kleptomania* into the search engine of my phone. I quickly read a couple of articles, and there was a lot of debate about whether it was inherited. People took things on impulse, and it was usually something they could afford.

Whoever the people were in the scrapbook, they could obviously buy their own luggage. An overnight case wouldn't have meant that much to them, and certainly the contents at the time wouldn't have been important. Back in 1922, Hemingway was a war hero and journalist. *The Sun Also Rises* wasn't published until 1926, so he wasn't the famous author that he is today.

I did another search on my phone. I read that after Hadley discovered the overnight case was missing, she and the conductor had searched the train high and low to no avail. But rich people would have private cars that probably wouldn't be searched. Now what to do?

I needed to talk this out with someone, but it had to be someone I trusted completely. As much as I loved Luke, this information might be too tempting for a reporter not to spill. Besides, this was all just speculation on my part right now.

Other thoughts started clicking into place. I thought about Mrs. Winthrop Granville's wild ramblings. I could imagine her babbling to the wrong person, telling them about her treasure. She'd talked to me about her love of Cracker Jacks, but it just as easily could have been the manuscripts.

The most logical person seemed to be Ruth because she was with her the most. Ruth could have known Kay and lied about it. But there were still other people involved. The person who'd threatened and chased Roger, another person who picked up the manuscripts in the woods and killed Kay, and who knew who else. If Ruth and Kay were in cahoots, they would have had to contact some kind of middleman to make the actual sale. The two of them wouldn't likely have those kinds of resources.

I decided to hide the scrapbook just in case someone else knew about it. I thought about hiding it in Kay's room, but it might be searched again by the police. Or some relative might show up wanting her things. I couldn't risk putting it there. I ended up emptying a box of the books I'd already priced. I put the scrapbook in the bottom of it and covered it with books. Then I set a couple more boxes on top. Hopefully, no one would come up here anyway, and if they did would think this was all books.

As a precaution, I found a notebook in my purse and wrote a note that said, "already priced." I tore it out and set it on top of the pile. What I wanted to write was *nothing to see here, folks, just keep moving on.* I sent Carol a text asking her to meet me for lunch. She said yes, if we ate at her shop. After trotting down the stairs to the first level, I found Miss Belle in her study. Roger was with her.

"I have a couple of errands to run," I said. Going to talk to Carol constituted an errand, didn't it? "I'll be back around two. Any luck on your end?" I asked.

Miss Belle shook her head. "We've searched high and low through this office. If that limited-edition book is in this house, it isn't in here."

"We can rule out the section of the attic I've been working in too."

"This house is a monstrosity," Roger said. He thrust a hand through his normally neatly coiffed white hair. "We may never find it, even if it is here."

"Are you doing okay, Roger? No more people chasing you?"

"I'm doing all right if you think not being able to go to my home or place of business is okay."

"So, not okay."

"I'm so sorry to have dragged you two into this mess," Miss Belle said.

"It wasn't deliberate," I said. At least I hoped it wasn't.

"I can't believe my life has come down to spending time with sketch artists, police, and state troopers," Roger said.

"How'd the sketch come out?" I asked.

"A darn good job, considering the little I could help out with. It's as if I blocked out the hooligan's face."

"Any luck with security cameras?" I asked.

"Not much, apparently. As Officer Bossum said, most cameras aren't that high-quality."

"Can I see the sketch?" I asked.

"Sure," Roger said. He pulled out his phone and found it.

It was kind of a generic-looking white guy wearing a ball cap, with no distinguishing marks or tattoos. Part of me had been hoping it would be Bull, and the police could track him down and get him out of my life. I passed the phone to Miss Belle.

"Do you recognize him?" I asked.

She studied the photo and then shook her head. "No. I don't know this man."

"I guess that would have been too easy." My phone buzzed. "My Uber driver is here. I'll see you in a bit."

I directed the Uber driver to the alley behind Carol's store. It didn't seem as if anyone was lurking around, and thankfully, there was no sign of Bull. A few minutes later, Carol and I had a roast beef sandwich from DiNapoli's she'd picked up spread on a table in her back room. Even half of one of these was too much for two people.

I dug in. "This is heaven," I said after swallowing.

"How do they make any money with their low prices and large portions?"

"I'm not sure," I answered. The meat was tendered and piled high, and there was provolone cheese and an au jus dipping sauce. I caught up on Carol's family's goings-on while we ate. After we finished, I decided to get down to what had brought me here. I filled her in on finding the scrapbook and its connection to Sebastian's family.

"What are you going to do?" Carol asked.

"I don't know. That's why I'm here."

"I'm not going to tell you what to do."

"But I want you to."

Carol shook her head. "Absolutely not."

"What about telling me what you'd do if you were in my shoes?" I asked.

Carol pointed at my shoes. A pair of pink Cole

Hahn flats I'd found at a sale for a buck. "I don't wear flats."

I wrinkled my brow at her.

"In other words, I'm not in your shoes, so I can't tell you what to do," Carol said.

"Some friend you turned out to be." I smiled at her to take the edge off the words.

"You're smart. You'll figure it out. In fact, you probably already know what to do," Carol said.

Did I? Not yet; not that I knew of. This was the joy and curse of being single. I made all the decisions; no one else told me what to do. But sometimes, like now, it wasn't easy.

"I've been thinking about something else. Something to do with CJ."

"What?" Carol's voice came out sharp.

I got that. She'd been through the wringer with CJ and me the past couple of years. There for every high and low. "In our divorce settlement, I ended up getting half his retirement pay."

"As you should," Carol said.

"I've been thinking about stopping it. I feel as if I'll never be completely free of CJ if I continue to take it."

"Are you nuts? Of course you're going to keep taking it." Carol jumped up and started gathering the remains of our lunch. "You earned it. You followed him around. Don't you even think about doing that."

"What happened to not telling me what to do?" I asked.

"This is completely different." Carol wrapped the leftover half of a sandwich and stuck it in her fridge. I got up and tossed our napkins and paper plates in the trash. "I always hoped you and CJ could work things out, but this last move of his was unconscionable."

It was. It had been the proverbial last straw, and it still stung.

"Taking what's yours isn't keeping you tied to him. Only you can do that. Think of it as the US government paying you for *your* service. For sacrificing your career. For helping a thousand strangers who crossed your path in all your moves. Being a commander's wife is a full-time volunteer job, with little recognition, no chance for advancement, and a bunch of people bitching behind your back no matter what you do. And what do you get out of it at the end? A certificate signed by the president thanking you."

"Wow. I didn't know you felt that way," I said.

"I sound bitter, don't I? You know I loved being a military spouse. Most of the time," Carol said. "My point is, you earned that money, and I don't want to hear another thing about it."

"Okay. I appreciate your input. What's on your agenda for the rest of the day?"

"Ironically, I have two military spouses' groups coming in. One at two and another at seven. Want to come?"

"No, I've got my hands full." I gave Carol a quick hug and left. My thoughts quickly turned back to the book and manuscripts. Who set all this up? And how the heck was I going to answer that question.

Chapter Thirty-Five

Luck was on my side. I managed to retrieve the Beetle and drive off without anyone spotting me. I needed to get back to Miss Belle's, but I decided to swing by the police station to see if I could track down either Pellner or Awesome. I'd rather talk to one of them than the state police, who might think I was making wild conjectures. I hoped I wasn't. I parked across the street from the police station near a tot lot. Red-faced kids were running around while moms sat watching in the shade. The whole scene put a smile on my face.

As I walked toward the station, one of the police SUVs pulled up beside me. The window rolled down. Pellner.

"Just the man I wanted to see," I said.

"Hop in," he said.

The SUV was cool despite all the equipment running in it. Police vehicles looked more like the inside of a spaceship these days, with their computers and communications equipment. Long gone were the radios on a long curly cord.

"What's up?" Pellner asked once I was strapped in.

Instead of just parking, he took off down past the town hall.

I didn't want to bring up the scrapbook yet but filled him in on Alicia Blackmore and my suspicions about Rena's conveniently timed inheritance.

Pellner whistled when I finished. "That's a pretty amazing story." He'd been weaving his way around some neighborhoods while I'd talked.

"I know. But between the missing manuscripts and the missing limited-edition book, we're talking millions of dollars. Her inheritance could have been a small investment really."

"I'll see if our web wonder woman can dig anything up about the inheritance. And we'll follow up with the Blackmore Agency. I know that a state trooper talked to them, but maybe he didn't ask the right questions or he asked the wrong person. Also one of the state troopers has been delving into Kay's finances."

"Has he found anything interesting?"

Pellner didn't answer.

"What have you found out about Kay?" I asked. "Does she have family?"

"I'm only sharing this because they've been notified, and it will be in the papers."

I nodded.

"She's from New Bedford. A middle-class family. Parents divorced when she was young. Her father died when he was fifty-six."

New Bedford was on the coast down near Rhode Island. "What did she do before she worked for Miss Belle?" I asked. "Does she have a record?"

He pulled back up to the station. "Here you go."

"In other words, you aren't going to answer me?"

Pellner flashed his dimples at me.

"Has anything come from the sketch of the guy who attacked Roger?"

"Nothing yet." Pellner opened a folder and handed me the sketch.

It was easier to see on an eight-by-ten piece of paper than on Roger's phone. I stared down at it, frowning.

"What, do you recognize him?" Pellner asked.

"I'm not sure." I grabbed my purse, dug around in it, and pulled out a pen.

"What are you doing?"

"Give me a minute." I drew dark-framed glasses on the picture and changed the baseball cap to some semblance of a tweed hat. Carol would be much better at this than I was.

"Who do you think it is?" Pellner sounded impatient.

"Trevor Hunter, one of the League of Literary Treasure Hunter members." I frowned at the picture. "He's the first of the group I met. Warned me off from another person, Bull Hardwick."

"Have you seen him since?" Pellner asked.

"No, but I've talked to him. I asked him to tell his group to quit following me."

"Did it work?"

"No." I turned in my seat so I was facing Pellner. "If Trevor is bad, does that mean Bull is good?"

"Not necessarily. Bad guys always know other bad guys. They might be from competing crime groups." Pellner took the sketch from me. "You're sure these two men are the same person?"

"Yes, but let me show you his picture from the League of Literary Treasure Hunters website." I found the picture and pulled it up. "Look at his nose and cheekbones. Shaving off his beard, waxing his eyebrows, and adding glasses doesn't change them."

Pellner studied both photos. "They do look similar. I'll take this back to the station to see what I can find out."

"I have his phone number."

"Send it to me." He stared out the windshield for a moment. "We might need you to come down to the station to call him to arrange a meeting you won't be going to. In the meantime, if you run into this Hunter character again, call 911."

I climbed out. "Thanks."

"Thank you," he said. He waved and drove off.

I got back to Miss Belle's house and went straight up to the attic to work. I wished I could turn off my brain and concentrate, but I couldn't, so I called Pellner again.

"I've been thinking about how all this happened," I said when he answered. "Say all those years ago, someone in Sebastian's family took the overnight case. It got stored somewhere until someday another family member realized what they had, the lost Hemingway manuscripts."

"Why didn't they shout it to the world or try to sell them?"

"I can think of a couple of reasons. If it's a prominent family like the Winthrop Granvilles, they wouldn't want to sully their reputation to admit they had a thief among them. Mrs. Winthrop Granville's family seems to be bibliophiles, so maybe having something so rare and valuable gave them some kind of hidden pleasure." I could just picture someone coming up to the attic to visit the manuscripts. Chortling with secret joy over owning them. "Who really knows what motivates people to do what they do?"

"So you think Kay just overheard you talking to Miss Belle and took advantage of the opportunity?" Pellner asked.

"No. It seemed too well planned for that." I launched into the theory I'd shared with Luke, that someone knew about the limited-edition book and that the manuscripts were just a bonus. "After Kay heard about the manuscripts, she must have accelerated the plan to meet a buyer in the woods. Otherwise they wouldn't have come back and searched the woods for them."

"Probably. But how would they know about the manuscripts?"

"Mrs. Winthrop Granville is having memory problems. What if she started talking about the manuscripts to Ruth after she'd already moved them to Belle's house? Ruth has a tough job and probably isn't well compensated. Maybe she decided this was her way of getting back."

"She couldn't have done it alone." Pellner rubbed the back of his neck.

"I agree. She teamed up with someone else along the way. Someone with enough money to bankroll the operation and get Rena out of the way. There must be some connection between Kay and Ruth that we don't know about. Get rid of Rena and put Kay in place." Now that I thought about it, Rena was lucky to be alive. "They could have just killed Rena."

"But that would draw attention to Miss Belle's house, which they wouldn't want."

I could tell Pellner was warming to my theory.

"So how did Kay end up dead?" he asked.

"Maybe she tried to cut her own deal with the middleman. Whoever fronted the money to get Rena out of the way. She hid the overnight case in the woods, after all. Or maybe it was Ruth out in the woods that day, waiting for her. Kay tries to up her cut of the sale of the manuscripts. Ruth wasn't happy and killed her."

"Now we just have to prove your theory," Pellner said. "Any thoughts on how to do that?"

He sounded a wee bit sarcastic. "Not yet, but between

me, the entire police department, and the state troopers, you'd think we could come up with something."

Pellner chuckled. "I'm sure we can. Just don't go off on your own."

"Do I ever?" I asked.

"I've got to go," said Pellner.

Chapter Thirty-Six

I couldn't concentrate on pricing books. So I Googled Ruth Stewart. There really wasn't much about her online. Ruth had a Facebook page but didn't post to it often. She'd gone to a high school in a small town in Maine. It didn't seem Winnie would approve of her using social media anyway.

Then I searched for Kay Kimble. She was almost twenty years younger than Ruth. Pellner had told me she grew up in New Bedford, a town known historically for its whaling, and currently for its commercial fishing. People there worked hard, and life wasn't always easy. So Kay and Ruth weren't from the same town, not even the same state. It made me wonder if I was wrong about a Ruth-Kay connection. I was getting nowhere, so I decide to talk to Miss Belle about my discovery in the scrapbooks.

I found her in her study, pulling one book after the other off the shelf.

"Still trying to find *The Sun Also Rises*?" I asked. "I thought you'd already searched in here."

She nodded. "Do you think it's a fool's errand? I

keep thinking it might have been missed, or it's wedged somewhere."

"I don't know. For all we know, Sebastian returned the book the week after he borrowed it."

"Roger would have gone through his brother's things when Harold died," Miss Belle said. "If it had been returned he'd have known it."

I nodded. "I supposed he would have."

"Of course his brother could have sold it at some point," Miss Belle said.

"Then why doesn't anyone know where it is? Although if it was a private sale there isn't necessarily a record." Again, I was struck with how many variables played into all of this. It was the worst jigsaw puzzle ever. None of the pieces fit.

"No one knew Harold had it, as far as I can tell. It's all very perplexing," Miss Belle said.

I nodded. When I told her about my suspicions about Winnie and Sebastian's ancestors, she'd be even more perplexed. "I found the old scrapbooks upstairs. They seem to be from Sebastian's family, not yours." Miss Belle raised her eyebrows. "I could see the resemblance between Mrs. Winthrop Granville and some of the women in the albums."

"I knew they were here. They were some of the things we moved over recently."

"Did she go up to the attic to look at them?" I asked. Maybe Winnie had used that as an excuse to visit the manuscripts.

"No. I don't think she knew they were here. I did enjoy Winnie's stories about traveling through Europe with her mother as a child. Apparently, her mother was something of a bon vivant."

"It doesn't have seemed to rub off on her."

Miss Belle laughed. "Not at all." She stopped and frowned. "How did she end up with the Hemingway stories in the first place? When did you say they were stolen?"

"In 1922 in Paris."

"She wouldn't have been born yet. She was born in 1927."

"What about her mom?" I asked. Maybe I needed to go up to get the scrapbook. But I was still hesitant. It seemed like evidence, although the statute of limitations would have been up years ago.

Miss Belle scrunched up her face. "I should know. The Winthrop Granville family history has been pounded in to me at every meal we've shared since Sebastian and I married." She took a moment. "Her mother traveled Europe after she graduated from high school. As I said, a bon vivant."

Miss Belle began pulling books off the shelf again. I went over to her. We'd take several books off and look in and behind them before setting them back.

"I might as well tell you, because you saw my mother-in-law take the paperweight. It's been a problem for years. But the family always managed to keep it out of the papers. If she was going shopping, there would be a discreet call to the manager of the store to make sure things that were taken were charged to their account. Or she'd have a companion who went with her and made sure to pay for whatever she took." Miss Belle shook her head. "It was an awful burden for the whole family."

"Why didn't she get help?"

"Help?" Miss Belle made a snorting sound. "And admit something was wrong with a member of the Winthrop Granville family? It's no wonder Sebastian wanted to move out here, and why we traveled so much."

We worked silently for a while. Moving from shelf to shelf, looking, clearing, reshelving. My phone binged, alerting me a text had come in. It was Tracy, asking me to meet her. I agreed to meet her at the tot lot across the street from the police station.

"I have to run an errand. I'll be back in an hour or so."

"Thanks for all you've done."

"Listen. Please don't tell anyone about my suspicions about your mother-in-law."

"Why?"

"Let the police handle it."

"They know about this?" Miss Belle's voice lost its soft Southern edge.

I nodded guiltily. "I talked to Officer Pellner this afternoon, when I started putting things together."

Miss Belle gave me a long look, and it wasn't a happy one. "Okay."

I let Frieda know I was leaving and headed out.

Tracy sat on a bench watching her kids run around the tot lot. She held up a water bottle. "Want one? I always bring extras when we're out and about on a hot day."

"Sure. Thanks. How are you doing?" I asked as I sat down next to her. I felt fairly safe meeting Tracy here. If any of the literary treasure hunters showed up, I could run to the police station for help. I'd checked around before I got out of the car but hadn't seen any. I wondered if they were still camped out by my house. I really wanted to go back home.

"I took your advice and talked to my husband's commander's wife. She suggested I visit the MFLC."

"The Military Family Life Research Center?" It provided anonymous, nonmedical counseling, and no records were kept of the sessions. It fell under the umbrella of the Airman and Family Readiness Center, which offered everything from counseling to financial advice to fun things like discounted tickets to sporting events and concerts. "Did you go?"

"I did, and they've been wonderful. I didn't realize how many other spouses had gone through similar experiences."

"I'm happy for you. I went through some tough times when CJ was deployed. And add to that your busy family life."

"And how messed up Eric's been since he got back. Admitting that was really hard. I just kept thinking he'd be okay. That we'd be okay."

"I hope you will be." I didn't want to sugarcoat what might lie ahead for them, or recite platitudes.

"I just wish more people knew about the kind of help that's available. That you don't have to tough it out alone."

It made me think of Luke. "If you're willing to share your story with a reporter, I know one."

"I don't know."

"It's my brother, Luke. He's had his share of tough times after serving, so he'll empathize with you." I took a drink of my water. Even sitting in the shade wasn't much relief from the heat.

"I'll think about it," Tracy said.

"He could interview other spouses too. I don't think many people realize how hard being a military spouse can be. Even under the best circumstances there's a lot of stress."

Tracy's littlest boy came running over. "I need water."

"Is that how you ask?" she chided him gently.

"Please may I have some water?" He had deep brown eyes. His dark hair was sweaty from running. Tracy got a water bottle from the cooler. He took a long drink before handing it back and running off.

"It's the only way I get some peace. I have to wear them out."

I nodded. It was quiet, but it was almost dinnertime. Tennis balls ponged as they bounced on the courts on the other side of the tot lot. But all the birds seemed to be taking naps. I only heard a desultory chirp now and again.

"How's Eric doing?" I asked.

"Lots of mood swings. He hopes the fund-raiser will work and worries it won't."

"It's going to be okay. We're going to bring King back."

Tracy turned to me. "I would like to talk to your brother. It's time we stop hiding behind our pride."

"Don't feel pressured," I said.

"No. Maybe it will help someone else too."

"Great. I'll give him your number."

As I drove back to Miss Belle's house, Alicia Blackmore called.

"I'm so embarrassed, I almost kept this to myself. But a woman is dead, so here we are talking."

"What's up?" I asked.

"One of my employees knew Kay and said she desperately needed a job. Kay had some minor legal issues when she was younger. Enough that I wouldn't have hired her. But Kay convinced my employee to give her this job."

"How did Kay know about the job?" I asked.

"Kay said she knew Miss Belle's former housekeeper, who'd told her about the opening. And that Miss Belle was working with us to find a replacement."

"But you said you didn't know about Miss Belle."

Alicia's lips tightened. "Apparently, my former employee was keeping a few things off the books."

This was disappointing. I'd thought maybe it would yield a lead to who was behind all this. Either Rena or Kay had been lying.

"Kay knew enough details about the job that my employee thought she was telling the truth and just a little down on her luck."

I still didn't have the answers I needed. "Thank you for calling. If you learn anything else, please let me know."

"Oh, I will."

I called Luke to update him on the situation. He hadn't found out anything remotely shady about Alicia Blackmore or her agency.

"I'm heading back over to Ellington," Luke said. "Where are you?"

"I just got back to Miss Belle's house. I'll talk to you later."

"Love you, Sarah."

"I love you too." I smiled as I hung up the phone. It was good to be able to say that to Luke instead of just thinking it, like I had all the years he'd disappeared from my life.

I let myself in through Miss Belle's kitchen. "Miss Belle?" I called as I walked down the hall. Her study was empty, as was Sebastian's library. "Frieda?" I listened, but no one answered. Something was wrong. Frieda's car was outside. There was a chance they were up in the attic and couldn't hear me, but something felt off. I walked to the main foyer and called again.

"Come on up, sweetie."

It was Frieda. She'd never called me sweetie or any other term of endearment. It wasn't her personality to do that. She was trying to send me a message.

"I'll be up in a minute. I left my phone out in the

car." Frieda didn't respond. I hustled back to the kitchen, pulled out my phone, and dialed 911. Fortunately, the dispatcher knew me and said she'd send someone. Not everyone would send a car on someone's suspicions.

I opened the kitchen door to let myself out. Bull stood there.

Chapter Thirty-Seven

Before I could scream, he clamped a hand over my mouth. His other hand landed on the back of my neck. My spinal cord seemed like a fragile twig that could be broken with very little effort.

"Be quiet," he commanded. "Someone has two women up in the attic."

Someone? At least the police would be here soon. He described the women. It had to be Miss Belle and Frieda.

"It's a man who goes by Trevor Hunter." He pulled me away from the house and toward the garage.

What would Trevor Hunter want with Frieda and Miss Belle? And Bull had said *goes by*, not *is* Trevor Hunter. My face was starting to sweat under his hand. I needed to do something.

"I'll uncover your mouth if you promise not to scream. It looked to me like a hostage situation. We don't want to scare him in to taking action."

I had no idea what Bull was talking about or whether to believe him, but I nodded even as I worried that this might be some kind of trick. It was getting hard to breathe with his massive hand covering half my face.

He slowly took his hand away.

"I know Trevor," I said. "What's he doing in the attic with Miss Belle and Frieda?"

"Like I said, it looked like he was holding them hostage."

I stared at Bull. "I called the police a few minutes ago because I felt like something was off," I said. "I need to call them back."

"I called them myself about twenty minutes ago. They're putting together the hostage rescue team. But call them again. The last thing we need is for wires to get crossed and have someone race up with their sirens on."

Though still uneasy, I decided if he didn't care if I called the police he must not be a threat.

I called 911 again, watching Bull as I did. After I updated the situation, I disconnected. "Why does Trevor have them?"

"I think he realized I was on to him." Bull shook his head. "I forced his hand, so he's making a last effort to find out if the manuscripts or the book are really still in the house."

"If his name isn't Trevor Hunter, who is he?"

"Trevor Berne."

Trevor Berne? "Why have you been following me?"

"I told you I wanted to talk to you."

"Talk, then," I said.

"I wanted to protect you."

"You have a really funny way of showing it. You scared me to death when you leaped on the back of my car."

"That's because you took off."

This was getting us nowhere.

"Why did you think I needed protection?"

"I've been working undercover, trying to unearth a group of very rich people who deal in stolen rare books and manuscripts."

"Are you a cop? FBI?" He didn't really fit my image of either, but if he was undercover, it would explain why.

"No." He sounded offended. "I'm with the security division of the League of Literary Treasure Hunters."

I stared at him. I couldn't have possibly heard that right. Worrying about Miss Belle and Frieda must have impaired me in some way. I wanted to shake my head or stick my fingers in my ears to try to clear them.

"You said the League of Literary Treasure Hunters has a security division?" I'm afraid I didn't hide my astonishment very well.

Bull looked hurt. "We don't broadcast it. One of our missions is to make sure the literary treasures of the world are available for all people to enjoy."

Pellner came around the corner just then. He put his fingers to his lips and gestured for Bull and me to follow him around the corner of the garage. A SWAT team milled about.

Bull quickly explained the situation as he'd seen it.

"You two stay here," Pellner said. "Sarah, what can you tell us about the house?"

I went over the layout of the house and attic with them.

Pellner looked at Bull. "Keep an eye on her. She had ended up in the thick of things more than once."

I held up my hands. "I'm not going anywhere." Contrary to what Pellner thought, I was more than happy to let the police do their job.

Seconds later, they were moving out, communicating with hand signals. When they were out of sight, I turned to Bull.

"Why didn't you just call and tell me you were on the side of good? Or send an email."

"I wasn't sure who to trust."

"You could have told the police."

"Again, didn't know who to trust."

"Then why trust me enough to want to protect me? Or for that matter talk to me in person."

Bull looked down at the ground. "Okay, maybe *protect* wasn't entirely accurate. *Watch* might have been more appropriate." He looked back up, one eye squinting, as if to gauge my response.

"So you thought I was in on it and wanted to keep tabs on me."

"I thought if I talked to you in person, I could gauge your honesty. According to the reports, you found the manuscripts and were around when they disappeared. Your whole story seemed off to me."

"How did you find me all the time? Tracking device?" I'd searched through my personal belongings looking for one, but never did find anything.

"No."

"Then how?"

"It's what I do for the League of Literary Treasure Hunters. I track things."

"That's how you found me at the hockey rink?"

Bull nodded. I frowned at him. "I don't like to be followed. It hasn't gone well for me in the past." It made me wonder what was going on with Seth and the trial today.

"Part of it was learning your patterns online. You were a little more challenging than some."

That was good to know. "How's that?"

"You don't ever tag the location you're in, and you don't tend to post where you are in real time, like a lot of people do. That will keep you safer. But you still have patterns of where you go. Almost everyone does."

"The hockey rink isn't part of any pattern I have." I still wasn't sure how much of what he was saying was true.

"Sometimes dumb luck plays a part in tracking," Bull said. His face got a little red like he was embarrassed to admit that.

"You said there was another part besides the online stuff. Drones?" I kept one ear out to hear if there was any activity coming from the house. But so far, nothing. I pictured the SWAT team moving silently for the house.

Bull laughed. "I wish."

"How'd you find me that day on the common?"

"I saw you were doing a fund-raising event there on Saturday. I figured you'd have to be there at some point, so I waited. Finding things isn't all jetting from continent to continent, roaming around in tuxes, and staying in exotic locations."

My eyes popped open a little more than normal. "But that's part of it?"

Bull nodded.

"I must be in the wrong business. I spend all my time in dusty attics and dirty basements." I thought for a moment. "If you didn't track me digitally, how did you find me the day I took the Uber?"

"Math."

"Math?" It hadn't been my strong suit in school. Thus the English degree in college.

"I searched a simple grid pattern. I figured out how far I thought you could get on foot, used a map to show me the blocks, and drove around. I was lucky to find you before you took off with the Uber driver."

"I could have gone to a friend's house."

"But you didn't, did you?"

Even though we were standing in the shade, the air felt like I was tucked in a teapot of steaming water. I kept listening for any sounds of action, but all I heard was the whirr of late-summer bugs and a garbage truck off in the distance. My stomach did a loop the loop before it crash-landed back in position. I grabbed Bull's massive arm to steady myself.

"You okay? Need some water?" Bull asked.

"The garbage truck. Today is garbage day, not Tuesday."

"Right." Bull looked at me like someone who'd just spotted a raccoon foaming at the mouth.

"Ryne told me he was on Nutley Street because it was garbage day. But that was on Tuesday."

"Could this Ryne person just have been confused?"

"No. He said he was near the woods because he'd found some great free chairs. That he was out driving around to dumpster dive." Ryne, with his charming, boy-next-door persona, his slightly sarcastic way. Maybe I'd heard him wrong. I wanted that to be it but knew it wasn't. "He lied to me. It's why he drove so slowly, not because he didn't want to follow the police. And he wouldn't let me out of the car to chase after the man with the case." It had all seemed so reasonable in the moment. But not now. Ryne, who'd been so helpful in the search of Miss Belle's house. I looked up to see if a cloud was passing over because the world seemed darker to me. "Ryne's in on all this."

Chapter Thirty-Eight

Bull kept staring down at me as if he didn't quite know what to do. Sweat beaded around his forehead and he swiped at it with his arm. "Are you sure?"

"I knew there had to be at least three people working with Kay. The person she was supposed to meet in the woods, the man who took the overnight case with the Hemingway manuscripts from the woods, and Trevor, who chased Roger all over town."

"How did she end up dead in this scenario of yours?"

"She must have tried to double-cross someone. To get a bigger cut or something, because why else would she hide the overnight case?"

Bull nodded.

"I think she met Ryne. Maybe he didn't mean to kill her. He shot, and the limb came down." I gasped. "That means he shot at me. Why would he do that? And then later act all buddy-buddy with me."

"He might have been trying to scare you away."

"Well, it worked. That doesn't explain why he circled back."

"To get information, or maybe he was going back to search for the overnight case."

I frowned. "Oh, he got information, all right. From me. I blabbed all the way back to Miss Belle's house about what went on the day Kay died. But someone other than Ryne and Trevor must have the manuscripts, or they would have left town. Right?"

"It might have drawn suspicion to them if they'd left. Or maybe they wanted to find the book too."

"Greedy jerks. But if they don't have the manuscripts, Kay must have called someone else she trusted. I wonder who that could be."

Bull lifted and dropped his left shoulder. I thought about what he'd said about Trevor, wondered how Ryne and Trevor ended up working together. "How do you spell Trevor's last name?"

"B-e-r-n-e."

"That's Irish, isn't it?" I asked. Bull nodded. A lot of Irish people had settled in Boston. There was an Irish mob for goodness' sakes. But who knows? They could have connected a million different ways.

A loud bang broke the quiet. I jumped back.

"They probably tossed a stun grenade into the attic," Bull said.

We waited quietly until Pellner finally came around the corner. "You can go in now."

"How are they?" I asked.

"Miss Belle and Frieda are scared. A bit dazed from the grenade, but that will clear up quickly."

"Pellner, I have something to tell you. It's about my neighbor, Ryne O'Rourke." I filled him in as quickly as I could. I was starting to worry about Stella's safety.

"And you're basing all this on hearing a garbage truck?" Pellner asked.

"I'm basing it on a lie he told me, and the information I fed him that probably helped him out."

Pellner's face was passive as he mulled over what I'd just told him. He finally nodded. "I'll check it out."

We headed toward the house, with Bull following. As I rounded the corner of the garage, two SWAT members brought Trevor out. He was cuffed and unresisting. Trevor glared at me.

"You would have done it too if you'd been in my shoes," he said to me.

I gave Trevor a long look. "I don't know what I'd have done in your shoes, but it wouldn't have been any of this." I started to walk away. "Are you working with Ryne O'Rourke?"

Trevor looked shocked but covered it quickly. But not quickly enough that Pellner, Bull, and I missed it.

"Never heard of him," Trevor said.

"You might as well admit it. This may be a small town, but the police know what they're doing," I said.

Trevor shrugged as a police officer put him in the back of a patrol car.

I sat and watched as EMTs checked over Miss Belle and Frieda. They had to shout questions to them because both had ringing in their ears due to the grenade. But both would be fine, given some time. I had a million questions for them, but it would have to wait until they felt better. Bull had taken off. Pellner was gone too. I hoped he was looking for Ryne.

Ryne. I hadn't liked or trusted him when I first met him at an estate sale in May. I'd tried to convince Stella not to rent the apartment to him. He was a handsome, oh so charming, single man who'd been living next door to me, but I wasn't ever interested in being more than a friend. Some part of me hadn't trusted him, even though I'd been letting down my walls a little because everyone else seemed to like him. Geez, he'd even fooled Awesome.

I went up and continued working on books. Miss Belle had a complete set of first-edition P. D. James books. I would love to spend some time with Adam Dalgliesh, James's police commander/poet protagonist. But my pricing duties kept me too busy.

At seven, Frieda came up. "Come on down for dinner," she said. "I'm sure you're full of questions. Roger has arrived too."

"Okay. I just have a couple more books in this box and I'll be down." I finished pricing and put my hand down on the floor to push myself up. I felt like the wood floor gave a little. I pushed again, and it definitely moved like the one had in Kay's room the day Awesome and I were in there. Miss Belle might need to do some maintenance on her floors. I hoped she didn't have termites.

I pressed down on the board next to it, and a piece popped up. I pulled up another piece and saw a tissue-covered package.

I took it out and unwrapped it. It was the limited edition of *The Sun Also Rises*, I opened it. A piece of paper fell out. It said, "To my good friend Sebastian. It was never a loan and always for you to keep. Harold." I set it aside and flipped to the title page. There was Ernest Hemingway's signature. I went through more of the pages, reading the notes he'd written in the margins.

I ran down the flights of stairs so quickly, I almost fell. I took the corner into the kitchen and slid across the floor like Tom Cruise in *Risky Business*, only I was fully dressed.

"Look what I found." I held up the book to show an astonished Miss Belle, Frieda, and Roger.

Everyone huddled over it, oohing and ahhing. Each of them took a turn looking at the note and the book. Roger looked a bit glum when he saw the note.

"Roger. It's as much yours as mine," Miss Belle said.

Roger's face brightened.

"Why don't you find a proper owner for it? Maybe a museum or library where it can be seen. We'll split the proceeds," Miss Belle said. "Because of Sarah, I know some very good causes to help veterans."

"Less my commission," Roger said.

We all stared at him.

"Gotcha," he said with a laugh.

We all joined in and laughed a lot harder than the moment called for. Then we took turns hugging each other.

After Roger left, Miss Belle and I sat at the kitchen table. She was still holding the book, leafing through it.

"How come you didn't know about this book?" It bugged me that she wouldn't know her husband owned something so valuable.

"From the date on the receipt, the exchange happened when I was spending a lot of time in Alabama while my mother was dying. Maybe Sebastian told me about it, but to me, it might have been just another book he bought. He died not so long after. We'll never know how it ended up in the floor."

I worried about Ryne still being out there.

"Miss Belle, do you know Ryne O'Rourke?" Part of me still hoped I was wrong about Ryne, that he wasn't involved in any of this.

"Not well."

I perked up. "But you know him?"

"I know his uncle much better."

"His uncle who runs that antique store?"

"Yes. We've known each other for years. He's been appraising the things at my mother-in-law's house."

If Ryne had been doing the appraising instead of his uncle, he would have been in a position to overhear Winnie talking about the manuscript and the book. My face flamed as I thought about him using an old woman like that. "Are you sure it was his uncle and not Ryne at the house?"

"I'm not sure," Miss Belle said.

"Then I'm going to call Ruth." Ruth, who I was silently apologizing to for thinking she was behind all or part of this.

Miss Belle nodded, so I dialed. After a brief conversation, I hung up. "Both of them worked there, but it's mostly been Ryne the past few months." My flare of anger receded, and I felt sad. "I need to call Pellner to let him know."

Chapter Thirty-Nine

At noon on Saturday the fund-raiser was in full swing. The air was scented with the hotdogs and hamburgers grilling on the north end of the town common. I stood near the church steps, watching over the event. Pellner showed up beside me.

"Any news about the manuscripts?" I asked.

"Nothing. We're tracking down people Kay had contact with, but they're like snakes that slithered back to where they came from."

"Do you think the manuscripts will ever be found?"

"I don't know. I talked to Bull this morning. He stopped by the station before he left."

"What did he have to say?" I asked.

"That he wouldn't rest until he found them. He's headed to New Bedford, hoping to find someone there who knew the people close to Kay."

"Any word on Ryne?"

Pellner shook his head. "No. Thin air so far with him."

"So he must have heard Trevor was arrested and took off." I sighed. "He's probably long gone."

"Maybe. Both his uncle and Trevor have been

blabbing about the whole plan. Ryne had overheard Mrs. Winthrop Granville talking about the limited edition of *The Sun Also Rises*. She was there when Harold Mervine gave it to Sebastian."

"Then why did Trevor threaten Roger and then chase him all over the place?" I wiped a bit of sweat from my forehead.

"Trevor thought Roger already had possession of it. Apparently, Kay misunderstood a conversation she overheard between Roger and Miss Belle. You finding the manuscripts was unexpected. No one knew about them. But they had already positioned Kay in the house by then. They took advantage of Rena's retirement, overheard Ruth recommend the Blackmore Agency. That set everything in motion."

"So a plan was quickly thrown together?"

"Exactly."

"How did Kay become involved?" I asked.

Pellner shook his head. "She knew Trevor and stopped by the antique store to meet Ryne. Ryne knew an easy mark when he saw one."

I didn't like what that implied about Stella and me. "And it was Ryne out in the woods? He killed Kay and shot at me?"

"Yeah. I'm sorry. According to his uncle that was a freak accident."

"And yet he shot at me anyway," I said.

"I pointed that out to him."

"Even though I was always a bit suspicious of him, I just thought it was because he was such a flirt. Not a criminal."

"He fooled a lot of people."

"It makes me wonder about my taste in men." I'd always accused Stella of having terrible taste in men, but maybe it was me.

"We're not all bad."

I nodded. Pellner left to join his family, and I decided to stroll through the vendor booths. A few minutes later, I stood running my hand along a shelf of a folding bookcase.

"Is this the same one I saw a few weeks ago?" I asked the woman I'd originally met at the flea market.

She nodded her head. "Yes. It's an original Larkin. Women in the early nineteen hundreds sold soap for the Larkin Company and earned these, or desks."

"I love that. I love it. But I live in a small place."

"Then it's perfect for you because of how it folds." She demonstrated by opening the two sides, swiveling up the shelves, and then folding the two sides back down. Then she quickly opened it all back up.

Maybe I could set it on the other side of the window from my grandmother's rocking chair. "You wanted two hundred for it?"

"Yes. They usually sell for a lot more."

"Would you take one fifty?"

The woman shook her head. "Like I said, it's worth more than two."

I'd been hoping she'd counter. "One seventy-five is the best I can do," I said.

The woman's husband came up behind her. He'd probably put the kibosh on the deal.

"We'll take it," he said. He pointed at his wife. "She put it aside after you saw it the first time. Said she felt like it was meant to be with you."

"Really? I get that feeling about things all the time. I'll buy something and then give it to someone who I think is really meant to have it." In fact, I'd recently purchased a vintage tablecloth with bowls of salad and jars of olives on it. I had a friend who loved olives, and I kept feeling I should send it to her. I paid them and told them I'd be back to pick it up later.

I weaved my way through the various booths until I spotted Miss Belle sitting at a table under a tree. She waved. I hurried over and sat down across from her.

"With all that's gone on, I never did donate anything for this fund-raiser," she said.

"It's okay. You're really stepping up for the library. They're a good cause too."

Miss Belle opened her purse and handed me a check. "I hope this helps out."

I stared down in astonishment and then threw my arms around her. "Thank you. This gets us halfway to our goal," I said as I released her. "How are you doing?"

"Frieda has agreed to stay on," Miss Belle said.

"That's wonderful news." I was happy for Frieda. Working for Miss Belle would be a lot easier than cleaning houses all day.

"And my mother-in-law is moving in with me sooner than we thought. Early next week. Ruth will be moving in too."

"Oh, how does that feel?" I asked.

"Like the right thing to do. I don't want to worry about someone else trying to take advantage of her."

"That will be a big adjustment."

"Thank heavens it's a big house and we can afford good care."

"Did you find out how the manuscripts ended up with Sebastian's family?"

"Winnie's explanation was a bit jumbled. She used phrases like *they were found* and *there was a mix-up with luggage.* It seems clear to me that her mother stole them. She might not have ever told anyone but Winnie." Miss Belle patted my arm. "And I'll see you on Monday."

"I can work tomorrow."

"I think you deserve a day of rest," she said as she turned to go.

I wiped a bit of sweat off my cheek. It was hotter than the blazes out here, whatever the blazes were. On the steps of the church, Stella was in charge of a sing-off. Votes were made by buying a ticket and putting it in a jar. The winning team was putting on a charity concert tonight in the old town hall across the common from my apartment. I was glad she was still willing to help, because she'd been pretty upset after hearing about Ryne's criminal enterprise. I'd managed to joke her out of it. Eventually, we laughed about the unlucky apartment next door, and the joys of finding a new person to rent the place. I was secretly hoping maybe it would be Luke.

On the church steps near the singers, there was a big wooden board with a needle on it that had zero at one end and $5,000 on the other. I handed off Miss Belle's check to James, who was keeping track of money.

"Look at this," I said as I handed it to him.

"That's fantastic," he said. He moved the needle to thirty-five hundred. "We're going to do it, aren't we?"

"We are. I told you we would."

I looked over at my apartment. Last night, Luke and I had moved back to my place after the police had said Ryne had cleared out. It was good to be home. I'd left a thank-you note for Seth, along with a nice bottle of cabernet sauvignon. Not only to thank him for letting us stay at his house, but because the assistant DA who'd helped prepare me for the trial had called. She'd told me that because of CJ's testimony, the defense lawyer had asked for a plea deal. I was so glad I didn't have to testify. I'd been a little disappointed Seth hadn't called me himself but hadn't had much time to dwell on it.

Luke had written an amazing story for the *Globe* about the manuscripts, *The Sun Also Rises* limited edition, and my role in the whole thing. I had talked about finding the manuscripts and shared the few lines I could remember. Miss Belle did the same. So, while there were still treasure hunters around and a few reporters, they weren't bothering me the way they had. Tracy had called Luke, and they were going to get together next week for an interview. Someone from Mike's organization had picked up the Volkswagen Beetle I'd been driving. Things were falling back into place.

The League of Literary Treasure Hunters were roaming all over the place, looking for books. I told them all they should stay in town for the library sale next week. I looked over the town common. People were laughing, singing, eating ice cream, and buying things. All of them out here to help someone they didn't even know. It wasn't easy having to make all the decisions about my life on my own. But the decision to stay in Ellington might just be the best one I'd ever made.

Luke came up to me. "Are you ready?"

I grinned. "You're on."

When we'd realized how hot it was going to be, Luke had suggested a town water balloon fight. Each balloon cost fifty cents, and all the money went to bringing King home. A group of teenagers from the base had been busy filling balloons with water for the last hour. An area of the town common had been taped off for the fight. We'd spread the word via social media.

People lined up to buy balloons, and they sold out in ten minutes. I bought the limit of five. Luke had found a bullhorn somewhere and announced the balloon fight would start in a few minutes. Everyone took up positions on the common. There were no trees to hide behind in this section. We all counted down with Luke. As soon as he said *go* and set down the bullhorn, I charged him. Splat, splat, splat. It was so satisfying.

I saw Tracy and Eric in the thick of things with their kids. They were all soaking wet and laughing. It lifted my heart to see them like that. A balloon landed in the middle of my back. I turned to see who threw it, but it was just a sea of people. I spotted the town manager. Laughing as she got someone with a balloon. She was usually dressed in a pristine suit, but today was in shorts and an Ellington Rocks T-shirt. I ran at her and threw. I was a little off, but it hit her in the leg. She pointed at me, laughing.

"You're going down," she said.

She took aim, but I threw my last balloon, then dodged behind a group of people. As I did, Luke hit me square in the chest with a red balloon. Water showered my face. I turned to run and smacked right into someone. Strong hands grasped my arms to steady me. I wiped the water out of my eyes but already knew who it was. Seth. He smiled down at me, and I threw my arms around him. Seth pulled me closer. Splat, splat, splat. Balloon after balloon pelted us, but neither of us cared.

Keep reading for a special excerpt of

I Know What You Bid Last Summer,

a Sarah Winston Garage Sale Mystery
by Sherry Harris!

FOUL PLAY IN THE GYM

When it comes to running a successful garage sale, Sarah Winston believes in doing her homework. She also believes in giving back. But when she agrees to manage an athletic equipment swap, she doesn't bargain on an uncharitable killer. The day of the event, the school superintendent is found dead in the gymnasium.

HAS SARAH PLAYING DEFENSE

Suddenly the murder suspects are the school board members—including the husband of a very difficult client who's hired Sarah to run a high-end sale and demands she do her bidding. In between tagging and haggling, Sarah studies the clues to see who wanted to teach the superintendent a lesson. But as she closes in on the truth, the killer intends to give her a crash course on minding her own business . . .

Look for **I Know What You Bid Last Summer**
on sale now where books are sold.

"I need your help, Sarah," Angelo said to me.

I'd rushed over from the Ellington High School gym, where I was in the throes of setting up an athletic equipment swap meet for the school board. The swap was in the morning, and I'd been up to my ears in ski poles when Angelo sent me a text asking me to stop by. Angelo never sent texts, so I had literally dropped everything and would have a mess of ski poles to clean up when I got back.

We sat in his restaurant, DiNapoli's Roast Beef and Pizza, at one of the wooden tables lining the far right side of the room. It was just after nine-thirty, and Angelo had closed for the night. His deep brown eyes crinkled with concern.

"Anything. What can I do?" Angelo and his wife, Rosalie, who sat next to him, had done so much for me that I'd gladly do anything this side of legal to help them. And maybe the other side of legal, if it was really important. They'd supported me when I'd moved to Ellington, Massachusetts, from nearby Fitch Air Force Base during a personal crisis over a year ago. The Di-Napolis encouraged me if I was down and celebrated my successes, like starting my Sarah Winston garage sale business. I leaned forward, shoving my glass of Chianti to the side.

Angelo looked at Rosalie. I thought I detected a slight roll of the eyes on Rosalie's part.

"You don't have to help," Rosalie said.

"Of course I will." In the past I'd found replacement tables and chairs for them if something wore out. This sounded more serious, and I was getting anxious. I wished they'd just spit it out. I looked back and forth between them.

Angelo cleared his throat. "Did you hear about the lasagna bake-off in Bedford next week?"

Bedford was the town next to Ellington. I nodded, mystified. While I was a whiz at setting up garage sales, my cooking skills were renowned for how awful they were. I hoped he didn't want me to enter. I thought the contest was open only to chefs at area restaurants.

"I signed up," Angelo said.

"That's great. You'll win," I said. "Do you need a sous-chef?" I could try, but it seemed like Rosalie or someone who worked here with him would be a better choice.

"I want to make sure I win," Angelo said. "I have to win." His hand fisted, but he refrained from pounding the table.

This time Rosalie definitely rolled her eyes. "You don't *have* to win. You want to win," she said with a shake of her head.

"So what do you want me to do?" My imagination was going wild. *Poison, sabotage, kidnapping?* What would making sure Angelo won entail? There were rumors his family was connected, that his uncle had more than just ties to the Mob. And I knew his cousin Vincenzo, an attorney, had gotten a few mobsters off racketeering charges. It seemed like Angelo had better options than me to make sure he would win. I grabbed my Chianti and took a big swig. Why did they call that Dutch courage—or in this case Italian?

"I need you to go to the top five competitors' restaurants and sample their lasagna and report back." Angelo leaned back in his chair.

That was it? He wanted me to eat pasta? Relief made my body feel like an overcooked piece of lasagna, saggy and limp. "I can do that."

"And bring me back a sample, without telling anyone what you are up to."

"Of course." Jeez, how hard could that be?

An hour and a half later I roamed up and down the long rows of tables in the Ellington High School gymnasium, using a hockey stick as a baton, making sure everything was ready. I pictured myself as a drum majorette being cheered on by a crowd in a huge football stadium. I could do with someone cheering for me. I probably looked more suited to leading the band from *The Music Man*, with my hockey stick and crazy march. Slaphappy. Giddy. Punch drunk. I was all those things. Maybe it was the combination of the Chianti from earlier with the DiNapolis and the caffeine I'd consumed after in the form of coffee, lots of it, from Dunkin's.

My stomach rumbled, and I thought about the lasagna Angelo had mentioned. I hadn't had much of an appetite since my ex-husband, CJ, left me six weeks ago, despite the rekindling of our relationship last February. I still couldn't believe he had chosen a job in Florida over me. But I couldn't think about that now. The lasagna project was something to look forward to, something to keep me busy. Busy had been my mantra since CJ left. I'd overbooked myself in the hopes that I'd be dead tired. But sleep, like my appetite, had all but disappeared. The lasagna would have to wait, though, because in nine hours the doors to the swap would open.

For the past week, people had been dropping off their gently used athletic equipment. Items they were tired of or that had been outgrown. Tomorrow other people would come and pick up what they needed. It was something that made everyone happy. The last of my helpers had left right after I returned from DiNapoli's around ten. Who could blame them? Some people had things to do on Friday nights. All the hard work getting ready for the swap was better than hardly working.

I twirled the hockey stick in my hand as I checked one last time to make sure all the equipment for the sports swap was at least somewhat organized. It hadn't taken long to learn that sports equipment didn't like to be arranged. It liked to roll or topple over. Baseball bats, lacrosse sticks, balls, pretty much all sports equipment. They were unruly and didn't lend themselves to neat arrangements. Except for the helmets. At least they cooperated by sitting proudly in rows.

I'd get zippo for doing this, so maybe it wasn't a smart business move. The last Saturday in June was primo garage sale season. I had turned down a lot of jobs, hoping that organizing this would up my profile in the town of Ellington and the surrounding suburban areas outside of Boston. It hadn't taken long to learn that sports equipment swaps were very popular in this area. Old and outgrown equipment was a big draw.

Most of the school board members had liked my idea of adding a silent auction to raise more funds for the school district. With all the sports teams in Boston, it had been easy to get items owned or signed by famous athletes and to prove their provenance. I'd even had a fan girl moment when I ran into Tom Brady the day I picked things up at Gillette Stadium, home of the Patriots. He was bigger in person and better looking. His smile almost melted my shoes.

I tossed the hockey stick up into the air as I twirled around, planning to catch it before it hit the floor. The lights went out, and I skittered to a stop mid-twirl. The hockey stick glanced off my shoulder and clattered to the floor by my feet.

"Ow," I said to the empty, silent gym. I felt around for the hockey stick so I didn't trip myself. After I picked it up, I shook my head, hoping the power outage wouldn't prevent the swap from taking place tomorrow. I shuffled in the general direction of my purse and cell phone, not wanting to knock over one of the tables full of equipment. If I could find my phone, I could use the flashlight app. Footsteps echoed on the gymnasium floor and they weren't mine.

"Hello," I called. At least I wasn't alone. Slow, deliberate footsteps headed toward me. "Who's here?" I couldn't make out anything in the dark.

There wasn't a response except for the echo of steps. I whirled, still clutching the hockey stick, and hurried blindly toward my cell phone. I knocked my hip into a table. Balls of all sorts, from basketballs to golf balls, spilled, bounced, and rolled around me. I stutter-stepped around them, slipping, hoping that they would slow whoever else was in here, too.

Footsteps pounded across the gym floor, growing closer. I veered away from my purse. Sprinted toward the only light in the gym, one of the glowing exit signs. Something hooked around my foot. Another freaking hockey stick. I sprawled as I slid across the gymnasium floor and landed in a display of skis. They thundered down, battering and bruising me. I started to shake off the skis, to get back up, to get away.

Something whacked my lower back, my kidneys. Another blow hit the back of my thighs. I collapsed and curled into a ball, making myself as small as possible. I flung my left arm over my head, protecting it. My right hand clutched the hockey stick. My eyes were adjusting to the dark, and I could see the outline of a shadowy person bending toward me. The person grasped my arm, wrenching my left shoulder, and dragged me. I tried to trip him with the hockey stick. He stomped on my hand. I let go of the hockey stick as I cried out.

I heard a door open. Hinges creak. The only doors that weren't exits in the gym were to the equipment room or the locker rooms. The door to the equipment room was the one with the creaky hinges. He shoved me. The door banged shut. Something was dragged across the floor, and it hit the door.

I huddled on the floor, trembling. I knew I should move, but couldn't. Too scared. Too hurt. Noises sounded from the gym, bangs and bumps, and I wondered what the hell was going on out there. I pushed myself up to a sitting position and listened. After a while I didn't hear anything. I got to my feet and stumbled forward blindly. I bumped into some kind of shelving unit. It rocked madly, but nothing fell on my head. I fumbled around for the light switch, running my hand up the rough walls, where it seemed like it should be.

I finally found it and flicked it on, blinking as the fluorescent light came to life. One of the long tubes blinked sporadically, crackling and sputtering. It created the perfect setting for a horror movie. The equipment room was full of creepy shadows. The doorknob turned easily in my hand, but when I tried to push the door open, it wouldn't budge. And every part of my aching body seemed to protest the action. Whoever was out there had blocked me in. I cursed when I realized I was stuck for the night, because no one would miss me until the morning. But what if he came back?

Connect with Us

Visit us online at
KensingtonBooks.com
to read more from your favorite authors, see books
by series, view reading group guides, and more.

Join us on social media

for sneak peeks, chances to win books and prize packs,
and to share your thoughts with other readers.

facebook.com/kensingtonpublishing
twitter.com/kensingtonbooks

Tell us what you think!

To share your thoughts, submit a review,
or sign up for our eNewsletters, please visit:
KensingtonBooks.com/TellUs.

Catering and Capers with
Isis Crawford!

A Catered Murder	978-1-57566-725-6	$5.99US/$7.99CAN
A Catered Wedding	978-0-7582-0686-2	$6.50US/$8.99CAN
A Catered Christmas	978-0-7582-0688-6	$6.99US/$9.99CAN
A Catered Valentine's Day	978-0-7582-0690-9	$6.99US/$9.99CAN
A Catered Halloween	978-0-7582-2193-3	$6.99US/$8.49CAN
A Catered Birthday Party	978-0-7582-2195-7	$6.99US/$8.99CAN
A Catered Thanksgiving	978-0-7582-4739-1	$7.99US/$8.99CAN
A Catered St. Patrick's Day	978-0-7582-4741-4	$7.99US/$8.99CAN
A Catered Christmas Cookie Exchange	978-0-7582-7490-8	$7.99US/$8.99CAN

Grab These Cozy Mysteries from
Kensington Books